# PRAISE FOR *THE MERMAID'S SISTER*

"This delightful fantasy novel . . . is widely appealing: there are elements of fantasy, romance, and adventure throughout. The book is a page-turner; the story pulls the reader in and the dynamic characters and plot twists keep interest levels high. The author's writing style is very descriptive, helping the reader truly visualize the sights, sounds, tastes, and adventures of the characters. A must read."

—*Publishers Weekly*

"This lovely, lyrical fantasy takes place in a mythical Pennsylvania mountain setting and tells the story of three foundlings—Clara, Maren, and O'Neill . . . Like all good fairy tales, this one touches on deeper themes of sibling rivalry, jealousy, insecurity, and questions of identity. Osbert the rambunctious wyvern is a particularly well-done character. VERDICT Noble's treatment of the mermaid theme is fresh and original, and even her minor characters are beautifully depicted."

—*School Library Journal*

CARRIE ANNE

## ALSO BY CARRIE ANNE NOBLE

*The Mermaid's Sister*

Amazon Breakthrough Novel Award Winner for Young Adult Fiction, 2014

Realm Award Winner for Best Speculative Fiction of the Year, 2016

# The Gold-Son

CARRIE ANNE
NOBLE

Published by Skyscape, New York

www.apub.com



ISBN-13: 9781477819678
ISBN-10: 1477819673

Cover design by M. S. Corley

Printed in the United States of America

*To Shirley*

A penny for your thoughts
A pound for your dreams
A kettle of gold for the secret you keep.

—"Song of the Leprechaun," as documented by J. E. Brown in *The Compleat History of the Tribes of Faerie*

## *An Crann gan Ainm*

## (The Nameless Tree)

***Ireland, 1811***

In the forest north of Loughgillan stood a tree so beautiful it could bring a grown man to tears—but few men ever saw it. The forest was a forbidden place, spoken of only in warnings and whispers. To go there was to risk your immortal soul, or at least your earthly existence.

The tree was neither oak nor ash, neither beech nor birch, nor any other tree named by humankind. Its trunk was wider than the town church, and its highest branches tangled with clouds. It blossomed for three days every spring, or so it was said, for a fragrance like honey and cake drifted into Loughgillan at that time, making stomachs rumble with longing that no mortal food could quench.

If you had followed Grania Kelly to that place on one particular blossom-scented March morning, you would have seen something you'd never forget.

And it was this:

Arms outstretched like a sleepwalker's, the nightgown-clad young woman stumbled over roots and fallen limbs, groaning and gasping and clutching her round belly. When Grania reached the Nameless Tree, she grazed her fingertips over its ridged bark as if it were the skin of her beloved. And then she lay down and rested her head upon a pillow of raised roots, letting her body sink into a fragrant bed of pale-pink petals.

After a few minutes, or perhaps hours (for time cannot be rightly judged in enchanted places), a wee man emerged from behind nearby twin oaks—a finely dressed fellow clad in a long-tailed coat and a peaked cap. He laughed at his good fortune just as loudly as Grania bemoaned her pain. Quickly, he rolled up his sleeves and knelt down at Grania's feet—just in time to catch the wailing child as it entered this world.

No matter how keen your ears, you could not have understood the words the wee man spoke over the babe before passing him to his half-laughing, half-weeping mother. No matter, for the words were meant only for the child.

Later, a few hours or a day after the man melted into the shadows from whence he came, the girl rose with her newborn pressed to her heart and began to walk slowly, gingerly, back toward the town.

If you had seen these things, you might have long wondered why she'd chosen such a place to bear a child. Indeed, she herself could never quite fathom it. Perhaps she'd felt sure to die in childbirth and wanted to see the fabled tree before she died. Perhaps, in her weakened state, dark forces had taken hold of her and lured her to that place.

It mattered not.

What was done was done.

# Part One

# Chapter One

## Pingin Airgead ar Mhalart ar Snagbreac

## (A Silver Penny for a Magpie)

***Ireland, 1827***

His given name was Tommin, but for as long as he could remember, his granny had called him nothing but Magpie. Indeed, it was the only word she had spoken since she'd been stricken with apoplexy thirteen years before, when Tommin was just three years old. That was the spring of the floods and the fever, the year he lost his mother, the year his father ran off without saying good-bye.

On this bright May morning, Granny eyed him from her chair beside the fire and accused him without opening her mouth. She always knew when he'd been up to mischief. She knew without making him turn out his pockets, without forcing him to confess aloud. Nothing in the world made him feel worse. He wondered if other sixteen-year-old boys melted so quickly under the gaze of their grandmothers. Perhaps it was an affliction only he knew. Perhaps it was because she was both father and mother to him, and the only one who loved him without restraint.

Tommin dropped a silver coin onto the kitchen table. To his ears, it resounded with an almighty clank, like the gates of hell slamming. Shame made his face hot as a demon's cook fire. Yet as much as he regretted stealing the coin, he loved the thing. It sparkled at him, wooing him, stirring his heart more than any girl ever had.

"Magpie," Granny said in such a way that he knew she pitied him.

"Landlord will be making his rounds today," Tommin said.

The old woman grunted. She patted her pocket, and the coins already inside clinked together. Tommin hadn't forgotten he'd given her the rent money days before when he'd brought home his honorably earned wages—and neither had she.

"Toward next month's rent, then."

Granny clucked her tongue. It was hopeless, his attempt at turning ill-gotten gain into innocent provision. He was no alchemist.

Trying to swallow his guilt, he ran one finger over the image stamped into the coin. A shiver of pleasure ran up his arm and spread throughout his body. This, he knew, was not normal. But that was *all* he knew of it: not *why*, not *how long*, not *who* had cursed him with the urge to steal, a compulsion that tortured him and then rewarded him for his crimes with immeasurable bliss.

Nothing satisfied him like stolen silver and gold. Only the crafting of shoes could quiet his greed—and that only for a short time.

Granny leaned forward to stir the pot of porridge hanging from its hook above the fire. The town clock struck seven as she motioned for him to bring his bowl. He had work to do, honest work, and Granny was not one to tolerate lateness or laziness. Her silent reprimands stung every bit as much as any shouted rebuke.

Tommin spooned his breakfast into his mouth and swallowed it without tasting it. It could have been wet sawdust and he would not have cared, still buoyed by the terrible pleasure of his recent theft.

Saints above, he hated himself.

Heaven knew he did *try* to be good, for Granny's sake even more than his own. No earthly sum could equal what he owed Granny for her years of raising him so lovingly. And now that she was old and weak, it was his turn to care for her and to provide for them both through his work with the shoemaker.

The truth was he had two lives, and one of them could not go on—unless he fancied swinging from the gallows or rotting in prison. Every theft carried him closer to his doom. But when the lust for treasure and the agony of wanting gripped him, he was too often helpless to resist.

There was no pretty word for it: stealing, thievery, robbery, burgling. Once a year when he was small, then twice. Every full moon by the time he turned ten, and now as often as once or twice a week . . . As he grew, the hunger inside him grew—a dark worm demanding to be fed treasure by his hand, gnawing at his resolve to be good.

It wasn't that he hadn't tried to cast off whatever curse or demon plagued him. A hundred times he'd prayed until his knees grew numb. He'd confessed to mostly deaf Father Dunn again and again, and he'd performed each act of contrition precisely. He'd sipped water from holy wells, tied good-luck charms to his wrists and ankles, slept naked in a moonlit field, eaten an array of bitter herbs, and consulted books of lore. Nothing ever worked.

"Magpie," Granny said, interrupting his bleak daydream. She offered her wrinkled cheek for a kiss—her way of shooing him out the door.

He kissed her, inhaling her comforting lavender-and-fresh-bread scent. "Do you need anything before I go? Your shawl? More tea?"

Granny shook her head and reached up to pat his cheek. With this gesture and the tender look in her unclouded blue eyes, she told him she loved him. "Well then, I'm off," Tommin said. "I'll be home before dark."

Passing the table, he retrieved the silver penny and slipped it into his pocket with one smooth motion. Such a pretty thing, of such a pleasant weight. A thing to be kept, to be hidden with its mates in the box beneath his bed, to later be buried deep in the meadow grass that grew between the lake's edge and the border of Lanty's Wood.

"Magpie!" Granny scolded as he slipped out the door.

Eyes like an eagle, Granny had. He stepped into the lane and let springtime's sun warm his face. The good, pure light lifted his heart and gave him a sliver of hope. Surely somewhere there was someone who could cure him of his problem. All he had to do was avoid getting caught thieving until he found whoever it was.

The faint aroma of gold tickled Tommin's nose and awakened a fierce longing in his breast. It took all his strength to turn away from the scent and to run in the opposite direction, but he managed it.

His feet pounded hard against the cobblestones. This time, he'd won the fight. Next time, he might not.

Panting, he scrambled into the shoemaker's shop. He gripped the doorjamb with one hand and silently thanked heaven for the not-so-small victory.

The old shoemaker looked up from his bench and smiled. "Just in time," he said.

"Truer words were never spoken," Tommin said. He inhaled the familiar scents of leather, polish, and dye, and found peace. Within the walls of Master Rafferty's shop, Tommin's lust for treasure seldom stirred. And that was a bit of luck a boy called Magpie never failed to be grateful for.

# Chapter Two

## *Printíseach Gréasaí*

## (The Shoemaker's Apprentice)

Down the lane from the shoe shop, a rooster crowed. At the sound, Tommin watched Conn Rafferty set aside his knife and leather and hurry to the open door. From his pocket, the old shoemaker took a pinch of salt. He flung the salt into the street, made the sign of the cross, and said, "God between us and all harm." He whistled three short notes before finally returning to his bench.

Tommin had witnessed this a hundred times, this strange ritual. Indeed, it was one of many the old shoemaker performed throughout the day. Some, Tommin had been told by his master, warded off wicked Faeries. Others were meant to prevent ill luck from settling on the shop or its owner. A few were done to honor saints (ones with odd names he never heard mentioned by anyone else). From throwing salt to setting out dishes of cream, from spitting into eggshells to whispering gibberish to passing cats—Tommin had seen it all.

If anyone apart from the Almighty deserved credit for the way the town of Loughgillan remained largely untouched by storm, famine, and subjugation, the master shoemaker did.

"Better to be cautious than dead for the rest of your life," Master Rafferty said as he resumed his work.

Tommin smiled. "Right, sir." He held up a dark-brown shoe and inspected it from all sides. Plain and sturdy it was, as Master Rafferty insisted every shoe from his shop must be. Deeply pious and humble as well as superstitious, Master Rafferty refused to be party to others' indulging in excesses or fripperies—no matter how much they offered to pay. Sometimes Tommin wondered why the man had chosen to be a craftsman instead of a clergyman.

*If he had any idea how wicked and greedy I've been, he'd toss me out onto the streets like so much salt,* Tommin thought. Fortunately, Master Rafferty did not have the gift of seeing a person's secret sins. Tommin did love his job.

And he was good at it. Better than good.

Tommin had started his shoemaking apprenticeship when he was eight years old, after asking for it himself like a grown man. Back then, he'd yearned to make shoes with a burning, soul-deep desire, almost the same sort of desire he felt for treasures now. On his first day of work, and with little instruction, Tommin had created a pair of slippers so fine that Master Rafferty had gasped at the sight of them, marveling at the delicate cutwork and declaring them fit for only the angels' feet. After the shock passed, Master Rafferty promptly doused Tommin with a vial of holy water to test whether the lad was the devil's disciple or the good Lord's gift. For how else could a mere child do such work? When Tommin failed to shriek and shrivel at the water's touch, Master Rafferty praised the Almighty with a shout and led the boy to the altar in the corner to light a candle of gratitude.

The next day, Master Rafferty instructed Tommin in the "proper" way to make shoes and boots, forbidding him to craft anything other than simple, durable footwear ever again. Men's souls, the shoemaker declared, stood in the balance. Coveting one's neighbor's finery could well be the first step on the path to greater sins.

But once, last summer, when Master Rafferty went on a pilgrimage to Saint Horgat's Well, Tommin had gathered discarded scraps of calfskin and cut and stitched the sweetest little pointy-toed slippers. They fit in the palm of his hand, perfectly matched, their seams almost invisible. He had embroidered them with swirling vines and tiny stars, using golden thread he'd found tucked away in a drawer.

Finished, he'd set them on his workbench. They were shoes for a Faerie, no question about it. The *something* in him—the same *something* that plagued him to steal—had driven him to create them, but at least they'd serve as an offering instead of a theft. At the end of the day, he'd left the slippers under a blackberry bush on the border of Lanty's Wood. He knew in his bones that they'd be claimed before the moon set that night.

After that, he hadn't taken the risk of making fancy shoes in secret again. Instead, in an effort to offset the weight of his sins and to enjoy his talents, he used the scraps he collected to make durable, practical shoes to send off to Dublin's needy children. He joined the odd pieces perfectly, with seams so minute that they could barely be seen with the naked eye. He imagined the little ones' delighted, dirt-crusted faces as they held out skinny arms to accept the first new shoes they'd ever owned.

Tommin's hammer slipped from his hand and hit the floor with a loud clatter.

"Daydreaming again, are you?" Master Rafferty asked.

"Sorry." Tommin bent to retrieve his hammer.

The old shoemaker squinted at Tommin. "Is something bothering you this day, lad? You're looking a bit off-color. Trouble sleeping, perhaps? I've a bit of lavender plucked from Saint Lucha's gardens that might do the trick, were your granny to brew you a tea at sunset."

"Thanks, Master Rafferty. That's very kind of you." He *was* kind, Master Rafferty. Kind enough to forgive Tommin for his wicked ways, surely. Tommin gripped his hammer tightly and made a bold choice. He would do it. He'd ask Master Rafferty if he knew what might be causing his affliction. If there might be some herb, ritual, or prayer to deliver him from his magpie tendencies.

By the saints, he felt foolish for not having asked sooner. The man loved him as a son, didn't he? And if anyone in Loughgillan knew the remedy, it would be Conn Rafferty.

Tommin fiddled with his shirt collar. "Sir? I was—" The bell above the shop door jangled, and Tommin closed his mouth to save the words for later. That is, if he could work up the courage to speak them later.

"Good day to you," a deep, unfamiliar voice said from the doorway. It was the kind of voice Tommin imagined a great king might have, rich and resonant. A voice fit to give grand speeches or to inspire men to wage war.

When Tommin turned and saw the voice's owner, he almost gasped aloud. Instead of the handsome giant of a man he imagined, before him stood a short, stocky, brown-haired fellow with a bearded face as ordinary as milk. Yet there was something unusual about the well-dressed middle-aged man, a peculiar twinkle in his green eyes that made Tommin shiver inside—and fervently wish Master Rafferty would fling salt or holy water.

"The name's Lorcan Reilly," he said, stepping up to the counter. "I have heard you make the best shoes in the county."

"I'm a modest man," Master Rafferty said, "but the truth is the truth, and I'll not speak against it."

Tommin glanced at the gentleman's exquisite shoes and wondered why he'd *really* come to Master Rafferty's shop. From across the room, Tommin could tell they'd cost more than he'd earn in six months—and that they were worth every penny. The highest-grade leather dyed pine green, tooled and assembled artfully.

A hearty sneeze drew Tommin's attention back to the doorway. *Today is full of surprises,* he thought, for never in a month of Sundays would he have expected such a loud sneeze to have come from a *girl.*

"My niece, Eve," Lorcan Reilly said without giving her a backward glance. "Pay her no mind."

But Tommin could not help himself. By his reckoning, the rail-thin girl was between fifteen and eighteen. A few strands of copper-colored hair clung to her freckled forehead, having escaped her brown headscarf. She wore a simple dress of fern-green homespun fabric, covered from shoulders to waist with an acorn-brown shawl—a strange contrast to her uncle's finely tailored outfit. Her sole adornment was a thin gold ring worn on her right hand. She met Tommin's gaze with blue-gray eyes that conveyed neither joy nor sorrow.

"Tommin?" Master Rafferty said.

He turned his attention to the old shoemaker. "Sir?"

"Did you not hear the gentleman's question, lad? Such a day-dreamer you've become lately!"

"I'm sorry," Tommin said. "I was thinking."

"Never mind," Lorcan Reilly said, picking a speck of lint from his sleeve as if it were a flea. "My time is too short for idle conversation with numb-minded boys."

"Well then, step this way and I'll take your measurements, sir," Master Rafferty said, gesturing to an upholstered chair in the back half of the shop. "We'll be finished in two shakes of a lamb's tail."

As soon as Master Rafferty's back was turned, Lorcan Reilly took three quick steps toward the girl and jabbed her in the ribs with his walking stick, hard enough to make her cringe. Tommin cringed as well. "You stand here and don't make mischief," he whispered just loud enough for Tommin to hear. "Or you'll bleed for it later."

"This way, sir," Master Rafferty repeated, and Lorcan Reilly sauntered off to join him.

As the old shoemaker rattled on about the likelihood of an afternoon rainstorm, Tommin left his workbench and made a pretense of going to the window near the door to inspect the weather for himself.

Standing close to the girl, he whispered, "Does he always treat you like that?"

Eve shook her bowed head, staring at her shoes. Did that mean he didn't, or that she was too afraid to speak of it with her uncle so close? He tried again. "Do you need help?"

Again, she shook her head. And then, warily, she met his gaze. The sorrow in her eyes moved him like the saddest of songs. He'd have wagered his dinner that her uncle had caused the yellow-brown bruise on her forehead.

He laid a sympathetic hand on her sleeve, and she jerked her arm away. Lorcan laughed loudly, falsely, from nearby.

"There. Almost finished," Master Rafferty said.

The girl gestured for Tommin to get away. She took a step backward, reaching behind her waist for the doorknob.

Quickly, Tommin glanced over his shoulder. Master Rafferty was leading Lorcan Reilly to the counter, blocking the gentleman's view of them. There was no time to hesitate. "Please let me help you," Tommin begged.

The girl bolted out the door.

Tommin shivered as he returned to his workbench, feeling Lorcan Reilly's gaze on the back of his head like a slow-creeping spider. As much as he wanted to go after the girl, he suspected it would only stir up more trouble between her and her uncle.

While Master Rafferty finished measuring, the customer spoke little, and then only to give instructions regarding the type of leather he required. Finally, Lorcan Reilly sauntered past Tommin's bench, coins jingling in his pocket. He chuckled low, as if he knew how Tommin's stomach fluttered with desire at the sound. Of course he didn't know, there was no way he could—but Tommin liked him no better for it.

He clutched his hammer and counted the seconds till Lorcan Reilly stepped outside. Then he stood and stared out the window, watching the disagreeable man stroll up the lane like he owned it. He wondered when the man would return, and if Eve would come with him. On second thought, he'd rather not see Lorcan Reilly ever again. There was something about him, *something* . . .

"Tommin!" Master Rafferty scolded. "For the love of the saints, boy! Have you lost your senses?"

"Sorry?"

"Did you not hear me asking you to fetch our order from the tannery? You're dull as soap today, I swear."

Tommin headed for the door, stopped, and turned to face his master. "Did you not find that man terrible and strange, sir?" Tommin asked. "Gave me the shivers, like someone walking over my grave."

"Seemed a nice enough fellow to me," Master Rafferty said. "And folks call *me* superstitious! Now, off with you, before I decide to cut your wages."

Tommin hurried to obey. With a sinking feeling, he knew he'd be doing more than fetching leather before returning to the shop. His palms itched as the lust for precious metal heated his blood and quickened his pulse. He blamed Lorcan Reilly's blasted coin rattling for sparking the wicked fire within him.

"No," he said aloud as he hastened down the lane. "I won't do it." Not in broad daylight. Not for a second time in one day. The risk was too great, as was the transgression.

Halfway to the tannery, without slowing his pace, he picked a man's pocket with as much skill as he imagined any big-city criminal might use. Tommin's fingers tingled as he tucked two silver coins into the leather pouch he wore at his belt. Two coins at once! He'd never done *that* before!

He ducked into a narrow space between two buildings as a thrill of ecstasy weakened his knees. He crouched in the cool shadows while little stars of pleasure burst in his chest and rode the tide of his blood to every part of his body.

He laughed because he could not help laughing, and he cried because he was ashamed. Wasn't he just as loathsome as Lorcan Reilly? They were both thieves in their own right: Lorcan had obviously stolen his niece's joy, and Tommin nicked whatever shiny thing he fancied. A sin was a sin.

After a few minutes or perhaps an hour, heavy footsteps approached. In his hiding place, Tommin hugged his knees and held his breath. The stout form of the town constable passed by, followed by the smaller figure of the man whom Tommin had pickpocketed.

"Some snot-nosed lad from Yew Street, I reckon," the constable said. "Long gone by now. Most likely just trying to put food on the table for ten or twelve siblings. Almost feel sorry for them, I do. But the law's the law. Thou shalt not steal and all that, eh?"

When the men were well away, Tommin crept out onto the street again. And then he ran.

He ran toward the tannery as if his life depended on it. He ran from who he was and what he'd done—and what he knew he'd do again, like it or not.

# Chapter Three

## Cailín ag Caitheamh Ciúnais

## (A Girl Wearing Silence)

When twilight settled on the meadow at the edge of the wood, Lorcan Reilly left Eve alone. The weight of his presence always made the air too heavy for her lungs, but as the slope of the hill erased him from view, everything lightened. Finally, she could breathe.

She sat in front of her little tent and watched the stars appear like grains of salt strewn across a cloth of deepening blue. She tried not to think, just to listen to the insects fussing in the grass and the birds twittering as they settled down for the night, and for a while, she was almost successful. Yet there he was in the corner of her mind: a thin, pale-skinned, dark-haired boy with serious eyes. The shoemaker's apprentice.

The boy her uncle had dragged her halfway across the country to find. The boy he'd mumbled of a few nights ago when drunk (*son of my past and prince of my future . . .*).

Tommin, the shoemaker had called him. *Well, Tommin,* she thought, *if you knew what was good for you, you'd run away and hide like the devil himself was at your heels.* He'd been so kind to her, so anxious to help. As far as she could recall, no one had ever given her a second thought or more than a passing glance—but today, Tommin had looked straight at her and noticed her suffering. Perhaps that was why she couldn't stop thinking of him; he'd reminded her that she was neither invisible nor insignificant. He'd offered her hope and asked for nothing in return.

Eve stood and tucked a loose strand of short hair behind her ear, cursing Lorcan Reilly for cutting it like a boy's. That was one thing she could remember clearly enough: how he yanked and hacked at her hair, tossing locks into the fire, creating a mighty stink that made her already teary eyes sting. Every few months, the same bit of torture. And for what? There must be a reason, but that information either escaped memory or had never been given to her.

Now tense with frustration, she began to pace. There was nothing else she could do. Uncle had marked off a circle with a radius of twenty steps from the campfire and sealed her inside with strong magic. She was trapped, as Tommin would be soon. They'd both be at his mercy.

But no. Uncle had no mercy in him. Only cruelty and greed. Only coldness and trickery. She had endured it for . . . how long? Her memory failed her yet again. Another one of Uncle's enchantments, no doubt. Her childhood was absent from her mind, her adolescence a mere jumble of oddments: a glimpse of the sea, sleeping on a fragrant bed of moss, watching Uncle dancing and fiddling amid a company of impossibly beautiful ladies and gentlemen, Uncle's firm grip as he pulled her—terrified—through dank earthen tunnels, the sharp sting of his belt or stick on her back or the smack of his palm on her face when she'd displeased him, being rarely alone but always lonely.

Tommin should be told that Uncle Lorcan had plans for him, plans to use him in some dark scheme. But she could neither write nor speak to give warning. Even rabbits in a trap could cry out; she could object only by waving her arms or stomping her feet. A fine lot of good that would do her or Tommin.

Her foot slipped on a patch of damp grass and touched the invisible boundary. Searing pain shot up her leg, and she fell to the ground.

Blood trickled down her calf where a thorn had caught her skin. She touched it and swore a silent oath, her eyes on the nearly full moon.

*I will escape,* she vowed, *and I will not let Uncle snare Tommin if it is within my power.*

She squared her shoulders, lifted her skirts to her knees, and started to run—careful not to touch the boundary again. Faster and faster she ran, circling the camp. When the time came for her to flee Lorcan Reilly, she would be strong and quick of body. He would never be able to catch her again.

# Chapter Four

## *Éin Uafásacha ó Ghar is i gCéin*

## (Terrible Birds from Near and Far)

The fever lit on the town of Loughgillan like a flock of Death's own crows, at first perching wherever their talons could grip easily—upon the very old and the very young. And then, the birds seemed to settle anywhere and everywhere.

The remote and unusually prosperous and peaceful town of Loughgillan had seldom known such ill luck. Or so centenarian Mrs. Grady told Tommin as he stood beside her in the rain-soaked churchyard following a group funeral for the blacksmith, the night watchman, and Mrs. Grady's twin granddaughters.

On the day Master Rafferty fell ill, his overheated brain cooked up all manner of reasons for the fever. First, he declared that the townsfolk ought to have scattered iron filings around the borders of the town to prevent the malevolent *Unseelie Sidhe* from trespassing. The next hour, Master Rafferty blamed roving tinkers for poisoning the wells. Finally, he concluded loudly that a lack of devotion to Saint Gurnesta of Colcrinny had brought down this plague.

Tommin spoke gently to the man who was as close to being his father as anyone alive, guiding him to his bed, removing his apron and shoes, and tucking the blanket under his chin. He promised to light a candle and to beg for Saint Gurnesta's mercy upon them all.

When the sun began to set, Tommin dabbed Master Rafferty's damp brow with a rag one last time before taking up his coat and slipping out the back door. He did not bother to say good-bye; the shoemaker was beyond conversation, lost in restless sleep.

He hated to leave Master Rafferty alone in his room behind the shoe shop. The old man had no family at all, and the trio of spinster sisters who usually cared for the town's sick were already overtaxed caring for others. But Tommin had to check on Granny. She'd been well enough when he'd left for work that morning, but he'd heard of several people going from good as gold to dead as doornails in the space of a few hours—a thought that sent a shiver through him for two reasons: fear and a sudden longing to steal.

The mere thought of the words "good as gold" had prodded the greedy magpie in him awake, curse them.

And curse his palms for itching and burning.

"Not now," he muttered. But then, weary as he was with worry, he decided he might as well get it over with. At least the touch of silver or gold would give him strength for a few hours and lend him joy on this joyless day. He'd repent later—unless the fever took him, and then . . . well, he'd have to answer to the Lord Himself in person. An unpleasant prospect, but there it was.

Stopping in the eerily deserted square, he sniffed the air like a hound. From the east came the faint scent of gold, and perhaps a precious stone of some kind. A ring or a brooch? Urgent desire stirred deep within his belly, and he hurried past the church and several houses, following his nose to his destination.

He knew the house from which the beckoning scent came. Bridget Sloane, a pretty girl his age, lived there with her father. She worked at the dairy farm south of town, making butter to be sent to the city. Funny enough, her hair was the very color of butter. He'd fancied her when he was fourteen, and they'd kissed behind the blacksmith's forge on the last day of the May fair. Her mouth had tasted of honey cakes and berries, and he'd thought of little else for a week. Finally, trembling with shyness and hoping for another kiss, he'd brought her a handful of daisies—and found her in the arms of Fergal Sullivan. He'd never spoken to her again.

Now he stood by Bridget's door, listening. He heard someone breathing, deeply and unevenly, and a male voice murmuring nonsense. Whoever was inside was ill. Was stealing from the sick any worse than stealing from the well? At least he was unlikely to get caught.

Tommin slipped inside. In the dimness, he saw the Sloanes: Bridget and her father, Jack, sweaty, sallow skinned, and sleeping fitfully on mattresses laid along opposite walls of their one-room cottage.

With his painfully itchy hand, Tommin groped beneath Bridget's straw-filled tick until he caught hold of a little wooden box. The gentle tingle in his palm assured him something lovely lay inside—even before he opened it.

He glanced at Bridget for a moment. Her chest heaved up and down like a set of bellows, and her skin looked fragile as old parchment. She'd be dead soon, poor Bridget, and would have no need of what he guessed was an engagement ring from Fergal Sullivan.

"I'm sorry, Bridget," he said, pocketing the box. "But you'll have better treasures in heaven, to be sure." He touched her hot shoulder, wishing he could pray for her soul but knowing he was unfit to speak to the Almighty.

"Is someone there?" Jack Sloane asked from his mattress, his voice slurred. "Bring me my harp, Lizzie, my darling. I left it in Declan's barn, and his cows might do it a mischief."

"Wait here and I'll fetch it," Tommin lied as he slipped back into the street.

While he walked, his fingers fumbled within his pocket to free the ring from its box. When the gold collided with his skin, a surge of pure bliss rushed through him. He knew he was smiling like a drunken groom, but couldn't bring himself to care.

*Joy now, sorrow later,* he told himself as he half ran, half danced the rest of his way home. Then again, maybe he'd *not* be very sorry this one time. Surely this episode of thievery was justifiable. How else could he stay strong enough to run the shoe shop, care for Master Rafferty, and look after Granny? Besides, the Angel of Death would carry Bridget off before she ever had a chance to miss the ring.

"Granny!" he called out cheerfully as he crossed the threshold into the kitchen. She looked up from her darning and met his eye.

"Magpie," she said, clucking her tongue and shaking her head slowly. "Magpie."

He turned away from her and poured a cup of water from the clay pitcher, a bit alarmed that Granny's scolding did not stir any guilt in him. But the feeling passed as quickly and harmlessly as a bit of dandelion fluff carried by the wind.

# Chapter Five

## *Bróga Maithe, Bróga os Fearr*

## (Good Shoes, Better Shoes)

Sleep eluded Tommin.

After a few hours of tossing, turning, and tangling in the blankets he'd put on the floor of Master Rafferty's shop, he gave up all hope of slumber. With his whole body still buzzing from the theft of Bridget's ring, he felt he'd be awake for days.

*Might as well work,* he thought, lighting the wick of an oil lamp.

First, he'd check on Master Rafferty. The old shoemaker lay flat on his back in bed. He'd kicked the blankets off, and his spindly legs stuck out the bottom of his long shirt like a pair of white twigs. Tommin held the lamp closer, terrified by the man's deathlike stillness. Suddenly, the shoemaker's arm twitched. Tommin exhaled with relief.

"You needn't scare me like that again," he said as he rearranged the blanket. "Now, if you'll excuse me, I'll go finish Lorcan Reilly's order for you."

And so Tommin did. For a little while, his worries faded, and he found himself humming as he shaped, stitched, hammered, and polished.

When pink rays of dawn light streamed through the window, he set the shoes on the counter and sized up his work.

He could not decide if he should be pleased or angry with himself, now that he'd recovered from his gold intoxication and could clearly see the results of its influence.

Of this he was certain: Lorcan Reilly had better come to claim the shoes before Master Rafferty left his sickbed, or there'd be the devil to pay—for Tommin had brazenly broken nearly every rule the old man had taught him.

The shoes were nothing short of magnificent.

# Chapter Six

## *Filleann an Coimhthíoch*

## (The Stranger Returns)

Tommin tapped the last wooden peg into place in the sole of Johnny Egan's boot. He set the boot and his hammer on the workbench, stood, and stretched. The days seemed to last much longer without Master Rafferty's jolly comments and funny rituals. But after the old shoemaker had spent a full week lingering in Death's courtyard, the good man was on the mend, thank heaven, and soon things could go back to the way they were before the fever came to Loughgillan.

The door opened, and the wind caught it and slammed it hard against the wall. Startled, Tommin turned to find Lorcan Reilly framed by the doorway. The stocky gentleman wore a coat of red velvet, a waistcoat of Oriental brocade, black breeches, and black brogues with silver buckles.

Silver buckles. Tommin's heart skipped a beat. *Silver.*

"Good day," Lorcan Reilly said in his deep, kingly voice. And then he chuckled. "Has the shoemaker's apprentice never seen a shoe buckle?"

"Sorry," Tommin said. "They're marvelous. I mean . . ."

"That they are. I do have a weakness for silver. The smoothness of it under one's fingertips, how it warms in the palm of the hand, the way it reflects the light."

Tommin swallowed hard. The way the man spoke of silver! A faint itching started in Tommin's tightly clenched left hand.

Lorcan Reilly strode across the room and leaned against the bookcase where Master Rafferty stored dozens of foot-shaped wooden lasts. The gentleman straightened one of the rows, aligning the toes just so. "Now, gold is another thing. Like sunlight forged into metal, so bright, so pure. Do you like gold, lad? Or has it never crossed your young palm?"

Torture, that's what it was. Like pouring whiskey in front of a newly reformed drunkard.

This friendlier version of Lorcan Reilly irked him more than the grumpy-customer version had. He was too charming by half, slick as a buttered eel with his fine manners and poetic phrases. But Tommin wouldn't let the man's charm deceive him; he'd not forgotten Eve's sad eyes and bruised forehead.

He grabbed the linen-wrapped shoes from beneath his workbench and clutched them to his chest. "Your shoes are done, sir," Tommin said in a loud voice tinged with annoyance.

"Excellent! Bring them forth, my fine fellow! And you must call me Lorcan from now on. I insist."

"Lorcan," Tommin said. With a queasy feeling in his gut, he carried the bundled shoes to the counter and set them down with a dull thud. Would Lorcan Reilly accept them—when they were obviously not what Master Rafferty had agreed to make? Lorcan picked them up and uncovered them slowly. *By the saints, the man knows how to torment a person,* Tommin thought.

A wide grin spread across Lorcan's face. "Ah, now that's a sight to savor." He turned the shoes over in his hands, examining every inch of leather, every tiny stitch and tack. "Your man Rafferty made these?"

Tommin's cheeks grew warm. "He started them, but he fell ill, so I finished them. Surely you've heard there's fever in Loughgillan."

"Indeed. Lucky for me, then. No offense to your master, but his apprentice has clearly surpassed him in skill. Has he seen these beauties?"

"No, sir. And I'd rather he didn't. I broke his rules. I'm only allowed to make plain, practical shoes, but I got carried away and . . ." Tommin looked at the floor, feeling convicted.

"Easy, was it? Like breathing?" Lorcan said encouragingly.

Tommin nodded and met Lorcan's gaze. He didn't want to smile, but he couldn't help himself.

"You have a gift," Lorcan continued. "Your talents are being wasted in this place, you know. You could be a wealthy man if you'd move to Dublin or London."

"My granny needs me here," Tommin said. "Perhaps someday, after she's gone, I'd consider leaving."

"I have connections. I could help you. And not just with the shoemaking. I can tell you're a young man of myriad talents, just in need of a little guidance from someone older and wiser. The things I could teach you! Well, you would not believe me if I began to tell you half of them."

Tommin made the mistake of looking down, and the shoe buckles caught his eye again. *Blast.* Now both palms itched, and it was spreading to his wrists. He had to scratch; he couldn't keep himself from doing it for one more second.

Lorcan sat down on Master Rafferty's stool, removed his buckled shoes, and slid his feet into the new pair. "Ah," he said, drawing the syllable out long. "They fit like a second skin. Well done, lad. Well done."

"Thank you, sir." The shame he'd felt for breaking Master Rafferty's rules diminished as pride swelled inside his chest. Why should he have been ashamed? He'd done something good and beautiful; he'd created something that made him happy—and pleased a customer, besides.

"Tommin? Are you there?" the old shoemaker called from the back room.

"One minute, sir. I'm with a customer," Tommin replied.

Lorcan bent and grabbed his buckled shoes from the floor. He stood, still smiling. Grinning like he knew the best secret in the world, or like a boy who'd just gotten away with something utterly delightful and forbidden. "Well, I'll leave you to your chores. Think about what I said, won't you? Try to imagine the possibilities outside this dusty room." He took a card from one of his coat pockets and pressed it into Tommin's hand. "My address, should you need to call upon me for anything." He laid a hand on Tommin's shoulder and looked him straight in the eye. "Anything. Anytime. Do you understand me?"

Tommin nodded. A strange shiver ran through him—not altogether unpleasant yet a bit disquieting. He closed his eyes for a moment, trying to calm his racing heart and somehow get control of the insufferable itching.

And for the first time in ages, he thought of his mother. He pictured her walking from shadow to shadow beneath tall trees. Strange to picture such a thing out of the blue . . .

"Tommin? Could you bring me some water, lad? I'm dry as Saint Peter's heel bone," Master Rafferty called.

The shoemaker's apprentice opened his eyes and started to bid Lorcan Reilly farewell, but the man was already gone.

# Chapter Seven

## *Beoir, Uibheacha, agus an Turgnamh*

## (Beer, Eggs, and an Experiment)

The moon hung directly above Eve's tent. She could hear her uncle before he appeared at the crest of the hill: sometimes swearing at the steep terrain, sometimes singing snatches of songs, sometimes laughing to himself. Eve wanted to laugh, too, for Lorcan Reilly was drunk. And this was a rare bit of good fortune for her.

If this bout of intoxication proceeded like most of the others, her uncle would be passed out by the fire within ten minutes of his return. And then she'd try out the idea she'd been mulling over since the last time he'd stumbled into camp with his belly sloshing.

"Eve!" Lorcan bellowed as he approached. "You freckled frog of a girl. Cook me an egg. Two eggs! Not burned, or I'll give you the back of my hand, so I will."

She nodded, smiling sweetly as she could. Best case: he'd fall asleep before the eggs were done and she'd eat them (her mouth watered at the thought, since he never fed her enough). Worst case: he'd gobble down the eggs, smack her for not cooking them properly, sing another song or two, and then fade into sleep within a few hours.

Her stomach grumbled. Stars above, she wanted those eggs—but not more than she wanted him asleep.

"Be quick about it now!" Lorcan said, reaching into his waistcoat pocket and pulling out the little brown bat he kept there during daylight hours. He tossed the creature skyward, and it unfurled its wings with an angry squeak before beginning its hunt for insects.

Eve hurried to Lorcan's wagon and grabbed the iron skillet from a crate, two eggs from a basket, and a lump of butter from a cracked china bowl. All the while, Lorcan sang and talked to the moon.

With her back to him, Eve set the pan over the fire and dropped the butter into it. She watched it melt into a dark pool and breathed in its comforting aroma. She cracked open the eggs. Her stomach growled like an angry dog, and Lorcan stopped reciting his ode to lecture her on dietary frugality, his words slurring and stumbling over one another.

And then, *silence*—except for the hissing and popping of eggs frying in butter. Eve looked over her shoulder and saw Lorcan Reilly passed out, flat on his back on a patch of grass. The bat swooped low, skimming the air a few inches above his body, chittering as if it shared her joy.

While the bat continued its antics, Eve ate straight from the pan. The hot yolk ran down her chin, burning like the devil, but the richness of forbidden food made up for the pain. *May all hens be blessed,* she thought as she scraped up the last crisp brown morsel.

She set the pan in the grass and wiped her mouth with her sleeve. It was time to try her idea.

Lorcan snored as she grabbed hold of his ankles and pulled him toward the boundary of the camp. He weighed more than she'd imagined he would. Soon she was sweating and grunting like a sailor loading a ship. Just a few more feet . . .

Now, the tricky part. Since she couldn't step onto or past the line without consequences, she'd have to maneuver him another way. She tugged and rolled him to where she imagined the invisible boundary was, and then she gave him one last shove.

There. She'd made a bridge out of him. If her plan worked, she could walk over him without getting hurt, since no part of *her* body would come into contact with the enchanted ground.

*No time like the present,* Eve thought as she set foot on Lorcan's finely clad leg. She scrambled along the length of him like a nimble deer navigating a fallen log. One foot on his knee, then on his thigh, belly, chest, shoulder—and with a hop, she was free.

With a shout of celebration, she took off running.

A few minutes later and halfway over the hill, she realized she ought to have planned better.

She'd brought nothing with her: neither money, food, nor shawl. She should have at least thought to bring her uncle's pet bat along—although she suspected Lorcan had bound the wee thing to himself with magic she could not undo. Anyway, she was sorry she hadn't tried; the bat was the closest thing she'd had to a friendly companion. But escaping had been her only thought, with no consideration of anything else. At least for now her stomach was full, her body warmed by running.

Arriving at the edge of town, she stopped to catch her breath beside an empty, thatchless cottage. She twisted the gold ring she wore on her pointer finger, as she always did when perplexed. Was this the way Lorcan had taken her when they'd visited the shoemaker's shop? As usual, her memory was hazy. Well, it was a small enough place. She'd move through the lanes quickly, find the main road out, and perhaps beg a ride from someone toward a bigger city, somewhere Lorcan would have a harder time finding her if—*when*—he came looking for her. Rounding a corner, she almost trampled a huge tomcat. It hissed its displeasure and ran off into the shadows. And then she looked up and saw the shoe-shaped sign above the door. This was the place Lorcan had brought her, she was sure of it.

Here was her chance, then, to warn Tommin, set before her as if by fate. Would she ever be able to forgive herself if she didn't take a few minutes to try—after he'd been so kind to her?

She peered into the window and saw only the dark shapes of workbenches and stools. She knocked, but no one answered.

She knocked again, harder. Her knuckles would surely be bruised purple come morning. But still no one answered the door. Well, she'd tried her best. She couldn't wait any longer. She wished Tommin all the luck in the world, but she had to go before her own luck ran out.

"Hey!" a man's voice broke through the heavy silence. "You're that fancy fellow's lass, aren't you? The one with the red coat, thinks he's so much better than the likes of us common folk? All la-di-da and 'fetch me another pint' and waving his thorny stick about." He approached quickly, with purpose, a broad man with a head like a melon, dirty breeches, and a sweat-stained shirt. Even bathed in the blessing of the moon's fair light, the man's appearance was vulgar and menacing.

Eve's body tensed as she looked for the best way to escape. The lane was narrow, and at its end stood a high stone wall. She was trapped.

"Ah, and I'd wager you think *you're* too good to talk to me, too." He came closer. "Well, I'll show you who's not good enough." His fat hands grabbed her at the waist and pulled her close. "There now," he said. "Just a little kiss and we'll be friends, eh?"

With all her strength, she stomped on the man's foot. He gasped with surprise but didn't loosen his grip on her waist. He shoved her hard, pressing her back into the wall of the shoemaker's house.

"So it's a wild cat you are." He laughed in her face and moved closer, smashing his moist mouth against hers.

She bit his lip hard, so hard she felt her teeth cut through his flesh and tasted his blood. He swore, slapped her face, and stumbled backward.

"Hey!" a young man's voice shouted from nearby. "Brendan Mulroney, are you bothering that girl?"

Cheek stinging, Eve dodged her attacker and began to run. As she ran past the young man, she recognized him as Tommin, but after what she'd just been through, she wasn't about to stop until she'd left this town far behind. She turned down an alley and then crossed a lane, lost among the maze of houses and shops, dogged by the sound of footfalls not far behind her.

"Wait!" Tommin shouted. "You're going the wrong way if you want to get out of Loughgillan."

Eve stopped and turned to face him. She pointed to an alley a few yards away.

"Not that way, either," Tommin said as he approached. He pointed to a wooden bench outside a one-windowed dwelling. "Come on. Let's sit over there and rest a minute. You're well out of danger now."

*If only I were,* Eve thought. *And if only you were, as well.* Because of his kind voice, and because her legs ached now that she stood still, she gave in to his request. But there was no way on earth she'd let down her guard completely; perched on the edge of the seat, she remained ready to run.

Tommin sat beside her and shimmied out of his jacket. He wrapped it about her shoulders. "Bit of a chill in the air once you stop running," he said, adding sheepishly, "He didn't hurt you, did he? Mulroney?"

She shook her head. The jacket and Tommin's kindness comforted her, taking the edge off the shock of the assault and her fear of Lorcan discovering her. She almost felt safe with Tommin. She could not recall the last time she'd felt safe.

"What are you doing out at such an hour? Is your uncle ill?"

She shook her head again. She pointed to herself and then made running motions with her fingers on her palm.

"You've run away from him, then?" Understanding dawned on his face. "*And* you can't speak. Well, that's another tack in the heel, isn't it?"

She nodded, although his turn of phrase puzzled her. Perhaps it was a shoemaker's saying. It didn't matter. What mattered was the concern etched on his brow, the way his clasped hands rested in his lap.

"It's good you've left him. Very good. But where will you go?"

She shrugged.

"Look," he said, "it's only an hour or two till dawn. Saints, you didn't bring a single thing with you, did you? Not even a bit of food or a blanket! Come back to my granny's, and we'll see what we can do to help you. It isn't far."

Eve wanted to go with him so badly that she felt the longing in the depths of her belly. She imagined his grandmother embracing her, heaping porridge into a bowl for her, wrapping her in soft shawls and sweet words. It would be heaven on earth.

Tommin stood and offered his hand. "Come on, then," he said. She looked up into his earnest face, and she had to shake her head in refusal. She had to run. She couldn't put this good-hearted boy and his old granny in danger by biding under their roof. When clever old Uncle Lorcan found her there, he'd surely murder them all.

"You won't make it far in the state you're in. Please let me help. We won't keep you long, I promise."

Eve reached out and put her hand in his. Gently, he pulled her to her feet. He led her down the lane, smiling faintly. "I'm glad I couldn't sleep and decided to go early to work," Tommin said. "Master Rafferty would say it was your guardian angel who woke me up and sent me. Do you reckon that's what happened, Eve?"

*I'm sorry, Tommin,* Eve thought as she shrugged out of his jacket and took off running.

"Eve!" he called after her. She ran faster. Past shops and cottages and chickens, past empty market stalls and sheds full of cows or goats, through a graveyard and someone's freshly manured garden. In the distance, the setting moon lit the stone bridge that led out of town. She urged her legs to carry her faster than they'd ever done in her life.

She tripped over something—a root or a rock?—and fell flat, all the air forced from her lungs by the hard earth.

"Gladys here has a few *more* things to say to you about your running off in the night, Niece," she heard Lorcan Reilly say as she lifted her head to meet his gaze.

How had he . . . ? More of his magic, probably. Or perhaps he hadn't been as drunk as she'd thought.

A wicked grin spread across Lorcan's face as he raised his stick above her body. Eve closed her eyes as he and Gladys delivered a dozen swift whacks to her back. The next thing she felt was her scalp burning as Lorcan yanked her to her feet and pulled her along by the hair. Bent double, she stumbled, simmering with anger toward herself for her failure and toward Lorcan because . . . well, because of how he *always* was.

"You'll not try that again," her uncle said as an unpleasant tingling spread throughout her body, some sort of enchantment that made her limbs weaken and her pulse slow. "By gold, the trouble you put me through—when you ought to be thankful for the future I've given you! Someday, child. Someday, you'll see."

As much as Eve wanted to fight back, she knew it would prove futile. Instead, she did her best to keep up as he dragged her through Loughgillan's empty streets and back into the hills.

Her day would come.

*Her* someday, and not whatever someday Lorcan Reilly had planned.

# Chapter Eight

## *An Doras gan Ghlas*

## (The Unlocked Door)

The day began as any other. Tommin splashed his face with cool water from the basin, dressed quickly, and ate breakfast with Granny (the usual thick porridge, topped with a dab of honey and a splash of milk). He offered up a prayer of thanks that he and Granny had escaped the fever, and that Master Rafferty was on the mend. He was grateful, truly grateful.

And after a week and a half of playing nursemaid to his master and keeping up with shop business, he was tired.

Perhaps he could rest on Sunday afternoon. A long nap beside the lake would do wonders for him. If he could get by for just two more days . . .

He kissed Granny good-bye and headed out. Instead of taking his usual route, he turned left at the Sullivans' cottage and shimmied through the passage between the candlemaker's shop and the tailor's house. The shortcut led to the tannery, where he needed to pick up Master Rafferty's order for cowhide.

While he walked, Tommin let his weary mind wander. And it wandered to Eve. Had she made it to safety? Would she find a life of joy away from her nasty uncle? Strange as it was after knowing her such a short time, he thought he might miss her a little.

When the gold lust came, it hit him hard, like an unexpected left hook to the nose followed by a punch in the gut. The world swayed before his eyes as he stopped to lean against the churchyard's stone wall. He recognized the sweet scent of gold in his nostrils and turned his head toward it. It was close, the treasure that beckoned him. If he'd had half his usual strength, he might have run away from it. But saints above, he was tired, and he was treasure hungry—and the gold smelled like a feast fit for King Midas.

With awkward steps, he followed the tantalizing smell to the constable's daughter's house at the edge of the main square. The nicest, newest house in town, for the girl had married the son of wealthy Dublin merchants. Tommin had never dared set foot inside before, fearing the many bright temptations he imagined perched on shelves and mantelpieces, arrayed in jewelry boxes and silk-lined coffers. Also, he'd never been invited to call. A fact that would not stand in his way now.

He looked about to make sure no one was watching and then skirted the perimeter of the house, making his way to the back door. There he paused and listened, but heard not a sound coming from within. Perhaps the family had fled Loughgillan at the onset of the fever, as a few other families had done. Wouldn't that be a grand stroke of luck for a thief like himself? He trembled with longing as he imagined exploring every luxurious room, stuffing every pocket with coins and necklaces, bejeweled figurines and heirloom brooches.

The door creaked softly when he opened it. The fact that it wasn't locked didn't distress him; Loughgillan folk were a trusting, law-abiding lot for the most part. His own thefts, when he'd heard them mentioned, weren't even blamed on thievery. It was always *Silly me, I must have dropped a coin in the street* or *I can't remember where I put my purse when I came home from the market.* Tommin owed much to the sweet naïveté of his neighbors.

Desire drove him quickly through the tidy kitchen and into a small parlor bedecked with china shepherdesses, plump-cushioned sofas, and gaudy wallpaper. The strong aroma of good gold beckoned him onward, through a dining room (hung with two crystal chandeliers as big as Granny's table), into a foyer, and up a well-polished set of oak stairs.

He passed by several doors, ignoring lesser temptations of silver and jewels. And then he thrust open the door where he knew he'd find his heart's desire: thick gold coins. He walked straight to a bureau, opened a drawer, and pulled out a wooden chest. The coins inside rattled as he clutched the treasure to his breast, and what a lovely song that was! Even through the wood and his layers of clothing, the gold affected him. Elation and strength surged through his body. Still, he wanted more: to feel the glorious metal with his hands, to worship it with his eyes—so he carried the chest to the velvet-draped bed. He knelt on the floor and opened the lid with all the care one might give a holy relic.

He reached inside and grabbed a fistful of coins.

*Heaven could not be better than two handfuls of gold,* Tommin thought. There could be no greater ecstasy, no higher pleasure than this. Laughter erupted from his mouth.

"Don't move," a man's voice said from behind him. "If you dare move so much as an inch, I'll shoot you dead."

# Chapter Nine

## *An Costas Óir*

## (The Cost of Gold)

When the little square of window above him darkened, Tommin wondered a great many things, for he had plenty of time for it now. Shackled to a heavy dresser in the back room of the constable's house (Loughgillan's infrequently used version of a jail cell), there was little else he could do.

He wondered if Granny had heard the news of his botched burglary yet, or if she was sitting in her chair, thinking he'd stayed late at work to finish an order. He wondered what she'd cooked for his dinner and if she needed more water lugged from the well.

He wondered what Master Rafferty had made of his absence from the shop, and if he'd have a job once he got out. *If* he got out.

With his wrists chained, he could not scratch his excruciatingly itchy hands. Nor could he wipe the beads of cold sweat from his forehead. Having the gold wrenched from his grasp had replaced his euphoria with a pounding headache, teeth-rattling chills, and a fierce craving to steal again.

The night wore on slowly. Tears trickled from the corners of his eyes as the needle-sharp, burning itch spread from his hands to his shoulders. Tentacles of fiery pain licked his collarbone. His tongue was dry as old leather.

"Boy." A deep whisper came in through the window. "Are you living?"

"Lorcan?"

"Him and no other. I've come to make a deal with you."

Tommin might have laughed had he not been so miserable. "I'm afraid I'm not able to offer much in the way of deals. I'm chained up here, in case you didn't know."

"Chains are little hindrance to me. Listen carefully now. I'm going to liberate you from this place. In return, you'll agree to go on a journey with me and do exactly as I say for a time. You see, I know what your trouble is, and I know the medicine for it."

Tommin gasped. "Medicine?"

"Yes, lad. So, what do you say?"

"My granny. Who will look after her? I can't just leave her and go off . . ."

"You've already done as much! Do you think you'll go free from here? I heard the constable's son-in-law say he'd use his influence to have you put in prison in Dublin for your crimes. Your granny won't be seeing the likes of you anytime soon, lad, whether you go with me or to prison."

Tommin's heart sank, for he knew the fellow spoke the truth. Granny might well be dead and buried before he regained his freedom. "Could I send word to her, then? That I'm safe, and that I'll send for her as soon as I can."

"If you agree to obey me without stint for the next few months, I'll make sure someone looks after your grandmother. So, what is it to be, lad? Rotting away in a Dublin prison or spending a season with me?"

"Get me out," Tommin said. "I'll do whatever you ask if you can help me stop this blasted itching."

Lorcan didn't answer, but thirty seconds later, he opened the door and strode to Tommin's side. Lorcan's teeth glinted in the dimness as he smiled. He knelt beside Tommin, whispered a string of unfamiliar words, and blew his hot breath on the shackle binding Tommin's right hand. The metal heated about Tommin's wrist and the cuff sprang open. Quickly, Lorcan repeated the ritual and freed Tommin's other hand.

"Look at the state of you," Lorcan said as he hauled Tommin to his feet. "You'd have been dead within two days had I left you here."

Tommin's knees buckled, but Lorcan held him upright. "I don't think my legs will carry me," he said. He scratched both his arms at once—which only made the itching worse.

"Hush. Once we're outside, we'll find a nip of something to fortify you for the rest of our journey. Now, one foot in front of the other. There's a good lad."

As the sky blushed at dawn's approach, they moved through the deserted lanes, Tommin leaning heavily on Lorcan. His body ached, and his vision shifted in and out of focus. Somewhere close, a rooster crowed. The sound ricocheted inside his head as if to forecast betrayal after betrayal.

"There now," Lorcan said, stopping and inhaling deeply. "You smell that silver, Tommin?"

"I do, sir." Perhaps he shouldn't have admitted such a thing, but didn't the fellow seem to know already?

"Just the remedy for what ails you. Now you see how we understand one another? So, let's tippytoe in and get your wee helping, and we'll be ready to face the day like the fine folk we are."

A few minutes later, Lorcan stood watch just inside the door of a shabby one-roomed house as Tommin raided a tin Big Joey Flynn had hidden behind a pitcher on a shelf—with Big Joey and his wife sleeping not ten feet away. This was possibly the stupidest thing he'd ever done, especially since he was almost too weak to walk. If Big Joey were to awaken, he'd have Tommin in a headlock quicker than he could say "mercy." Big Joey could crack Tommin's neck like a twig.

Big Joey snored. Tommin claimed two silver coins, and elation and strength threaded their way from his fingertips to his toenails. By the time he followed Lorcan back outside, he was good as new. Better than new.

"Not half-bad for a beginner," Lorcan said. He patted Tommin on the back.

For a fleeting moment, Tommin wondered what Lorcan meant by "beginner." But the thought flitted away. He didn't care now, not while the world wore such incredibly bright colors. Not while his blood sang the song of the stars inside his veins. He was happy just to walk on the dew-dampened grass, to listen to the birds' good-morning symphonies, to feel the breeze caress his unitchy skin. Happy to be a free man again.

Lorcan said nothing as they hastened out of town and into the hills. He swung his thorny walking stick and took long, confident steps like a fine gentleman out for a stroll.

At the edge of the forbidden forest, Tommin stopped. The trees loomed like giant sentries. Every warning he'd heard from his cradle days till now echoed inside him, urging him to turn away from the place. Here was the line, according to the good shoemaker Rafferty, the border that hemmed in Loughgillan's good fortune, secured by decades of the Rafferty family's offerings and rituals. Beyond this place, anything could happen.

Any bad thing.

Tommin pointed. "Do you truly mean to go in there?"

Lorcan stopped and faced him. "Yes. You've been there before and lived."

"I have?" Tommin could remember nothing of the sort, but even in the afterglow of his post-theft high spirits, he hesitated to argue with Lorcan. The fellow had freed him from his shackles using magic; what spell might he use if Tommin crossed him?

"Relax, lad. Everything will make sense soon enough," Lorcan said, slipping an arm around Tommin's shoulders. "Besides, you promised to do as I say."

Tommin saw Eve approaching then, taking slow steps as if in pain. The poor girl hadn't gotten away from her uncle after all. As she drew closer, he noted (with his still-sharpened senses) a bruise on her cheek (the color of a ripe plum) and a rip in her skirt (lightning shaped). Were these wages she'd earned for sinning against Lorcan Reilly?

"My niece, Eve, is a clumsy girl," Lorcan said as if reading Tommin's mind. "And none too clever. Poor lass can't speak a word."

Eve met Tommin's gaze for the briefest of moments, her eyes full of despair. Her short coppery hair caught the sunlight. Her freckles were red-brown stars on the pale sky of her face. He knew this flight of poetical thoughts sprang from the silver's influence, but it didn't keep him from enjoying them.

Eve shook her head like Granny often did, in that "poor Tommin" sort of way. And then she lifted a pair of heavy-looking packs and turned to follow her uncle into the forest. Tommin filed behind them onto the narrow path that began abruptly between two oaks.

Although the lush trees, ferns, mushrooms, and patches of moss dazzled Tommin with their colors and aromas, he felt it was wrong to be there—and especially wrong to be following Lorcan there. Slowly, his misgivings multiplied. The forest was forbidden for a reason. Lorcan Reilly knew *actual* magic, and judging from how he treated his own flesh and blood, he was not of a benevolent nature. If only he'd memorized some of Master Rafferty's protective charms, or had armed himself with a pocketful of salt and iron filings, or a jar of holy water . . .

Tommin looked over his shoulder. He saw no sign of where they'd entered the forest, nothing but tree after tree. Tall trees, ancient trees, trees that gave the impression they knew something.

With all his heart, he wished he'd not promised to follow and obey Lorcan Reilly.

A bird shrieked above him. At least he hoped it was a bird. He refused to consider what else it might have been. Instead of looking up and possibly seeing some terrible winged monster, he focused on the back hem of Eve's skirt, concentrating on how it brushed over moss and twigs as she walked, like a cloud gently passing over a mountain. Nevertheless, fear was beginning to overtake his euphoria.

"Keep up, lad," Lorcan said sharply. "We've no time to waste admiring the scenery. Gah, I'd forgotten how ridiculously drunk a wee bit of coinage makes you Newlings. Like cows staring at daisies."

"Newlings?" Tommin said as a pine branch slapped him in the chest.

Lorcan turned his head to glower at Tommin. "Never mind that for now. Just keep walking."

The path bore to the left, then to the right. Up a steep, pebbly hill and then across a trickling stream. To the right, to the left. With every step, Tommin grew more sober. With every step, he fought the urge to run back the way they'd come.

When Eve stopped abruptly, Tommin looked up. Before him stood a tree that might have been as old as time itself. Its silver-gray branches spread wide in graceful curves, ending in heart-shaped leaves so green that they defied greenness. A breeze rustled its highest branches and coaxed a sweet moan from the barely swaying trunk. This tree was the most beautiful tree he'd ever seen. Who could bear to look upon anything more beautiful?

Eve sat down among the ferns and sobbed, and although Tommin clenched his fists and bit his lip in an attempt to ward off his own tears, he fell to his knees and wept like a little child.

# Chapter Ten

## Siúl sa Choill

## (A Walk in the Wood)

"Get a hold of yourself now, lad," Lorcan said, squeezing Tommin's shoulder hard enough to make him flinch. "And you, girl. Get up. Change your clothes and get ready to go among the People."

Scowling and wiping her tears on the back of her hand, Eve grabbed one of the bags and disappeared behind the massive trunk of the tree.

Tommin dragged a sleeve over his wet cheeks and stood up on wobbly legs. He started to ask where they were going and what people they'd be visiting, but Lorcan put a finger to his lips.

"Hush. Not another word until I say so," Lorcan said. "Now, come this way and I'll show you a wonder." He led Tommin in the opposite direction from where Eve had gone, forced to lift his feet in a strange dance in order to navigate the thick, trailing roots. Stopping, he pointed to a place where the roots encircled a patch of verdant moss to form a perfect circle. "Just there. That's the very place you were born, Tommin Kelly."

"I was born by the lake," Tommin said. "Not here. My mam told me so, the summer before she died. She showed me the place, under a willow tree on the eastern shore."

Lorcan's expression darkened. "Do not dare to call me a liar, Tommin Kelly. You were born here, and I caught you myself. So we're bound. You to me and me to you, for all time." He stood face-to-face with Tommin and placed his hands on his shoulders. "It's time you knew the truth. It's time for you to become all you were destined to be. You, lad, are my own gold-son."

"Godson?" Tommin's stomach churned, and cold sweat formed on his brow. "Granny never said—"

"*Gold*-son. Chosen and sealed for all time. My own progeny and pride."

Lorcan Reilly was nothing but a madman speaking nonsense. Of course he was. Or perhaps this was just a bad dream. The worst dream ever.

But when Tommin's knees gave way and Lorcan caught him under the arms, his touch felt all too solid and certain to be a thing of dreams.

"Come on, my lad," Lorcan said, moving to Tommin's side and coaxing him to walk away from the huge tree. "There's a stump just over here for you to rest on while you get your bearings."

For a while, Tommin sat on the stump. He wanted to try to make sense of things, to get a grip on what was real and what was imagined, but his mind had gone numb and dizzy at the same time.

Eve returned and stood a few feet away from Lorcan. Dressed in tan breeches, a green coat, and a dark-gray flat cap, she made a convincing boy. She stared at her shoes as if to avoid meeting Tommin's gaze. The detached look on her face worried him more than anything. Would he end up like that? Resigned to a life ruled by a violent lunatic? He had to get away. This was all wrong. He stood, and quick as lightning, Lorcan blocked his path and gripped his upper arms.

"Now, I remind you that you did swear to obey me. So, when I release your arms, you will walk until you're standing close enough to kiss the Nameless Tree, and then wait for me. Walk slow and steady, mind. And keep your eyes on that knot six feet up the trunk. And if you're thinking of asking why, don't. You'll know soon enough."

Tommin nodded. Walking to the tree meant putting distance between himself and Lorcan, which seemed like a grand idea. Once he got to the tree, perhaps he'd take off running. He might find his way out of the forest, or he might end up as supper for wolves. He'd made so many bad choices; why not make another? He almost laughed at his own dark humor.

"Go," Lorcan said. "Now!"

The shrieking bird cried out again as Tommin took his first step toward the tree. The thick moss sprang beneath his feet. The scent of soggy leaf litter and rotting wood crept up his nostrils. The dampness in the air chilled his skin.

Were those eyes peering at him from the underbrush?

Again, the bird shrieked. Again, Tommin thought of Master Rafferty and wished for salt and charms. Anything to protect him in this not-right place. Would he ever see the shoemaker again? Yes, he thought. Of course he would. He hadn't promised to stay with Lorcan *forever*. Soon, he'd sit with Granny by the fire once more, a hundred times more.

He'd make plain shoes as he was taught. He'd never steal again. He'd be good. Perfect.

"Don't dawdle," Lorcan said. "Eyes straight ahead."

Tommin focused on the knot. He was almost there. A few more steps . . .

The ground disappeared from under him, and he fell. His arms beat the air, grabbing wildly for anything to stop his fall. Down and down he plummeted, past layers of earth and roots and fat beetles that clicked as if to mock his desperate flailing.

"That's the way of it!" Tommin heard Lorcan call from far above. "We all must fall before we rise!"

Tommin hit the ground hard, and everything went black.

# Chapter Eleven

## *An Domhan Thíos*

## (The World Below)

"Granny," Tommin said, eyes shut. He couldn't quite muster the energy to open them. Every bone and muscle in his body throbbed and burned. He must have finally fallen victim to the fever. He hoped Granny wouldn't catch it from him.

"I'm not your granny," a young boy's voice said.

Tommin opened his eyes and found himself abed in a candlelit room with stone walls and an earthen ceiling. A boy no older than ten stood beside him, his mouth pursed like a grumpy old man's and his sky-blue eyes narrowed with disapproval. A thatch of ginger hair failed to cover his saucerlike ears.

"Sit up, will you," the boy said, jiggling the wooden tray he held and rattling the dishes. "Do you think I have all day to stand here with the likes of you?"

"Sorry." Tommin shimmied into a sitting position. His head pounded like a dozen bodhran drums.

The boy shoved the tray onto Tommin's lap. "Your breakfast, Your Majesty," he said, rolling his eyes. "Mushroom bread toast, fried mushrooms, and mushroom tea. It all tastes like dirt, but that's what you get down here in the Faerie Neathlands, unless it's a holiday or you're one of the king's cronies. They eat beef twice a day and drink wine from breakfast till bedtime, or so I hear. The name's Copper, on account of my hair and on account of the Leps like to name folks after stuff like coins and such. Now, eat your food and be quick about it. Master'll be back soon, and then you're done whether you're done or not. And don't think you'll get to sleep in that cozy bed again. It'll be a mat on the floor for you till you're all trained and make the change."

Tommin frowned at the brown and gray meal. Hadn't Master. Rafferty taught him that Faerie food was irresistibly attractive as well as dangerous? Well, he wasn't going to chance eating it, no matter how ugly it was. He lifted the tray and motioned for Copper to take it, but the boy shook his head. Tommin said, "You might as well have it back. I know that if I eat this, I'll have to stay here forever. So, thank you all the same."

Copper laughed. "You're a rare one. That stuff's not magical. See, the Leps are different from the other Faerie types. No magic food, no seducifying humans, no living in flowers and trees. They're not even put off by iron and salt like the other kinds. Proud of being different like that, the Leps are."

"Why should I believe you?" Tommin asked.

"I don't care if you do or you don't," Copper said, lifting his chin proudly. "But I'll tell you this: the master's been known to give beatings to them that wastes food in his house. And that's all I'm saying."

Convinced by the boy's speech and suddenly hungry in spite of the food's appearance, Tommin took a swallow of the scum-coated gray-brown tea. It tasted exactly like it looked. He gagged.

"Oh, come on. Just swallow it down like a big boy," Copper said. "Now, I'm going back to the kitchen to clean up the mess making *your* food caused me. Although you ought to be the one to do the washing up, if you ask me."

"Copper, wait. I need to ask—"

"Oh no you don't!" Copper said, hands on slim hips. "No more questions. I'm not supposed to talk to you, remember? If Master catches me jabbering, he'll give *me* the stick again, and I'm still bruised from the last time."

"But—"

"No. I'm not telling you a thing. Only this. Seeing as you're down here, you must've been chosen and cursed. Next, they'll be teaching you their secrets, and after that, they'll give you this blue, fizzly drink. It's magic; the 'elissker,' it's called. Anyway, they'll give it to you three times, and if you drink all three Cups of it, you're doomed to be one of them forever—or however long the blasted devils live. Always tricking and stealing and then getting innocent people like you involved to keep it going. They can't breed, you see. So they do that thing with the boy babies, touching them before they're baptized and cursing them with Lep enchantments. Then when the boys get old enough and show they're good at thieving and shoemaking, the Leps bring them down here. Like they did with you, right? Me, I'd rather be dead than one of them greedy sots. Not like you've got much choice, anyway. Last one that tried to escape got burned at the stake the hour after he left his master's house. One before that got beat almost dead and then sold to the meanest Troll in the Neathlands. You'd never find the way out before you got caught, not even if you tried for a hundred years. Now don't ask me anything else, because I'm through talking to you. By Croesus, you'll get me tossed to the cats with all your questions and refusing food and all. You're trouble, that's what I think." Copper rushed out of the room and slammed the door behind him.

"What? Come back! What's a 'Lep,' anyway? Copper? You have to tell me that much!" Tommin shouted to no avail. Left alone, he flopped back against the pillows, upsetting the teacup onto the toast and soaking the grayish-brown square with brownish-gray liquid. It didn't matter. He didn't think he could swallow the stuff—not even under the threat of a beating.

He clutched his aching, muddled head. Was any of this real? *Please let me be dreaming,* he thought. *Let me wake up and see Granny and go to work.*

The door opened, and Lorcan Reilly sauntered in, swinging his thorny walking stick. "Good day to you. I see Copper has given you breakfast."

"I want to go home," Tommin said.

"Ha! Not a chance, lad. You're bound to my service, remember? Besides, we haven't even begun to have fun yet." Lorcan smacked the stick against the blanket. Tommin jumped. "Now, a few rules. Firstly, you will obey me as you've sworn, or Gladys here will make you wish you had." He held up the stick and looked at it lovingly. "Gladys is very persuasive. Second, you'll speak to no one unless I give you permission. Third, you'll tell no one that Eve is not a boy. I call her Eevar here, and that's all you need to know on that front."

"But . . ." Tommin could not think of one question that seemed safe.

"Now, you need not look so disturbed. You've been given a gift. A grand destiny. Few are chosen for this life. The gold and silver we'll reap together! Your human mind can't fathom the kind of Bliss I'll lead you into."

At the word "gold," Tommin's palms itched. "Please," he whispered. "I don't want a 'grand destiny.' I just want to stop needing to steal. You said you would give me the remedy."

"And I will! The remedy is this: you shall not be slave to the wealth of the world, but its master. It's all rightly ours, the birthright of our People. To be free of your ridiculous guilt and shame, you must accept who you truly are: a chosen gold-son of the Leprechauns, created to collect and bury what is ours, and to send up the rainbow in rapturous celebration. Trust me, lad, and forget your silly human principles and the short, sorry life you had planned. I offer you riches and pleasures and immortality."

Tommin gripped the blanket with both his cold, sweaty hands. Lorcan Reilly was a *Leprechaun*? That's what the servant boy had meant when he'd spoken of "Leps"? He tried to recall any tales he'd ever heard of Leprechauns.

*Lovers and hoarders of gold. Clever tricksters. Faerie shoemakers.*

"Heaven help me," Tommin muttered, his throat burning with bile.

"Heaven is for humans, not our kind," Lorcan said, smirking. "After you drink your First Cup of Fortune, you'll come around quickly to the right way of thinking. And once you've fully converted, you'll look back and count yourself lucky not to be a common, pitiful son of Adam."

Clenching his eyes shut, Tommin raged and despaired inside. He'd spent years longing to know the truth of why he stole, expecting the knowledge would bring him some comfort. But knowing was far worse than wondering had ever been.

It was far worse knowing that he, Tommin Kelly, had been doomed to become a thieving Leprechaun from the hour of his birth. That he'd never stood a chance against the curse that drove him, and that the remedy Lorcan offered was no remedy at all, only outright surrender to wickedness.

"That's right. You rest," Lorcan said. "A good sleep cures a thousand ills."

Tommin listened to Lorcan's footsteps retreating and the sound of the door slamming.

As the hours dragged by, he kept his eyes shut, but he did not sleep. The whirlwind of thoughts and questions tearing through his mind kept him more wide awake than he'd ever been in his life.

Copper had made escaping sound impossible—but what if, by some great miracle, Tommin did escape and return home? Prison, likely—but whether locked up or free, had he any prospect of leading a good, honorable life? Wouldn't he be forced to live as he had been, secretly lying and stealing to satisfy the curse's demands? And when his body's need surpassed his ability to provide, what then?

He didn't know much about his problem, but he knew it would be the death of him one way or another.

He ought to have confessed to Master Rafferty years ago and called upon the man's expert knowledge on curses and Faeries and all. If anyone might have known how to help him . . .

Perhaps he still could, if Tommin could get back to the shop.

Bolstered by hope, he sprang out of bed and tried the door. The doorknob stung his hand like a fistful of nettles. "Blast," Tommin said. "Blasted magic. Blasted Leprechauns."

He moved quickly from one end of the room to the other, running his fingers along the walls in search of hidden windows or doors, or some weakness through which he might escape, but it was no use. This was it, then. Until he figured out another plan, he had no choice but to obey the Leprechaun as he'd promised.

A few hours later, the door flew open, and Copper stepped in. He flung a pile of clothes onto Tommin's lap. "Get up and dress yourself, lazybones. Master's taking you and the other one for your schooling. He's been waving old Gladys about like mad this morning, so unless you fancy your backside tanned, you'd better hurry."

Tommin stood. "Wait," he said as Copper started to leave.

"You know I'm not allowed to be talking with you," Copper said. He turned and glared.

"Do you know a way out of this place?"

Copper's eyes widened. "Are you daft? Were you not listening before when I told you what happens to them that tries to run off? About the Trolls and stake burning and all? Well, I'll remind you, then. If the Leps don't catch you and kill you dead, their blasted Faerie-blooded cats will. And if you get past the cats, you'll likely end up in the Trolls' lands or the bad Faeries' country. Dead is what you'll end up. Dead before you have time to change your mind and run back here all sorry! Dead or *wishing* you were!"

"Cats?"

"Just shut your gob," Copper said, throwing his hands up in exasperation. "I'm through talking with you. You'll get us both sent off to the Trolls." The boy's cheeks were just-slapped red. "Nothing but trouble, that's what you are." He turned to the door again.

"Wait," Tommin begged. "Please."

Copper heaved a great sigh and put his hands on his hips. "Your Majesty?"

"What should I do, then?"

"Do I look like a fount of wisdom to you? Would I have been a slave here for a hundred years if I knew how to get free? Everybody looks out for themselves hereabouts, and so will you. There's nothing else for it." Copper's blue eyes welled with tears, which surprised Tommin not a little.

"I'll help you if I can." Tommin's heart ached for the boy. *Imagine,* he thought, *a hundred years underground with a cruel master and no hope of escape.*

Copper sniffed and then set his jaw. "Don't waste your breath with such blabber. You just act obedient, keep yourself alive, and try not to drink the blue stuff if you can help it. And maybe someday you'll be allowed to go Above again."

"Copper!" Lorcan shouted from the next room. "Come here at once!"

The boy scrambled out, slamming the door behind him.

*Act obedient.* Tommin had planned to do as much before the boy's speech. To start with, he dressed in the linen shirt and breeches Copper had left for him, replicas of what Eve had put on before he'd fallen down the hole. Perhaps the clothes were a uniform of sorts; at least they were clean and comfortable.

Somewhere outside the house, a deep bell sounded.

"Tommin!" Lorcan called. "Hurry or Gladys will make you wish you had!"

"Coming." He tucked in his shirt and prepared to face whatever the day held. He resolved to earn the Leprechauns' trust and to learn everything he could so he'd be able to outsmart them and escape. If all went well, before long, he and Copper would be sitting with Granny at her kitchen table, breaking *real* bread and telling tales. Of course, there was the problem of his burglary and jailbreak . . . Well, he'd cross that bridge when he came to it.

He grabbed the doorknob, but it didn't sting him as before. Instead, a faint itching began in his palm. A bad omen, that was. How long could he put off stealing? Was there anything *to* steal in the land of the Leprechauns, or did they bury their crocks of gold elsewhere?

"Tommin!" Lorcan scolded. "Don't stand there idling." He grabbed Tommin by the collar and pulled him out of the bedroom and through an orderly candlelit kitchen. When they reached the kitchen door, there stood Eve, as serious as a Sunday sermon. Lorcan released Tommin's collar and took Gladys the stick down from a hook. "The pair of you had better not bring me shame today," Lorcan said. "You may find Gladys unpleasant, but what she offers is the kiss of an angel compared to what you'll get if you cause me a speck of trouble."

"Yes, sir," Tommin said. As usual, Eve said nothing. She simply nodded and avoided Tommin's gaze.

"This way, my Newlings," Lorcan said, stepping out into the dim street and turning left. "Your fortune and my fame await."

# Chapter Twelve

## *Ceachtanna do Leipreacháin*

## (Lessons for Leprechauns)

Although Tommin was a few inches taller than Lorcan, he struggled to keep up with the Leprechaun's swift stride. Eve trailed behind them, her footsteps silent on the pebbled street.

At first glance, the underground town imitated the world above: houses and shops made of bricks or stone, with regular windows and doors—some even roofed with slate shingles. But Loughgillan's streets were never this eerily silent. And in spite of an abundance of lampposts and hanging lanterns, this place was cloaked in heavy shadows and gloom. Worst of all, there was no sky—only a jagged, high ceiling of dark rock, with roots dangling down through cracks, dripping slowly and endlessly.

As they walked, Tommin noticed gardens of pale mushrooms and ghostly-looking fungi growing in rock-edged beds and window boxes. With a pang of homesickness, he remembered Granny's window boxes—filled to overflowing with bright flowers and leafy herbs, the envy of her neighbors. He offered up a prayer for her health and comfort, although he doubted his prayers would pass through the barrier of soil and stone above his head.

Scratching his palm, Tommin inhaled the cool, damp air. Mingled with the smell of mildew and mud was the unmistakable aroma of gold.

He glanced over his shoulder and spotted the source: the thin gold band on Eve's finger. The ring glinted in the lantern light teasingly. His gut twisted with longing.

Saints above, he wanted that ring.

A smack to the back of the head made Tommin cry out. One of Gladys's thorns caught in his hair. Lorcan yanked the stick, and Tommin winced as a clump of his hair left his scalp.

"I'm thinking it's the ring and not my *nephew*, *Eevar*, you're smitten with," Lorcan said. "Neither one will be yours, regardless." He dug in his waistcoat pocket and removed what looked like a pocket watch. He pressed a button, and it sprang open. Lorcan held it out to Tommin. Inside the watchcase, a dozen little golden pills sparkled. "Go on, lad. Take one," Lorcan said. "Hold it under your tongue till it melts. It will tide you over for now."

Eager to end his cravings, Tommin did as he was told. The pill was both sweet and sour, like the wild berries that grew beside the lake. As it dissolved, warmth and happiness spread throughout his body.

"I've never seen a Newling so besotted before the First Cup," Lorcan said with amusement. "It's a portent of greatness to come. I've had five other gold-sons before you two, but they never amounted to much. Ordinary Leprechauns they are, keeping their quotas and abiding by our laws. But you, Tommin. You'll be a prince among the People. Mark my words."

Exhilarated by the pill, Tommin grinned. His gold-strengthened eyes caught sight of other eyes peering at him from the shadows and the dark spaces between buildings. They glowed amber, green, and gold. He pointed to one set. "Lorcan?"

"The *Cait Sidhe*. Faerie cats," Lorcan said. "Wild and wily they are. The king's clowder. Bred to keep the rats in check. Keep your distance if you want to keep your fingers. Respect the beasts if you don't want to face the king's wrath."

A fat orange tabby with long, pointed ears sauntered out of the shadows and sat in a pool of lamplight. It hissed and bared its knifelike teeth. Tommin moved to Lorcan's other side to avoid it, and almost collided with a glowering Leprechaun clad in green velvet and ruffled lace.

"Good fortune to ye," the Leprechaun said to Lorcan, tipping an emerald-studded top hat.

"And a full crock for you before the day's end," Lorcan replied without slowing his pace. After the velvet-clothed fellow ducked into a stone house, Lorcan said, "That's our standard greeting here. Of course, if we meet Above, we never speak to one another at all. You'll learn these things in your manners and morals class, so don't bother pestering me with questions, Tommin Kelly. I smell you thinking."

The fact of the matter was Tommin wasn't thinking much of anything. He was far too busy enjoying the effects of the pill. His bruised bones no longer ached, and by the saints! Didn't everything suddenly look lovely and fascinating?

A trio of sleek black Faerie cats slunk by. Their shiny fur caught and held Tommin's attention. Like midnight lake water, it was. Undulating and resplendent.

He stumbled on a cobblestone, and Lorcan put an arm out to steady him. "By Croesus, lad! Half a pill for you next time!"

The thought of *half* a pill didn't please Tommin. The little thing had been so delicious and invigorating. Like someone had condensed the thrill and satisfaction of an act of thievery into tablet form—without the impending guilt.

"Here we are," Lorcan said, stopping suddenly and pointing with Gladys. A sign hung over the door of the brick building: NEATHGILLAN ACADEMY. Below the letters Tommin recognized were a set of strange, scraggly symbols he assumed said the same in some Leprechaun language.

The door opened, and a man wearing a long black gown stepped out. A black mortarboard sat atop his close-cropped brown hair, and his brown beard came to a point just under his chin. With an inscrutable smile, he spread his arms wide and bowed slightly. "Ah, Lorcan Reilly," he said. "You've brought your Newlings just in time. Sixth and seventh gold-sons, aren't they? Well, leave them to me. Class ends precisely at eighth bell, in case you've forgotten."

"I forget nothing, O'Ferrell, you son of a spendthrift!" Lorcan said gruffly—but then he chuckled and reached out to shake the schoolmaster's hand. "Now go inside with the schoolmaster, Tommin. Eevar will join you in a moment. We have a bit of business to discuss between ourselves."

The schoolmaster put an arm around Tommin's shoulders and guided him into a long room with a podium and blackboard at the front. Five straight rows of crude, slate-topped tables were lit from above by a dozen hanging lamps. The lamps hissed and spewed a noxious gray haze into the air, and although Tommin tried his best to stop himself, he couldn't help coughing.

Most of the seven students turned to gawk at him. Teenage boys with hungry eyes dressed exactly as he was. Two of them looked on the verge of tears; one trembled like a frightened animal. Stolen boys. *Kidnapped boys.* If he hadn't been high as a kite from the gold pill, he would have felt sorry for them.

As it was, he felt nothing but perfectly fine with everything. And a bit dizzy.

"Choose a desk," O'Ferrell said. "Class will begin at the next sounding of the bell. Welcome to the Neathgillan Academy for Leprechaun Newlings."

# Chapter Thirteen

## *An Fháinne Ciúnais*

## (The Ring of Silence)

Just outside the academy door, Lorcan Reilly grabbed Eve's hand roughly enough to make her gasp. "Now, don't fight me and don't start fussing," he warned. "Or else you'll pay dearly later. Understand?"

He glanced about as if to make sure no one was watching. And then he took hold of the thin gold ring she'd never once removed since her mother had given it to her. He swore and yanked, grumbled and pulled until it grated over her knuckle, crushing bone and scraping skin.

Lorcan kissed the ring before dropping it into his pocket.

Inside Eve's throat, something shifted and made a little pop like a soap bubble exploding.

"There now," Lorcan said smugly. "Your voice is returned to you."

She looked at her bare, bleeding finger. She touched her throat. She opened her mouth but found she was too overwhelmed with emotion to speak. Too angry, too dazed by disillusionment, too full of hatred for Lorcan Reilly.

Lorcan flicked a piece of gravel off his shoe with the end of Gladys. "You need not look so alarmed, child. It was just a bit of magic bought from a Trooping Faerie. No permanent damage done. You'll likely find your thoughts a bit clearer now as well, but be sure not to use your mind for mischief."

Light-headed, Eve stretched out her arms to steady herself, to find some balance in a world gone topsy-turvy. It was not the loss of the jewelry that clawed at her heart and weakened her knees, but the loss of its meaning.

Ever since she was a four-year-old child, she had cherished the ring as a memento of a mother whose face she'd all but forgotten. She'd believed the ring was a gift given to her just before her mother breathed her last. The tender scene had played in her mind over and over as she grew up in Lorcan Reilly's care. He'd used the tale as a bedtime story, portraying himself as the hero who had been there to comfort her, the savior who had rescued her from a bleak, parentless state.

The ring had been a shackle, not a treasure.

Suddenly, she remembered Copper's words from the previous night, words she'd forgotten till now. *Lies are the native tongue of the Leprechaun,* Copper had whispered as Eve washed dishes and he dried. *Among the Faerie folk,* he'd said, *there are few tribes who can tell a lie. The Leps are best at it by far—and Master Lorcan has got to be tops among them.*

Eve had dropped a mug into the basin of sudsy water, splashing herself and Copper. She'd eyed Copper disbelievingly.

*Steady now,* Copper had said. *You mean you really didn't know he's not your uncle? That he's a thieving Leprechaun trickster? By gold, he's been using more magic on you than I thought! Got your mind all scrambled up like eggs in a pan, the swine!*

She'd gripped the edge of the counter as if holding on for dear life.

*Well,* Copper had continued. *Also explains why you never seem to remember me when you come back here, even though you've lived in this very house alongside me for most of your life.* Copper had offered her a towel and a sympathetic look. *I would have told you, you know. I would have helped you if I could, one of those times we were Above in the good clean air. But up there, I can't talk any more than you can. Blasted Leps. Worse than Trolls, if you ask me. Leastwise you know what to expect from a Troll.*

Lying flat on her back in bed later, Eve had turned the idea over in her fuzzy-as-usual mind. The more she'd thought about it, the more she'd believed Copper's declaration. If Lorcan was indeed a Leprechaun, everything peculiar about him made sense: his frequent disappearances, his great love for gold, his talent for making shoes, and his uncanny ability to charm his way out of trouble.

And what did Copper mean about being with her Above? Was her memory so utterly wrecked that she could forget such a rare and spirited boy?

Lorcan interrupted Eve's remembrances by poking her knee with Gladys. "You have nothing to say? Well, that's a surprise," he said with smug amusement. "Perhaps I never needed to remove your voice!"

Eve's face grew hot, and she glowered at him. "Why did you do it? Why did you bother with me at all?" she asked. Her throat burned as she spoke for the first time in thirteen years.

"You're an anomaly, child," he said. "A spectacular abomination of my making. According to our laws, I ought not have claimed and gifted you at birth. There are no female Leprechauns. You'll be the first woman blessed with the green blood of our People once you've taken the Cups. Perhaps even our first queen, if I deem you worthy to share the throne with me."

Eve clenched her fists at her sides. She wanted to punch him, to tear his hair out, to knock every tooth from his head, but somehow she stayed still. She knew a time would come, and not soon enough, when she would kill Lorcan Reilly for what he'd done, but that perfect moment had not yet arrived.

"You're angry with me about the enchanted ring," Lorcan said gently. "But I only kept you quiet to protect you. Children do chatter, and although the ring also hobbled your mind a bit, you still saw and heard things that might have gotten us both executed by the Faerie authorities if you'd mentioned them to anyone. With you subdued and silent, I could pretend you were my niece or servant Above and my mute

Newling when in the Neathlands. But I suppose you don't remember your other visits here Below."

She shook her head. She looked past Lorcan at the brick wall, not wanting to meet his eye lest he enchant her again somehow.

"Patience, Eevar. My plan will bring us both glory, but you must be patient and obedient." Lorcan rapped Eve's shoulder with Gladys's thorniest side as he spoke, punctuating his words with pain.

She reached up and pushed the stick away. "No. I will not be patient, *Uncle*. What I will be is your ruin. You made a mistake in restoring my speech. I'll tell everyone what you've done."

"Ha! If I go down, so shall you. The king and the Leprechaun High Council might excuse me for a price, but they'd most certainly kill you. They'd never let an aberration like you continue living." He lifted his chin and looked down his nose at her. "I have the advantage here, as always."

Eve swung her fist at his jaw. He blocked her punch with Gladys and taunted her with a look of haughty amusement.

"Go to class now," Lorcan said. "Schoolmaster O'Ferrell must find you fit to take the Cup of Fortune. That is why I gave you your voice, to aid in your success at the academy. So you can do your gold-father credit."

Again, Lorcan scanned the area for eavesdroppers. Finding none, he continued his lecture. "Now, mind your manners and your mouth at all times. Once you drink the Elixir of Fortune, you'll forget all your petty grievances and rejoice that I chose you. And when we attain our future glory, I reckon you'll even be grateful—as unusual as that sentiment may be among us Leprechauns." He prodded her with Gladys. "Go on, then. I happen to know the schoolmaster dislikes tardiness."

Without wasting another word on Lorcan, Eve entered the academy. Her knees trembled as she walked; she was so full of simmering rage that she could barely see where she was going. She slid into a seat in the front row and bit down hard on her lower lip to keep from crying. It seemed ridiculous to be so close to tears. After all, she wasn't *sad*. Angry, disgusted, resentful—yes. But not sad. Sadness would not help her retaliate against Lorcan Reilly. There was no sadness in revenge.

In her lap under the desk, Eve rubbed the indentation left by the magic ring. She stared straight ahead, planning her own version of "future glory," vowing to ruin the Leprechaun who had stolen her past.

# Chapter Fourteen

## *An Scoil Nua*

## (The New School)

Tommin sat at a roughly made desk behind a plump, curly-haired fellow. The boy turned around and looked him over. At one edge of his smiling mouth was a smear of something mushroomy gray.

Out of the corner of his eye, Tommin saw Eve—Eevar—walking up the aisle toward the front row of desks. Was she paler than usual, or was it a trick of the hazy light?

"Hello," the boy said more loudly than necessary. "Name's Alby. Pleasure's all mine—and so's the treasure. Ha!" He reached back to shake Tommin's hand. "You feeling all right? Your eyes are a bit glassy."

"Well enough," Tommin said. The truth was his head felt a bit floaty, in a pleasant way. His eyes wandered up the slope of Alby's snub nose, crossed over the ridge of his brow, and then followed the curves and whooshes of the boy's sand-colored curls. Around and over, waves of hair on a wavy hair sea.

"You sure? I mean, you look a little . . . *Oh*, I understand. Slow as treacle, I am. You've just had one of the gold pills. My master gave me one yesterday, and whoa! Knocked me flat for a while, didn't it? Flat and happy, that's what I was. Started feeling normal again around bedtime." Alby tipped his head and dug his finger into his ear. When he'd finished digging, he said, "Had a powerful itch. So, how old are you?

I'm seventeen. Master Owen says we'll likely look about the same for a good long while, as Leprechauns only age when stealing and burying up among the humans. So you know if you see a Lep that's all wrinkle faced or bald, he's probably rich as anything. Still, what's a few wrinkles when you get to live forever, eh?"

"You there," the schoolmaster said from the front of the classroom. "Alby, is it? Quiet down. Idle conversation between students is strictly forbidden."

"Sorry, sir," Alby said. He winked at Tommin before turning to face O'Ferrell.

A deep bell sounded, and the schoolmaster tapped a long, thin stick on the podium. "Let us begin," he said. "You Newlings have been brought to the Neathlands for the purpose of induction into the ancient tribe of the Leprechauns. This is the greatest honor in all the realms of Faerie, and not to be taken lightly. You were chosen at birth by your gold-fathers, blessed with sacred words, and left to grow among the humans until your progenitors deemed it time to bring you here to fulfill your eternal destinies. My name is Master O'Ferrell, and I will teach you the laws, ways, and illustrious history of the Leprechauns. When you leave my classroom at term's end, you will be fit and ready to drink the first sacred Cup of Fortune."

At a second-row desk, a boy with black hair sticking up from his head like burned grass raised a grubby hand. "Pardon me, Master O'Ferrell, but I find this a wee bit confusing."

"Sit, Flanagan. All will become clear in time."

"Yes, sir." Flanagan sat. The back of his neck turned red as a radish.

O'Ferrell removed his mortarboard and set it on the podium. He leaned forward on his hands, his expression stern as a storm cloud. "There will be no whining, no back talk, and no tomfoolery in my classroom. You will give up any hope of going home to mammy or sweetheart. You will train hard and well to become a credit to our People, and you will learn to love gold above all things and find the highest pleasure therein."

A boy sitting near the front of the room sobbed. O'Ferrell slapped his stick against the podium with a loud crack.

"Dare to do that again, lad, and you might not live to hear my first lecture," O'Ferrell said. He laid the stick across the podium and continued. "If any of you are unwise enough to disobey me, fail my examinations, or openly reject the glorious opportunity given you to become Leprechauns, you will be sent to the Trolls posthaste. Does anyone know what becomes of boys sent to the Trolls?"

Alby stood and said, "My master told me Trolls usually like boys slow roasted rather than raw, but it's a matter of personal preference. And if they're not feeling so hungry, they'll take off an arm as a snack and have the rest of the boy later, maybe bit by bit for a fortnight or two. Some Trolls, them that's more peaceable, use boys for slave work instead of food, making them dig tunnels by hand or skin rats for stew or whatever else the Trolls want till they wish they were dead anyhow."

"Correct, Alby," O'Ferrell said. "Although your account falls short in describing the true terror that awaits failed Newlings at the hands of the Trolls. But do not worry, my lads. Chapter sixteen in your textbooks covers the subject well enough to give even a full-blooded Leprechaun nightmares."

O'Ferrell picked up his stick and pointed it toward Eve. "You. Eevar, is it? Come forward and distribute the textbooks."

Eve stood and walked to the front. Tommin noted her deliberate footsteps and the proud tilt of her chin. She didn't seem at all frightened by O'Ferrell and his threats—but then, hadn't she been raised by Lorcan and his stick, Gladys?

Straightening the fat tome on the podium before him, the schoolmaster said, "Those of you who are unable to read, see me during the first break for a literacy potion. For now, perk up your small ears and absorb my words."

Eve dropped a book on Tommin's desk with a thud. He smiled at her (the gold pill's influence mostly, although he couldn't deny he thought her pretty), but she moved on without acknowledging him.

And so class began. O'Ferrell described the subjects they'd study: Leprechaun rules and customs, histories and legends; principles and magical qualities of the various Faerie tribes—including Elves, Ogres, Pixies, the dreaded Trolls, and other beings Tommin had thought imaginary until now.

*Now* he could believe almost anything.

Tommin flipped through the pages of the textbook, thankful Master Rafferty had taught him to read and write. After Copper's warnings about drinking the blue stuff, he was relieved he'd not need the literacy potion the schoolmaster offered. Hadn't Master Rafferty told him a hundred times that all magic was dangerous and unpredictable?

If Master Rafferty could have seen him now, taking Faerie classes from a Leprechaun in an underground schoolroom, the man would have dropped down dead.

O'Ferrell droned on and on about sacred coats and types of hats. Tommin's feelings mellowed as the effects of the pill faded. His human reasoning returned bit by bit, and he realized he'd need to be careful to stay as sober as possible. If one pill had so strongly affected him, what might he do or become after a *few* of them?

He swallowed hard. He knew in his heart he wouldn't be able to resist taking another gold pill or two if Lorcan offered them when the gold lust struck. Truly, if he was suffering from an agonizing bodily need for treasure, wouldn't he be foolish not to accept such a simple remedy?

Did taking the Leprechauns' medicine make him any more one of them than stealing had?

Perhaps . . . or perhaps not.

The way he reckoned, he had two serious battles ahead of him: the first, a campaign against being completely transformed into a Leprechaun; and the second, a struggle to defeat the part of him that was *already* like them, the part of him Granny had rightly called Magpie.

# Chapter Fifteen

## Beacáin agus Ainnise, Tae agus Dóchas

## (Mushrooms and Misery, Tea and Hope)

In a world with no sun and no moon, where passing hours were marked only by the sounding of bells, Tommin lost track of time. Had he been in the Neathlands for a few days or a few weeks? Months, perhaps?

Today, he'd spent all of his so-called afternoon sitting on the Persian rug in Lorcan Reilly's parlor, with books strewn about him in all directions. Bleary-eyed from reading and mesmerized by the crackling of the fire in the grate, he ignored the hefty textbook balanced on his knees and stared into the flames. After what he reckoned were weeks of diligent study, he'd memorized all 127 of the Leprechaun commandments; he knew by heart the 77 laws held in common by all Faerie Peoples, and could describe in detail the Sacred Rite of the Burying of Treasure (with accompanying single or double rainbow). He felt almost prepared enough to pass the upcoming examination, the one that preceded the Ceremony of the First Cup.

Of course Tommin had not forgotten Copper's warning against drinking the blue elixir, but he could find no way around it. To advance to second-level status and earn the right to go Above again, he'd have to drink the First Cup.

Second-level students got basic maps, field trips, and practical lessons in using Glamour and Charm.

Second levels could, conceivably, escape the Neathlands and never return.

Somewhere in the house, a door slammed. Door slamming happened often, with Lorcan's temper, Copper's temper, and Eve's temper in residence, so Tommin did not flinch at the sound. He turned the page and began to review the names of the Leprechaun kings, in order of their reigns.

Copper appeared in the doorway, *smiling*—and never before had Tommin seen even a hint of such a thing on the boy's face.

"You look bright as a penny. Is it Christmas?" Tommin said.

"Good as. Himself has gone to a council meeting at the pub, and when he goes to one of those, he's sometimes gone for days." Copper held Gladys the stick high. "Left me in charge, too. I'm to beat you and Eevar if I like!"

Eve squeezed past Copper, shoving the stick aside. "Perhaps you could make tea instead, Copper. The mint kind Lorcan never shares."

Copper pointed Gladys at Eve. "I should beat you for saying that. Excepting it's a good idea. We'll make a wee party of it, eh? Maybe I'll sneak a few of the master's jam cakes onto the tray, too." Whistling a tune, Copper retreated to the kitchen.

Eve sat on the carpet beside Tommin. She took the book from his lap and dropped it to the floor with a thump. "You don't need to study. You're already at the top of the class."

"I have to pass the examination," Tommin said. "No sense taking risks by being lazy."

"You *want* to join them?"

Tommin shrugged noncommittally. "Well, it's that or the Trolls, isn't it?" He looked into her face. They'd not had a chance to speak more than five words to each other since arriving in the Neathlands—in spite of living under the same roof. Mostly because the Leprechauns didn't tolerate chitchat among the Newlings (Tommin's knuckles still bore a purple stripe from the crack of O'Ferrell's ruler, for which he rightly blamed Alby), but partly because she'd led him to believe she was mute. Apparently, she wasn't. He'd nearly fallen off his chair when she'd answered in class the first day, and now here she was ordering tea and telling him what to do.

"I don't believe you want to be a Lep," she said. "Not really. In fact, I think you hate them as much as I do." She rubbed her finger in the place where she used to wear the lovely little gold ring. The thought of gold made his stomach flutter. And he noticed, as he did rather often, she looked especially pretty in the firelight. Not as attractive as gold, but pretty enough to make him wonder if his hair looked funny or if he had mushroom stuck between his front teeth.

As Master Rafferty had taught him, Tommin took a moment to consider his words before he spoke. Could he trust Eve, or had Lorcan (and Gladys) manipulated her into keeping watch over him, instructing her to weasel out any traitorous notions he might have? If she was Lorcan's spy, she was a good one, for something in her eyes and earnest expression made him want to tell her everything: his every last fear, failing, sin, and hope.

He ran a hand over his hair, attempting to smooth the cowlick in back, and then said slowly, "Does it matter what we want? It seems to me we have to do whatever they say."

She looked him square in the eye. "I've done Lorcan Reilly's bidding since I was younger than Copper looks. I don't intend to obey him forever. Besides, I *can't* become a Leprechaun. Their magic isn't meant for girls. If the Cup doesn't kill me, the High Council will, once they get wind of Lorcan's scheme."

Behind them, a spoon hit the floor with a clatter. Tommin glanced at Copper standing in the doorway openmouthed, tea tray tipping at a dangerous angle. "Girl?" he squeaked. "You're a *girl*? How could I not have noticed before now? Am I as stupid as that?"

"I would never call you stupid, but for someone over a hundred years old, you are very easily shocked," Eve said. A little smile formed at the edges of her mouth, a thing as rare as flowers in wintertime. "Ah, don't blame yourself. You probably did notice, lots of times, only Lorcan made you forget with his blasted magic. Now come and sit, Copper. I think you and I could be of help to one another, and perhaps to Tommin—if he wants to go home again, that is."

"I do," Tommin said, giving in to his instinct to trust her. "I want to go home." Admitting the truth felt good. Having others on his side felt good.

"You might have to kill old Lorcan if you want to get away," Copper said. "I never could, myself. Not that I know how, since there's not many ways to kill them monsters. No, don't think I could anyway."

"I could," Eve said without hesitation.

Tommin held his peace. Stealing was bad enough. That was something his cursed body demanded. Murder was something he doubted he could do, even on his worst day.

Copper knelt and set the tray on the floor. He poured the tea and passed the cups, blushing when he handed Eve hers. The aroma of mint swirled in the rising steam; Tommin inhaled it like a swimmer coming up for breath. Suddenly, his eyes stung. He missed Granny every day, but this simple brew brought memories of her strong enough to make his heart ache in his chest. He took a sip and hoped no one would notice his tears.

"We need a plan," Eve said.

Copper set his cup on the floor. "Good luck," he said. He bit into a mushroom biscuit, and crumbs rained onto his shirt. "Me, I've been trying to come up with a plan to run off since before you were born, and here I am. Mushrooms and misery, that's all I've got for all my hoping and dreaming."

"I think it can be done," Tommin said. "Second levels are taken up to train. We could slip away when they aren't paying attention. We'd have to leave Ireland fast, though. There are too many Faerie folk watching, and most of them would turn us in just for the fun of it. Perhaps in a less enchanted country, we could start new lives."

"I'll never be second-level anything," Copper said. "And you, Tommin. Even if you do escape, you'll always hunger for gold, no matter where you go. It's in your blood, and it will only get worse the longer you live without fully changing over. For some reason, conversion helps the Leps control their cravings better. That's what I've heard, anyway."

Tommin had no illusions about throwing off his magpie ways, but he wished Copper had not mentioned it. Or said the word "gold." To keep from scratching, he swallowed the dregs of his mint tea and then concentrated on refilling everyone's cups. He'd taken half a little gold pill before Lorcan left, and it should have satisfied him for hours, but the mention of thievery always made him itch, the way someone itches when they hear mention of head lice or bedbugs.

"I promise I'll get you out, Copper," Eve said, laying a hand on the boy's thin shoulder and making him blush scarlet.

"I don't want to live Above," Copper blurted. "I hate eating bugs more than I hate eating mushrooms. And having to squeak and chitter instead of speaking proper. It's awful, that's what it is."

Tommin raised his eyebrows and looked at Eve. She shrugged.

Copper groaned with exasperation. "Quit looking at me like I'm mad, will you! I'm after telling you I'm one of the Underantrim Faeries. A shape-shifter."

"You're what?" Tommin set down his teacup with a clatter.

"Did you learn nothing in school?" Copper rolled his eyes. "For the love of gold, I'm not human! Whenever I go Above, I turn into a blasted bat!"

"I remember you now," Eve said, eyes wide. "The little brown bat. Lorcan keeps you in his pocket."

"His stinking, scratchy pocket. I'd rather kiss a Troll's hindquarters than go back in there once more. But Lorcan never would leave me home here when he goes roaming, seeing as how the Leps think my kind makes the best household servants and they steal us from each other any chance they get. I'd be snatched away quick as anything."

"Well then, we'll help you get home to Underantrim," Eve said. "To your tribe."

"Yeah, well, I won't hold you to that," Copper said. "Nice as it sounds. It's been so long since I left, I probably wouldn't even recognize the place."

Tommin took a biscuit from the plate. "What about your family, Copper? Don't you miss them?"

"All carried off by the Leps on the same day, we were. Stolen and bound into their service with magic, right down to the baby. Still, I wouldn't mind going back if I could, I suppose. It was lovely there, and green. And we had berries all year, big as my fist."

"So, we're together in this?" Eve asked. "We'll keep our eyes and ears open for ways to break Lorcan's hold on Copper and get him home to Underantrim, and also try to come up with a plan for Tommin and me to escape?"

Tommin and Copper nodded.

"Good," Eve said. She set her cup on the tray and stood. "Well, if I'm to pass the examination and avoid being sent to the Trolls, I need to go study. I never even started reading *Ways of the Woodland Faeries and Elves*, and it must be three hundred pages long."

"Three hundred and eighty," Tommin said. "Not including the appendices."

Eve moaned. "Tell me this will all be worth it someday."

"That's my dearest hope," Tommin said.

"Cake," Copper muttered as he hefted the tea tray and headed toward the kitchen. "I hope for cake. By gold, you haven't lived till you've had cake made by Underantrim Faeries. Makes your mouth go all tingly and happy, it does."

After Eve retreated to her room off the parlor, Tommin sat still and thought for a long while. Running away with Eve seemed possible;

freeing Copper from some Leprechaun spell and returning him home to another part of the Faerie Neathlands did not. Well, if anyone could figure it out, he believed Eve could. She was clever and determined, and had had the dubious benefit of living among the Leprechauns for years, observing their habits and magic.

Tommin opened his copy of *Leprechaun History*, volume three. His eyes were drawn to a vivid illustration of a wild-haired, pointy-nosed fellow wearing a bejeweled crown that must have weighed more than Copper. The caption read, "King Aureus I, son of the Underclare tribe, righteous gold-father of seven mighty converts, including the avaricious princes Niall the Light-Fingered and Hugh of the Triple Rainbow. Reigned for ninety-two human years, slain and succeeded by King Silverknuckles (see page 578)."

*Princes.* The word struck him like lightning, illuminating a memory of something Lorcan had said to him when they had first walked the streets of Loughgillan: *You'll be a prince among the People.*

Tommin's heart raced as Lorcan's intentions became clear; the vile fellow was planning to become king of all Leprechauns—which, Tommin knew from his studies, could not take place unless every last one of his gold-children fully converted.

Including himself. Including Eve.

But what of the fact that Eve was a girl? If Lorcan Reilly could accomplish what everyone in Faerie history had deemed impossible, would that not make him the most powerful, fearsome Leprechaun king ever?

*It couldn't happen,* Tommin thought.

Lorcan was mad to attempt to make a female Leprechaun. Madder still to think she'd help him gain the throne. She'd sooner slit his throat and leave him for the Neathgillan cats to feast upon.

Warmth spread through Tommin's body as if he'd just stolen a handful of silver. Only this was a *good* warmth, kindled by hope and not theft. If, as Master Rafferty had been wont to say, knowledge of the enemy is a sure and ready weapon, then Tommin was no longer unarmed. He knew his enemy's grand plan—and its weakness.

Tommin rose, anxious to go share his revelation with Eve. At that moment, the all-too-familiar creak and slam of the kitchen door echoed through the house.

"Copper!" he heard Lorcan shout in the next room. "Sleeping at my table! Worthless lout! Get up and make me some toast before I pummel the stuffing out of you!" The sound of a chair tipping over and dishes breaking followed Lorcan's drink-slurred commands.

Quickly, Tommin tiptoed down the short corridor and into the narrow, furnitureless room he and Copper shared. He dove under a mound of rough blankets and feigned sleep—the best way to avoid conflict with his drunken master.

Conversation with Eve would have to wait.

# Chapter Sixteen

## A Bróga Gránna

## (Her Ugly Shoes)

In her room, Eve tried not to listen to Lorcan's ranting and Copper's cries for mercy. How many times would she have to bear witness to this selfsame scene, knowing that to interfere would only make things worse for Copper and herself?

Setting her textbook down, she paced the room, humming loudly to cover the sounds as much as she could. After a few minutes, she turned to the shelf above her wardrobe. She reached up and retrieved a pair of unfinished shoes.

Cradling the shoes against her chest, she crossed the narrow room and sat on the edge of her musty, straw-filled mattress. As Copper quieted, she set one shoe beside her and lifted the other to inspect it.

As part of the final examinations, Master O'Ferrell had instructed each student to prepare an example of his finest work, done in brown or black leather, with buckles or laces, high heels or low. It was only a matter of tradition, of course. Any Leprechaun-cursed lad could make perfect shoes in his sleep. But the brown shoe Eve held was clunky and crookedly sewn. Evidence that she was not a Leprechaun-cursed lad at all.

Unless Tommin agreed to help her, O'Ferrell would find out her secret—and she'd be as good as dead.

Eve ran her fingers over the uneven stitches, imagining all the care Tommin put into the shoes he made. The pair he'd made for Lorcan had been a work of art. He had skilled hands, that boy. And he was kind—but perhaps not so very wise. She'd caught him stealing looks at her. He fancied her, most likely. And perhaps in another world, in another time, she might have returned the sentiment eventually. Perhaps he might have found a way to soften her stony heart. But in the Neathlands, tender feelings could cause nothing but harm to them both.

This was no time for folly.

Besides, she had no desire to be entangled with anyone. She'd never been free in her life, and she meant to taste freedom. To gulp it down by the barrelful. Truth be told, it rankled her greatly to have to ask for Tommin's help with the shoe project—but it was that or fail . . . so ask she would. Lucky for her, there were still a few days left before the shoes were due to be placed on O'Ferrell's desk.

Once she passed the exams, another predicament loomed, and she'd been unable to think of any way around it. Soon, the day would come when she'd have no choice but to drink the Cup of Fortune, the enchanted elixir that altered Newling boys into full-fledged Leprechaun blackguards. She might be able to bluff her way through school and Lep society, but she couldn't fool magic into believing she was male.

Drinking the Cup might kill her.

And probably not politely. Probably in some spectacular, agonizingly painful way, melting the flesh off her bones or exploding the organs within her one by one.

A faint rapping came at her door, and she heard Copper say, "Master's passed out, so you needn't be afraid to go to the kitchen if you need something. Good night to you."

"Thank heaven," Eve said, feeling some of the tension evaporate from her body. The beatings and scoldings were over for the day. She set the ugly shoes on the floor, lay down on the mattress, and, miraculously, fell asleep.

When the morning bell sounded, she gasped and sat straight up.

"Blast," she said, realizing that she'd dozed off before she'd finished studying for the first day of the week-long course of written tests.

"Well, good luck to me," she said as she raked her fingers through her hair in lieu of a comb. "And good luck to you, Tommin Kelly, while I'm at it."

Nothing else could help her now.

# Chapter Seventeen

## *Luach Saothair gan Iarraidh*

## (Unwanted Rewards)

The next Monday, all over Neathgillan, sheets of parchment listing the results of the first written examination were nailed to shop doors and lampposts. Before the third bell of the morning, every Leprechaun in town knew that Tommin (gold-son of Lorcan Reilly) had scored highest and that Malachy (gold-son of Bernard O'Hagan) had failed and would be transported to the border town of Neathmulltagh and auctioned off to the Trolls within the week.

Outside the door of the Ha'penny Public House, Lorcan Reilly slapped Tommin hard on the back. "Well done, lad. I knew you'd make me proud the first time I watched you on a Take."

The "Take," Tommin had learned on his first day at the academy, was the Leprechaun term for common thievery—a title that made Tommin feel no better about the criminal behavior.

Lorcan pushed Tommin a few feet to the side so he could open the pub door. "Go in, then. You deserve a pint of our own strong Leprechaun brew as a reward. No mushroom juice for you this auspicious day, Tommin, my lad."

Tommin looked over his shoulder at Eve. She shrugged. "Master Lorcan?" Tommin said. "Can Eevar come in with us?"

Lorcan grunted. "He may. But no pint for him. He's third from last on the list, and he'll get nothing but a good smack from Gladys from me. Later, though. No need to spoil our time of celebration with his whining."

Eve followed close behind Tommin. Her pleasant scent always gave her away, the faint hint of newly unfurled ferns. He wondered why none of the Leprechauns ever noticed it. Maybe their own personal odors kept their noses occupied; Leprechauns were infrequent bathers, after all. If every Lep could have smelled like Eve, the Neathlands might have been a bit more tolerable.

Lorcan chose a private table in a far corner of the room and held up two fingers. A minute later, a serving boy (Copper's age, but golden haired and plumper than any other servant Tommin had encountered underground) brought two large stoneware tankards topped with fizzling foam and set them in front of Lorcan. "Anything else, sir?" the boy asked, eyes lowered.

"Not now, boy. For the love of gold, don't stand there idling," Lorcan said. The boy scurried away, and Lorcan pushed a tankard toward Tommin. "Drink up, son. You've earned it."

Tommin lifted the heavy tankard to toast his master, as Leprechaun manners required, and said, "May your brim-full pots be buried deep and may your rainbows hold up the sky." The foam tickled his nose as he took a sip. He smiled as the beer settled into his belly like swallowed sunshine. Out of the corner of his eye, he noticed Eve's pout. He wished he could share his tankard with her—because the beer tasted good, and also because he knew he'd be drunk if he finished it all himself. By the saints, the stuff was powerful!

"Don't be shy," Lorcan said. "There's more where that came from."

"You'll have to carry me home if I drink all this," Tommin said meekly.

Lorcan laughed. "You need to build up a tolerance, that's all. Drinking is one of the honored traditions of our tribe, lad. Did Schoolmaster O'Ferrell forget to teach you that?"

"He did mention it, sir," Tommin said. The room seemed to tilt a little, and he gripped the edge of the table.

"Lorcan Reilly," a curly-haired, bushy-bearded gentleman called from the bar. "I've something to discuss with you if you have a moment."

"Stay here and enjoy your reward," Lorcan said to Tommin, "while I have a quick word with Nick Duffy." He glared at Eve. "And you, Eevar. No tricks. You already have an appointment with Gladys, and she'd be glad to add a few extra swats to those you have coming."

Eve bit her lower lip and kept her gaze directed at the tabletop until Lorcan could be heard laughing with the other Leprechauns at the bar. Amid the noise of Leprechaun bragging and storytelling, Alby could be heard loudly introducing himself to one of the other patrons: "Name's Alby. Pleasure's all mine, and so's the treasure! Ha!"

Eve rolled her eyes heavenward, and Tommin groaned.

"Have some," Tommin said, sliding the tankard across the table to Eve. *"Please."*

"Not for all the cats in Neathgillan," she whispered. "Not even for all the *dead* cats." She wrinkled her nose and pushed the tankard away.

"Hush," Tommin said. "You know better than to insult the king's clowder in public." Was it his imagination, or were his words coming out slurred? It didn't matter. Eve smelled wonderful.

"'Clowder' makes them sound far too innocent. 'Band of furry demons' would be a more fitting title."

Her wry smile made Tommin's half-pickled heart melt a little. Her hair was red gold in the candlelight. Impulsively, he reached beneath the table and touched her hand.

"Hey!" She smacked his hand hard and slid her chair away from his. "You should never drink again," she said, her whisper as effective a rebuke as any shout. "Do you want to get us both sold off or killed? By all the stars, Tommin!"

Sobered, he blushed. "Sorry. The beer . . ."

"Yes, the beer. But now that we're on the subject, I'm telling you this: you need to get any silly romantic notions you might have about me out of your head. All I want is to be free of men—human or otherwise. I'm as attracted to you as I am to the blasted cats. Understand?"

Tommin nodded, wondering what it would be like to kiss her angry mouth. He stared at her lips, admiring their dark-rose color and perfect shape. Deep in his daydream, he failed to notice that she'd picked up the tankard and was pouring it into his lap until he was drenched.

"Hey!" He stood and brushed the liquid off his breeches.

"Understand now?"

"Yes," he said, sitting again, hands raised in surrender. "I should never drink."

"Right." She offered him a handkerchief to blot up the rest of the beer. "I need to ask a favor, although I wonder if you're fit to make any decisions in your state."

Tommin blotted his clothes. "I'm all right. And it might be a long time before we get a chance to talk alone again." He sat up straight and tried to appear serious. But by the saints, he still wanted to kiss her.

"True." Eve sighed. "Well, you know I'm terrible at shoemaking, and our projects are due soon. If I don't pass, I'll be sent to auction before the First Cup of Fortune ceremony."

"You want me to finish your shoes." He held out her soggy handkerchief, but she shook her head in refusal. He dropped it onto the tabletop.

He met her gaze. She'd never looked so humble. In the softest of whispers, she said, "I know it's a big risk. We'll both be in trouble if we get caught."

"Lorcan's magic didn't work on you at all, did it? When he cursed you, the enchantment must have bounced right off. Tell me, have you ever stolen anything? Have you even wanted to?" Tommin's words still slurred slightly, but his mind had cleared a bit since his beer bath.

She shook her head. "I care nothing for gold or silver. I have a vague recollection of Lorcan coaxing me to nick a brooch from a shop once. I was four or five, I think. I cried and he dragged me into the street by my hair. Gladys left scars that night." She pointed to a pale stripe on the side of her neck. "I think he's only kept me this long because he believes the Cup of Fortune will give me magic he can use. Beside the fact that he's always seemed to enjoy kicking me about like a mongrel."

"He's a monster," Tommin said, pitying Eve for her wrecked childhood. He'd never been more thankful for his gentle, loving granny and the kind, fatherly figure of Master Rafferty.

"And here he comes," Eve whispered.

"Well, my children," Lorcan said. "I must see you home and attend to other business." He twirled Gladys between his fingers. "No dawdling, no chitchat."

Eve's face changed before Tommin's eyes, reverting to an emotionless mask. She followed Lorcan outside, and Tommin trailed behind them. He realized (as he frequently stumbled over nothing) that Eve lived two lives, just as he did. If anyone could understand her, he could. He would have liked to have tried. But she was right. This was no time for romantic fancies. If they were to survive as humans, they needed to focus entirely on their plan to escape.

He veered to the edge of the street and clung to a lamppost. *And by all the saints,* he thought as his stomach rejected everything he'd drunk, *I swear I'll never touch the Leprechauns' beer again.*

# Chapter Eighteen

## *An Searmanas Naofa*

## (The Sacred Ceremony)

Built of gray stone and topped with a steeple that disappeared into the dirt sky, the building in Neathgillan's center was a close copy of Loughgillan's church. When Tommin passed through its arched doors, he half expected to see Granny kneeling at the altar. Instead, he saw his schoolmaster and a stern-faced, green-robed Leprechaun standing on a raised platform, flanked by six-foot-tall brass candelabra. Behind O'Ferrell and the officiant was a table covered in embroidered linen, adorned with a heavily engraved gilded pitcher and a large gem-studded chalice.

The fabled Cup of Fortune.

"Did you ever see the like?" Alby said from behind Tommin. "That Cup! I could fit my whole face in it."

"Hush, Alby," Eve said. Tommin thought he heard a quiver of fear in her voice, and who could blame her for it? So much could go wrong today. In all the books he'd read, he'd never found a single report of any female partaking of the Leprechaun's sacred elixir; who knew what might happen when Eve drank it?

There was a fair chance she'd not have a tomorrow.

He turned his head to gaze at her. He had to. Just in case. But saints, she looked brave, the way she held her chin up and her shoulders back.

"To your seats, lads," said a squinty-eyed usher. "Front row, like you practiced. Take the aisle nice and slow, and no more talking."

The Newlings lined up, two by two. Daniel and Alby first, then Tommin and Eve, Joseph and Flanagan, Marcas and Osheen—all dressed in long ceremonial robes of scarlet silk. They took solemn steps down the aisle, passing pews filled with Leprechauns dressed in their finest clothes. Somewhere in the sanctuary, someone played a somber tune on a harp.

Out of the corner of his eye, Tommin saw Eve shiver. His own fear had his guts tied into knots. If he could have done so without risking transportation to the Trolls, he would have offered her a kind word. *He* would have appreciated hearing a kind word from someone. But Leps weren't ones for goodwill, were they?

Finally, they slid into the front pew, and Eve glanced his way. In spite of the risk, he offered her what he hoped was a smile of encouragement—a difficult thing to do with the war of the apocalypse raging in his stomach.

A deep bell sounded. The officiant lifted his hands and said, "All rise for the singing of the sacred anthem of the Cup."

Hands on hearts, the Leprechauns sang lustily.

After the last note faded away, everyone remained standing. Eerie silence filled the domed sanctuary. And then Tommin saw *them*: cat after cat padding silently down the aisle. Ten, twenty, thirty . . . he lost count as they formed a semicircle behind the great table holding the Cup. They held their pointed ears at attention. He felt their eyes on him. He wondered what they knew, and if they'd be the ones to reveal Eve's secret. They were *Faerie* cats, after all. And hadn't Master Rafferty mistrusted even regular old stray cats?

After the cats sat, the Leprechauns followed suit. The officiant turned and poured blue liquid from the pitcher into the chalice. The elixir sizzled and glowed inside the Cup. Tiny sparks leapt from its surface. It was beautiful, and Tommin wanted it.

He gripped the front edge of the pew and clenched his eyes shut, barely hearing the chanting of the officiant, hardly noticing when the schoolmaster called Daniel and Alby to come forth, trying with all his might to keep from running up and grabbing the Cup.

Something jabbed him in the arm, something he reckoned was Eve's pointy elbow. He opened his eyes just in time to see Daniel sip from the chalice. The boy's face flushed pink, and he sighed as if satisfied to the deepest deep of his soul. He bowed slightly to the Cup and the officiant (according to custom, as described on page 289 of *Ways of the Leprechaun, Ancient and Modern*) before practically floating back to his seat in the pew.

Eternal minutes dragged by as Alby recited the oath, sipped from the chalice, and returned to his seat. And then it was time for Tommin and Eve to go to the altar. Tommin wanted to hurry, but Eve walked slowly, very slowly, in front of him. The fair skin on the back of her neck had paled to a shade that would have made new snow look dirty. Her shoulders trembled beneath her crimson gown.

They stopped before the officiant. Tommin heard Eve take a deep, shuddering breath, and then he watched her seem to take command of herself. Hands folded at her waist, she stood tall and proud as a queen. This was it, then. Eve's live-or-die moment.

Tommin shut his eyes and tried to pray.

# Chapter Nineteen

## *An Chéad Chupán*

## (The First Cup)

When the time to swear the oath came, Eve felt certain she'd drop dead from fear, or at the very least forget the sacred words she had to speak. But no, she surprised herself by lifting her chin and declaring boldly, "I, Eevar, gold-son of Lorcan Reilly, take this First Cup of Fortune for the greening of my blood and the impartation of the magical gifts of Glamour and Charm unto me. Let this blessed elixir do its work, diminishing the human within my body and increasing the Leprechaun. I swear by all the gold and silver to be true to the Leprechaun tribe until the last cinder of the world is eaten by the final flame."

As she placed her hands around the Cup, her heart stopped cold—then set to racing. With the eyes of a hundred Leprechauns upon her, there could be no turning back. She pressed the cool rim to her lip and tipped the contents into her mouth. The elixir bubbled on her tongue, sweeter than honey, richer than buttered cakes. She swallowed once and waited for pain to punish her, for death to seize her with frozen fingers, or for the wily Faerie cats to attack.

Seconds passed as slowly as hours as she waited.

"Psst, boy," the officiant whispered through clenched teeth. "Finish it."

Beginning to doubt the Cup would have any effect on her, she gulped down the rest.

But then, as the liquid filtered into her belly, something stirred deep within her.

It was nothing like the books had described; she saw no swirling colors, no visions of gold. Instead, a warm glow unfurled inside her like a flowering vine, spreading its tendrils through her being and choking out all weariness and fear, replacing them with strength and a quiet sort of delight—and something she could not name.

No, she could not name the *something*, but as surely as she lived and breathed, she knew this: it was magic, and it was hers to wield.

She bit her lip to keep from laughing.

The officiant lifted the Cup from her hands and nodded, signaling her to step aside.

Everything within her wanted to dance and shout—for not only had she survived the Cup, she'd gained power. Power she just might be able to use against Lorcan Reilly.

# Chapter Twenty

## *Olann Sé*

## (He Drinks)

The look on Eve's face as she moved aside to make way for him . . . Tommin couldn't quite figure it out. It lay between peaceful and smug—and he didn't really need to decipher it. She'd lived, and that's all he needed to know for now.

Tommin took a step forward, and when he saw the fizzing blue liquid mere inches away, he almost fainted with longing.

"The oath," the officiant whispered, scowling.

"Yes," Tommin said. He took a greedy gulp of air and then let the speech pour out of him, his eyes fixed on the Cup and its bubbling contents. The tantalizing aroma of the elixir beckoned him, and he had no inclination to resist its call.

Tommin clutched the Cup between his hands and sucked in a great mouthful of the liquid. The elixir effervesced and tickled his palate, chilling and burning in turns. It tasted of every good thing he'd ever eaten, and of things he'd only imagined: the victuals of angels, the devil's own cake, and fruits from Faerie gardens. It danced down his throat, filling him with pleasure so intense he thought he might die from it.

Music resounded within his bones; stars pulsed in his bloodstream.

Somehow he managed to bow appropriately before accompanying Eve back to their pew.

The remaining Newlings took their turns while Tommin sat still as stone, mesmerized by the colors of the tapestry behind the altar, the flickering candles, and the sound of Eve's breathing. Time slowed to a halt.

"Stand up," Eve whispered through clenched teeth, tugging the sleeve of his robe. He obeyed, grinning as he trailed behind her up the aisle and out the door. It was sad, he thought, that the Cup had not given Eve the same Bliss it had given him. He wanted to ask her if she felt even the slightest bit different, but the rules (which she'd already broken) stated that Newlings must keep silent for twelve bells after drinking the sacred elixir. And by the saints, he'd not be one to disobey and jeopardize his chance to taste the Second Cup!

Once he could speak again, the first thing he planned to ask Lorcan was how long he'd have to wait for that next dose of the elixir. He licked his lips, hoping to gather any remaining trace of it.

At the corner of Spendthrift Lane and Miser Street, Lorcan stepped in front of Tommin and Eve to lead them the rest of the way home. He strutted like a peacock—like the king Tommin knew he wanted to be.

When they reached the house, Lorcan fumbled noisily with his keys and swore at the troublesome lock. Eve reached over and pinched Tommin's arm so hard he knew it would bruise, yet the pain didn't bother him one bit. He'd not stopped smiling since the ceremony; he was that overwhelmed by happiness.

"Get hold of yourself, you fool," she whispered.

He said nothing, still loath to break the rules. The Leprechaun inside Tommin insisted that everything was grand, that Eve was the foolish one for not basking in the blazing afterglow of the Cup. But in the far, far recesses of his mind, the human boy Tommin quietly agreed with Eve; this reveling in Leprechaun magic was dangerous.

Tommin brushed past Eve, senses assaulted by a jumble of mouth-watering aromas. The kitchen table was full of platters and bowls of *real* food: a fat pink ham, pies, buns, cheese, potatoes fried crisp! Copper coaxed a dish of herring into the last open space and then wiped his hands on his grubby apron. Pride—and a smear of gravy—shone on his usually somber face.

"Good lad," Lorcan said, patting Copper's unkempt hair. "You've outdone yourself with this feast."

Copper beamed at the praise. Tommin's stomach rumbled loud enough for all to hear.

"Sit, sit," Lorcan said. "We shall celebrate your advancement, my Newlings. No mushrooms for you tonight!"

Tommin heaped food onto his plate and began shoveling it into his mouth. Compared to the elixir, it tasted bland; compared to mushroom mush, it was heaven served piping hot. Between bites, he noticed Eve eating slowly from a plate of modest portions. Lorcan drank cup after cup of wine, nibbling now and then on a slab of ham the size of his hand.

"You can do better than that, lad," Lorcan said, shoving a serving of steak pie onto Tommin's plate. "Try that now. Mushrooms are our sacred food here Below, and when we're well satisfied with our Takes, we Leprechauns could be happy eating sawdust . . . but a good feast on the Days of the Cup is a fine reward for one and all." He poured more blood-red wine into his cup and lifted it high. "To my sixth gold-son, Eevar, and to my seventh gold-son, Tommin. Long may we prosper, and long may our rainbows touch the sky."

Eve and Tommin lifted their cups of watery mint tea (apparently Lorcan's culinary generosity had its limits) and saluted silently.

The high-pitched end-of-the-day bell rang out, and Lorcan tossed his napkin onto the table. He stood and patted his belly. "Full as a tick, I am. Clean this up before you go to bed, Copper. If I find one crumb on the floor come morning, Gladys will skin your hide."

"Yes, Master," Copper said.

"And you two: no talking till morning, remember. It's bad luck, besides being against the law." Lorcan wobbled and wove his way across the kitchen and into his private rooms. He slammed his door so hard the dishes shook.

Eve stood and began to help Copper clear the table. The grim line of her mouth and the crease in her forehead gave away the still-simmering disgust she held for Tommin and his elixir-induced behavior. As his mood mellowed, he began to worry about the permanent effects the elixir might have, and to regret upsetting Eve once again. Wanting to make things right, Tommin laid a hand on her arm, but she swatted it away.

"I'll have no dealings with you while you're in such a state. It would do neither of us any good. Go to bed, Tommin."

"You talked!" Copper said. "It's bad luck! You heard the master."

Eve slipped a stack of plates into the basin of soapy water. "There's nothing in the Neathlands *but* bad luck, Copper."

"True enough," the boy said. "But there's bad luck, and then there's *worse*."

Tommin shook his head, still reluctant to speak. Anyway, he doubted he could say anything that would please Eve or Copper.

"Just go," Eve demanded.

The last bit of Tommin's elixir-given joy evaporated as he turned away from her and took slow steps toward his room. Before his eyes, colors dulled until everything looked as dingy as it had before the Cup . . . yet something inside him felt different—and that frightened him more than all the cats in Neathgillan.

# Chapter Twenty-One

## *Ealaíona Draíochtach na Trádála*

## (Magical Tricks of the Trade)

After breakfast (soggy mushroom toast with sludgy mushroom tea), Tommin followed Eve into the parlor. There, Lorcan Reilly sat in a wingback chair, smoking a pipe. A haze of blue-gray smoke hovered a few inches above his head.

Eve sneezed.

"Ah, my gold-children," Lorcan said, setting his pipe on a side table. He pointed to a wooden chair and a cushion-topped stool. "Sit there and there." He waited for them to obey before continuing. "As your gold-father, and since you have become second-level Leprechaun Newlings, it is my great responsibility and honor to teach you the ways of Glamour and Charm—two tools of our trade we call upon regularly in our dealings with humans."

Eve perched on the edge of the stool, unsmiling as usual. Tommin reckoned she expected to turn out to be a failure at Glamour and Charm, just as she'd been a failure at shoemaking and stealing.

"You did study this with O'Ferrell, did you not?" Lorcan said. "Usually my Newlings are excited to learn these magical skills, but you two look as overjoyed as dead rats."

"We studied it," Eve said. Tommin nodded in agreement.

Lorcan stood and paced the room as he spoke. "So, you will recall that neither Glamour nor Charm have any effect on other Leprechauns, as far as persuasion goes. The same holds true for most of the Faerie tribes. They can detect trickery as easily as we can tell soil from silver."

Lorcan gestured for Tommin to come join him in front of the fireplace. "Now, imagine you're out on a Take, and the lady of the house catches you in her kitchen. What would you have done before you studied our ways?"

"I would have run like mad," Tommin said.

"And now?"

"I'd try to strike up some Charm and confuse her a bit. Maybe make her fall in love with me enough that she couldn't care a straw that I've broken into her house and got my hand in the money box."

"Good. Very good. Now show me."

"But I can't Charm *you*," Tommin said.

"Correct, but I can feel the Charm's presence and intention, in spite of the fact that it will not affect me. Focus your mind on how you want me to feel toward you."

Tommin thought, *You find me handsome and sweet. You want to give me whatever I desire.* He focused all his energy on Lorcan. Deep in his chest, something stirred, vibrating like a hive of newly awakened bees. It didn't hurt, but it didn't feel nice, either. He repeated the thought he wanted to send to Lorcan, and the buzzing within him multiplied. His blood pumped hard through his veins as if he'd run a mile uphill, and his head grew light as he sent the thought a third time.

With a great gasp for air, he stopped.

Lorcan smiled. "A worthy attempt. You'll improve with practice. Your turn, Eevar."

Tommin slumped in the wooden chair, drained. Using Charm did that, but its use *was* meant to be followed with an energizing Take. His palms itched vaguely as he watched Eve walk to Lorcan's side. She said nothing, but after a moment, Lorcan shivered and put a hand over his heart.

"By the Great Himself," Lorcan said, eyes wide. "I've never felt such strong Charm from anyone, let alone a Newling."

"Truly?" Eve's astonishment was written all over her face.

"You'll need to be careful, child," Lorcan said. "Too much Charm can be deadly to both the Charmer and the Charmed, or so the old tales tell us. It must be used only when necessary, as a tool but never a weapon. Understood?"

Eve nodded. "And may I try Glamour next?"

Tommin yawned. "You aren't too tired?" If it weren't for the excitement of seeing Eve succeed, he might have dozed off by now. And his hands definitely itched.

"I'm not at all tired," she said.

"Fine," Lorcan said. "So, to be clear: Charm is the use of persuasion to bend the will of a human, and Glamour is a form of magic by which we cause a human to see us differently than we are. The caveat being that we must put on the Glamour *before* the human sees us in the first place. Glamour protects a Leprechaun from being recognized as a Leprechaun. With the use of Glamour, one can appear to be an average-sized blacksmith or a rather tall clergyman. This is a defensive tool, meant to prevent humans from calling us out and demanding three wishes or our precious pot of gold."

"But an un-Glamoured Leprechaun looks like a wee Faerie man to a human?" Tommin asked. "That's what Master O'Ferrell taught us."

"That's correct. In most cases, humans perceive us as under four feet tall if they catch a glimpse of us. Indeed, we *are* that height when Above after conversion unless we're purposefully covered in Glamour. It makes it easier to hide and to slip through small spaces. It's one of the gifts of the blessed Third Cup, and part of the Leprechauns' magical constitution. Our blood is green tinted, our bodies small, our minds sharper than shoe tacks."

Eve crossed her arms. "Yes, we did learn all that in class. And now I'm ready to actually try the Glamour, if we're done with the gabbing," she said. Tommin saw a twinkle in her eye that he'd never seen before, one that forecast mischief.

"Go ahead," Lorcan said. He took a few steps back and kept his focus on her face.

Eve closed her eyes for a count of three. Tommin neither blinked nor breathed as he waited. And then, around Eve's body, he saw a shimmering cloud of pale light. Another faint image overlapped the real Eve, this one the very likeness of the shoemaker Rafferty.

"Excellent," Lorcan said with a deep chuckle. "Perfection, in fact. This afternoon, *you* shall teach Tommin and I shall observe."

With a loud yawn, Tommin scratched his hands and wrists. With his eyes, he beseeched Lorcan for relief in the form of a little gold pill. Lorcan opened his watchcase-shaped pillbox and passed Tommin two tablets. "Eevar? Have you desire to partake?"

She shook her head.

Lorcan said, "Well, we'll make a Leprechaun of you yet. I haven't the slightest doubt."

Tommin put the pills under his tongue and leaned back in his chair, relishing the warm, tingling happiness that spread throughout his body.

"Tomorrow, we'll go Above and you'll learn the time-honored way to perform a Take," Lorcan said. "The pills don't provide enough nourishment for a second-level Newling, no matter how many you might take in a day, Tommin, my lad. You're bound to fall ill if you don't lay hands on some good gold or silver soon."

"Gold," Tommin muttered, smiling as if besotted. "And silver."

Lorcan said, "And you, Eevar. The things you might do among the humans with your rare talents! You are a treasure, child. Do not doubt it."

"Never, Uncle," Eve said sweetly. Too sweetly. Even in his happily drugged state, Tommin noted the promise of revenge in Eve's voice.

He'd think about that later. For now, he was sated and content. He stretched his legs out straight and crossed his ankles. His thoughts, as slippery as minnows, refused to be caught for long—but he did manage to hook onto the bright thought of eventual freedom, of going home to Granny and taking Eve and Copper with him.

Tomorrow would be a big step in the right direction. Tomorrow, above ground, in the good air and bright sunlight, Eve might realize freedom was better than revenge. *Anything* might happen tomorrow, Tommin told himself. And then he slipped into a dream of swimming among silver-scaled fish in a sea of gold.

# Chapter Twenty-Two

## *An Domhan Thuas*

## (The World Above)

The route from the Neathlands to the world above was as tricky as the Leprechauns who had built it. There were long tunnels carved through rock, a great many doors to be opened by a puzzling array of identical-looking keys, and dark, muddy passages so narrow Tommin's shoulders became caked with dirt. Torches held high, Tommin, Eve, and Copper followed Lorcan across stone bridges straddling underground streams and through caverns of slowly dripping stalactites. Upward and downward they trudged, and then upward again.

"You're sure this is the shortest way?" Tommin asked, panting.

"Never said that," Lorcan replied without stopping. "Keep up. We'll reach the portal soon enough."

"Don't know what you're complaining about," Copper said, passing Tommin. "You're not the one lugging the water jug and your weight in baggage."

Eve slowed to match her stride to Tommin's. "All this back and forth is so we can't memorize the way out," she whispered.

As if he'd heard, Lorcan looked back over his shoulder and said, "After you've imbibed the last of your three Cups, you'll be given your own keys and a complete set of maps. Of course, I haven't had need of a map in centuries."

They rounded a sharp bend and waited for Lorcan to insert an age-blackened key into a wide wooden door. When the door swung open, bright light poured in. Tommin shielded his eyes with his hand. Squinting, he saw a ladder ahead, a ladder lit by a shaft of *real* sunlight.

How long had it been since he'd seen an actual sunbeam? "Beautiful," he said—because it was, and because he couldn't help himself.

"I'll go first, and take Copper with me," Lorcan said. "Wait for my signal, and then you may follow." He placed his torch in a metal holder on the wall and took Copper by the hand.

"Wish I didn't have to come every blasted time," Copper said, dropping his pack and setting the jug in the dirt. "If you knew what it feels like when the light hits me and all my bones go wrong—"

Lorcan smacked Copper's cheek. "Enough." He pulled the boy to the foot of the ladder. When the sunlight touched Copper's ginger hair, he collapsed, his body shrinking until all that remained of him was a pile of clothes on the ground. Lorcan reached inside and fished out a little brown bat. The bat squeaked and wriggled until Lorcan stuffed it into his waistcoat pocket. Without another word, Lorcan nimbly scaled the ladder.

Once he'd disappeared from view, Eve turned to Tommin and spoke fast and low. "Pay attention to every detail. Everything Lorcan says and does—landmarks, rituals, unusual gestures. Any little thing might prove useful when our chance comes to run."

"We're running today?"

"Of course not. Unless you've got some secret plan to help Copper?"

"Not yet, I don't."

"All is well," Lorcan called, popping his head down the hole. "Come Above. And no more talking or you'll have an appointment with Gladys as soon as we get home. You think I can't hear you chattering like birds down there?"

Eve took Tommin's torch from his hand and set it in a holder. "Go on. I'll follow," she said.

Tommin ascended the ladder like a squirrel scampering up a tree. At the top, he climbed out of the hole and fell on his hands and knees. With dew-dampened grass under his palms, sunbeams stinging his eyes, and warm, fresh air in his lungs, he felt *new*.

"On your feet, lad," Lorcan said. "No need to crawl about like a wild animal."

A moment later, Eve jumped out of the hole. Tommin thought he saw a hint of a suppressed smile on her freckled face. The sight of her in the pure sunlight made him want to laugh and cry at the same time, made him remember what it felt like to be young and human and a little bit in love. When he managed to take his eyes off her, he found that everything that had once been ordinary to him now captivated his senses—the towering oak trees surrounding them, the birdsong, the curves and points of fallen branches, the hint of smoke on the breeze.

"This way," Lorcan said, pointing with Gladys. "Over the next hill lies gold for the Taking. Or at least silver. Tell me when you catch the scent of treasure, Eevar; that will give me the measure of your Leprechaun senses. Tommin's proved himself already in that regard."

As they walked, Tommin breathed deeply, smelling nothing but green plants and burning peat. He scanned his surroundings and found them vaguely familiar. Could that be the very tree he and his friend Sean had climbed to hide from Sean's mother after they'd eaten the pie she'd been saving for supper? Could that patch of woods across the valley be the forbidden forest he'd entered with Lorcan on his last day Above?

Was that curl of smoke in the distance ascending from Granny's chimney? How he wanted to run and see! He took a step forward, but Lorcan grabbed his elbow firmly. "Now is no time for foolishness," he warned. "Be calm, unless you want to wind up sharing my pocket with Copper."

Tommin glanced at Eve. She rolled her eyes, obviously sharing his disbelief that Lorcan had the power at hand to change him into a Faerie bat.

When they reached the bridge, Tommin knew for certain he'd come home to Loughgillan. Yet things were out of place. He'd not been gone long enough for all those new houses to be built, or for Farmer Walch's apple trees to have grown so tall . . . but there they were, plain as day.

"Time to put on a bit of the Glamour, Newlings," Lorcan said. "Let us array ourselves as merchants stopping on our way home to Dublin, a father and sons. Imagine yourselves respectably dressed, with friendly faces. Yes, that will do nicely. Now, we'll avoid people as much as we can. To escape notice is always the best course of action. We'll go in, have our Takes, and then return the way we came. Keep up your Glamours and no one will suspect you of being anything other than a human visitor."

After they crossed the bridge, Lorcan lifted a hand to signal Tommin and Eve to stop. "Eevar? Have you any idea where the treasure lies?"

She shook her head. "Not an inkling."

Lorcan grunted with disgust. "Well then, Tommin?"

Tommin inhaled deeply. "To the north," he said. "Silver coins, I think."

"Good," Lorcan said. "You may take the lead."

Tommin's desire for treasure grew, threatening to consume his thoughts, and keeping up the Glamour proved challenging. Using the magic was sapping his energy as rapidly as an uphill footrace would have. To make matters worse, his hands itched and burned like the devil.

He almost passed by Granny's street—*his* street—without noticing. Just in time to cast a glance in the right direction, he turned his head. Someone had painted the little house, and fresh thatch roofing glowed golden brown in the sunshine. A woman stood on the doorstep, holding a tiny baby in her arms. She had black curly hair and beady eyes like Eliza Harkin, a girl who lived on the far side of town. But Eliza was shorter, thinner, and twelve years old at most.

From the house next door, someone called out, "Eliza!"

Tommin stumbled, lost his Glamour, and hit the ground hard. As the breath rushed out of him, despair rushed in. He scrambled to his feet and ran toward the young mother.

"Where's Nora Dolan?" he shouted. "Where's my granny?"

"And who wants to know?" the neighbor asked, brandishing a broom and hurrying to the rescue of the shocked-looking young mother. "Dirty beggar! Get away with you!"

Tommin rushed into the house. The table was the same, but not the dishes. Granny's favorite chair wasn't beside the fire. Her knitting basket had been replaced by a wooden cradle.

"Where's Nora Dolan?" he shouted to the old walls.

"Nora Dolan's been in the churchyard five years or more," the young woman said behind him. "I'm sorry."

Tommin's knees buckled. A sound came from his throat, a moaning cry that made the baby howl.

He felt himself yanked to his feet by the shirt collar. "Pay him no mind," Lorcan Reilly said to the mother. "My son is unwell. We'll trouble you no more. You needn't tell anyone we were here."

Tommin didn't fight as Lorcan dragged him out of the house and around the corner.

"Fool," Lorcan said. "Pull yourself together, and get your Glamour back in place."

Hot tears spilled from Tommin's eyes. He wriggled out of Lorcan's grasp. "How long? How long have you kept me underground? Five years? Ten?"

"Time means nothing," Lorcan said. "You know Faerie time doesn't align with human time. 'Tis naught to be grieved over. You don't belong here among the humans anymore. You never did belong here, truth be told."

"Truth? How dare you talk about truth?" Tommin raised a fist. Eve grabbed his arm and held it tightly.

"Tommin," she said. "Think."

Slowly and reluctantly, he lowered his fist. Still, his heart beat fast and wild.

Lorcan smiled coolly. "There now. The Take will make you feel better. A bit of wealth in one's pocket puts everything into perspective." He patted Tommin's cheek. "You did come with me from that jail cell of your own free will, you remember? Every favor has its price, especially among the Faerie folk."

"You tricked me."

"I wouldn't put it that way at all, my lad. We made a bargain, you and I, for mutual benefit. If you weren't half-starved for mammon, you wouldn't be so confused and unsettled. Come, let's be on our way. We're close now. Smell that?" He waved one hand in front of his nose and inhaled. "Silver. High quality. At least four coins of a respectable size."

Yes, Tommin smelled it. Yes, he wanted it, and badly. But he would not say so and give Lorcan the satisfaction.

Eve continued holding Tommin's arm as they fell into step with Lorcan. Perhaps she thought he'd run. Perhaps she meant to soothe him with her touch. He was too angry and too full of sorrow to try to work out anyone else's intentions.

Intentions, he thought, were hard horses to ride. Even his own. And what were his intentions, anyway? Here and now: to steal the silver and satisfy the starving, fiendish magpie within him. Ultimately: to be free from the need for gold and free from the Leprechauns altogether—and to help Eve and Copper find freedom as well. And perhaps to see Lorcan Reilly punished for his wickedness somehow.

"This is the place," Lorcan said, stopping by a newly built house. "Deepen your Glamour a bit and go 'round to the back door, lad. We'll wait here."

Tommin did as he was told, but only because he had to. Only because the pain of longing was unbearable, like a thousand little knives scraping his skin again and again.

He crept into the kitchen, where an old woman dozed over a lapful of knitting. The sight of her dove-gray hair and wrinkled apron, so like Granny's, wrenched his heart. She snored lightly as he passed by her. Half-blinded by tears, he tracked the silver scent into the next room.

A minute later, when he laid hands upon the coins, his blood rejoiced. His body regained strength, and much of his pain vanished. But he did not think there was enough treasure in the world to erase the agony of being forever parted from his dear granny.

He had lost the only person who had loved him no matter what, and he blamed Lorcan Reilly for it—even more than he blamed himself.

# Chapter Twenty-Three

## *Boghanna Báistí agus Dorchadas*

## (Rainbows and Darkness)

In a shallow valley tucked between mountains, Eve stood beside Lorcan to watch Tommin bury a small crock of gold and silver coins. Eyes closed and arms raised to the skies, Tommin recited the ancient Leprechaun words that sealed the earth above the treasure to secure it from man, beast, and Faerie folk for a thousand years. Finally, he pricked his finger with a golden pin and shed a single drop of blood onto the dirt. A rainbow sprang from the ground and soared into the clouds, its bright colors blazing as it bridged the gap between the earth and the heavens.

"Fine work," Lorcan said. "Far better than that wee stripe of colors Eevar managed earlier."

Eve shouldered their bag and stuck her tongue out at Tommin. He grinned in reply, obviously intoxicated by the joy of sending up a rainbow. Pitiful, that's what these Leprechauns were, stealing wealth and then burying it forever. Sure, the Take and the rainbow setting gave them a few hours of ecstasy, but those thrills faded fast and left behind nothing but more hunger for treasure.

She had to get Tommin away from Lorcan soon, before the Leprechaun overtook whatever was left of the human boy. Heaven knew he wasn't going to be able to save himself if he went much further down the pathway to conversion.

"Back to the portal," Lorcan said. He gave his pocket a pat. "Copper has promised to cook us a fine supper when we get home. Mixed mushroom pie and chanterelle hot pot for my rainbow setters. And perhaps a bit of port I've been saving for a special occasion."

Eve and Tommin walked side by side in Lorcan's shadow. Tommin's face still glowed with pleasure. Eve reached over and pinched him hard. "Get hold of yourself," she mouthed.

"And, you may ask, what is the special occasion?" Lorcan said, twirling Gladys between his fingers as he walked. "The occasion is this, my Newlings: you have succeeded in passing my rainbow-setting test, and tomorrow you shall demonstrate for O'Ferrell, after which he'll approve you to drink the Second Cup of Fortune. Once he signs your advancement papers, we'll head straight to the cathedral, and the officiant will give you the elixir."

"Truly?" Tommin asked too eagerly. Eve pinched him again, and he brushed her hand away.

"Ah, greedy boy," Lorcan said with a chuckle. "I chose well when I chose you as my seventh gold-son." He stopped before an ancient yew tree and inserted a key into what looked like a hole bored by insects. A door swung open. He turned and said, "And you, Eevar. You should thank me. Your Take skills are barely adequate, not to mention your sorry rainbows. However, since your use of Glamour is exceptional, I'm willing to recommend you for advancement."

"Thank you, Uncle," Eve said sweetly as she stepped past Lorcan to enter the tree. She froze when she found herself at the top of a flight of steps that descended into utter darkness.

"Do not fear the dark," Lorcan said. The tree's door shut of its own accord, blocking every last bit of light.

*I'm not afraid of anything,* Eve thought, running a hand along the wall as she moved down the stairs. *Not anymore. It's you who should be afraid, Lorcan Reilly.* As a little girl, she'd had a great terror of the dark—and she did not doubt that Lorcan meant to torture her by calling upon it now—but since the elixir had awoken the magic within her, she'd changed.

She wasn't sure what she could do with the gifts the curse and the Cup had imparted, nor did she know the limits of her power. That was for her to discover—and for her to conceal from her false uncle until the great day came . . .

Something flashed from behind her. She turned to look up the stairs. There stood Lorcan, holding a black candle in one hand. Copper lay curled up at his feet, moaning and naked.

"I have everything under control, as usual," Lorcan said.

Eve dug into the bag to retrieve Copper's clothes. "Of course you do, Uncle," she said.

# Chapter Twenty-Four

## *An Dara Chupán*

## (The Second Cup)

The great bell sounded three times as Tommin and Eve stood before the altar with Lorcan and the officiant. *Nine o'clock,* Tommin thought—or what he'd come to think of as nine in the morning, Neathlands time. In his mind, he divided the number, multiplied it, drew it upside down and backward—futile attempts to calm his galloping heart.

The officiant chanted, lifting a dark glass bottle above his head, blessing the liquid and those who were about to imbibe.

Tommin's mind was unusually clear this morning. He weighed his options and his feelings. He wanted to drink the Cup, and he didn't. Mostly, he did. That was the problem. Things had gotten out of hand. He'd changed too much, given over to the Leprechaun in him too often. If he drank, would he lose the last remnant of his humanity?

But his choices were limited. Drink, or get sold to the Trolls. Drink, or die at the hands of the Leprechauns. Death by Gladys might also be a possibility. And then there was the option of making a run for it—which could end in being eaten by cats, lost in the endless maze of tunnels, or set ablaze by a mad Leprechaun mob.

When he heard the pop of the cork and the fizzling of the elixir, he quit debating with himself. The scent of the stuff and the memory of its effects taunted him, seduced him. *Magpie,* he heard Granny say in his mind, the word an urgent warning. *Magpie.* But he could not turn away from it now.

Eve drank first, draining the entire Second Cup as Leprechaun law required. Tommin watched, his breath held, eyes unblinking. He saw her shiver as she handed the chalice back to the officiant. He heard her exhale softly. She'd lived through another dose, and as far as he could tell, the drink had done nothing but make her cheeks rosy.

The officiant refilled the chalice, singing a sacred song as he did so. The flickering candlelight reflected off the jeweled Cup, and little bubbles popped on the surface of the blue liquid inside it. Tommin took the Cup and drank, swallow after blessed swallow of effervescent deliciousness. The more he drank, the more he loved the stuff. He felt as if he were drinking starlight and galaxies, imbibing bright universes of infinite happiness.

Tommin handed the empty chalice back to the officiant, noting the faint green glow of the skin on the fellow's face, how his white beard flowed like a stream made of dandelion fluff down the front of his embroidered robe, the glint of gold in his eyes. Surely he was centuries old, wise in the ways of all men and every Faerie tribe. He was a glorious, magnificent creature.

Lorcan cleared his throat. With a start, Tommin stopped staring at the officiant and realized that he had forgotten to follow Eve back up the aisle. She stood in the doorway, glaring at him and tapping her toe. Honestly, could a fellow not take a minute to enjoy himself? Perhaps even a *few* minutes on such a rare occasion as this?

With a nod and a grateful smile, Tommin left the officiant and sauntered up the aisle. Lorcan caught up to him, put an arm around Tommin's shoulders, and said, "'Tis a good omen, Tommin, your love of the Cup. A sign you've got an extra measure of Leprechaun magic in you. Your strong gold lust, your perfect rainbows—you remind me of myself as a Newling. We're headed for the top, my lad. All the way to the top, and woe betide the fool who'd try to stand in our way."

Eve shook her head as they passed her in the wide doorway. Sometimes she was so like Granny, Tommin thought, with all her eye rolling and silent pity. But Granny was dead, and so was the boy he'd been. With the glorious elixir greening his blood, his every limb sang out with Leprechaun Bliss.

# Chapter Twenty-Five

## Cait agus Coinnle

## (Cats and Candles)

A few days—or perhaps weeks—after the Second Cup ceremony, Lorcan sent Tommin on an errand to fetch candles from a shop at the far edge of town. Walking alone through the dim, mostly empty streets, Tommin had a rare chance to try to straighten out his jumbled mind. The Cup had satisfied his physical need to Take, so the lust for gold did not skew his other thoughts. Being away from Lorcan also seemed to help him focus better on non-Leprechaun things.

He turned left onto Auld Bank Street. A trio of cats slunk across his path, peering at him with glowing, demonic eyes. By the saints, he hated the Neathlands cats. He was certain they knew more than cats ought to, that they were simply waiting for the right time to launch a revolution or to slaughter every last nonfeline citizen of Neathgillan.

The time-keeping bell tolled eight times. In the shadows, a cat yowled along. Tommin shivered, pulled his green jacket tight around him, and picked up his pace. A few more blocks and he'd reach Avarice Lane—one of the best-lit streets in town, thank heaven, and one the wretched cats avoided.

The thought of avoidance led him to remember how badly he'd treated Eve in recent days. Or weeks. He'd ignored her, dismissed her whispered requests to meet clandestinely, and generally acted like a grumpy old man. Or a grumpy old Leprechaun. His face burned with shame as he realized just how ornery he'd been to one of his only friends.

Blast the elixir. Blast the greening blood flowing through his brain and making him more of a Leprechaun with every heartbeat.

Tommin's life had become like mad badgers caught in a whirlwind, his Leprechaun nature clawing and biting at his human desires in a never-ending, swirling frenzy. Lorcan kept him busy with frequent, chaperoned trips Above to Take and bury treasure. He studied every book he could get hold of, mourned his Granny, hungered for food not made from fungi, practiced Charm and Glamour, ran errands, and memorized the words of the pledge he'd have to recite at the Ceremony of the Third Cup. He had wanted to speak with Eve and not wanted anything to do with her . . . Saints, it was a mess, his life.

At this moment, all he wanted to do was apologize to Eve. To make things right with his best friend. He swore he would do so the minute he got back to Lorcan's house.

*If* he could remember to once he got there.

He hoped she'd not given up on him and their plan to escape.

He turned onto Avarice Lane and spotted the candlemaker's shop. The short, fat Leprechaun stood in the doorway, smoking a long-stemmed carved-ivory pipe. From the deep shade of his green-tinted skin, Tommin guessed the fellow to be well over two hundred years old.

"Quit your gawking," the candlemaker said. He pointed his pipe at Tommin and squinted his beady eyes. "You be Lorcan's seventh gold-son, isn't you? The one what he brags about when he's been downing the *poitín*."

"Yes, sir," Tommin said. "Master Lorcan's sent me for his order."

The candlemaker gestured for Tommin to follow him into the shop. The old Leprechaun moved at a snail's pace. "I'd of thought you too good for fetching and carrying from the way Lorcan goes on about you and your 'rare talents' and all," he said as he piled candles into a small wooden crate. "'Strongest gold lust I ever saw,' 'nose for the good stuff like's out of legends,' says Lorcan Reilly. Even said once you be the key to him getting the throne of the Great Himself. Glory to gold, he was drunk that partic'lar night, so ol' Lorcan Reilly was."

"Hmm," Tommin said. He reckoned it the wisest reply.

The candlemaker shoved the box into Tommin's chest, and he grabbed it just in time to keep it from falling to the floor.

With lowered brows and snarling lip, the candlemaker said, "I'm thinking to myself that you isn't got the brains of a dried-up turnip. I'm thinking you be one of them *stupid* Leprechauns what gets caught by a human soon as he drinks the Third Cup and goes Above alone, that's what I'm thinking."

"You may be right, sir," Tommin said.

The old Leprechaun kicked him hard in the shin. "Of course I'm right, you wee dog turd. Now get away with you! And tell Lorcan Reilly the bill's due tomorrow, and I'm adding another five guldens onto the tally since he sent the likes of you over to vexate me."

Shin smarting, Tommin clutched the box of candles to his chest and hurried out of the shop. As he left Avarice Lane, he imagined Copper's voice saying, *See? That's what'll become of you if you drink the Third Cup. That's your future, being a rude and selfish old crank, fond of nothing but gold and your own green-blooded self.* And he knew this imagined Copper spoke the truth. He just couldn't figure out a way to avoid it, having come so far. He'd read every book in the academy library about Faerie curses and come up with nothing. No remedy, no spell of liberation, no record of anyone ever having left the fold to rejoin the human race.

Tommin turned onto Drachma Street. Several of the lamps had gone out, leaving great portions of the street in deep shadow. He hastened his footsteps, trying not to think of the giant rats and the surly cats who tracked them.

"Get off!" Tommin heard a familiar voice cry out. "Go on! Get!"

"Copper?" Tommin said.

A terrible yowling and hissing echoed between the stone buildings, followed by the servant boy's blood-curdling scream.

Tommin dropped the box of candles and ran toward the sound. Behind a monument to King Gladpenny IV, he found Copper writhing on the ground, hands shielding his face from an attack by three Faerie tomcats almost as big as he was. Their claws shredded his sleeves and tore at his scalp as he cried, "Stop! You can have the bloody sausages! Just get off!"

Heart thumping, Tommin grabbed one of the cats and tossed it aside and then yanked another off the boy. The animal dug its claws into Tommin's arm, and panicking, he pulled it free and flung it hard. It shrieked as its body flew through the air and slammed into an iron lamppost, and then went silent. The remaining cat hissed and retreated into the darkness.

"You all right?" Tommin helped Copper to his feet. Blood ran from the boy's scratched head and neck onto his tattered shirt.

Copper wiped his face with his sleeve. "I'll be all right," he said. Shaking, he bent and picked up a paper-wrapped parcel. His face was grim. "But you're in a heap of trouble." He pointed to the lamppost. At its base, the tomcat lay perfectly still. "My gold, Tommin, you'll be dead as that when the high-up Leps find out what you've done."

"Saints above," Tommin muttered. "I didn't mean to kill it. I didn't even know they were killable! We'd better run. As fast as we can, Copper."

Tommin grabbed Copper's hand and pulled him along behind him. Only after they had reached the safety of Lorcan's kitchen did Tommin realize he'd left the candles behind as evidence of his presence at the scene of the crime.

It would not take long for the Leprechauns to figure out who was responsible for the murder of one of the king's precious felines. Tommin knew the punishment for tampering with the cats: an excruciating death by a Faerie-brewed poison that took three days to do its work.

Eve walked into the kitchen. "Tommin? What's wrong? You look as if you've seen the devil himself."

Tommin collapsed into a chair and held his head in his hands. "Not yet. But I'll be seeing him soon enough if I don't get away from here," he said.

Copper poured a cup of water from a pitcher and set it before Tommin. "It's all my fault," he said tearfully. "You should have let them have me."

"What are you talking about, Copper?" Eve asked, putting an arm around the boy as he began to sob.

Copper swiped away his tears with his shirtsleeve. "The blasted cats. Tommin's gone and killed one, and now he's doomed—and so am I, when the story comes out."

"Tommin!" Eve exclaimed, condemning him with a look.

"They were going to kill him," Tommin said. "And I only meant to scare them off. Things got out of hand."

"Tell me no one saw you," Eve said.

Tommin shook his head. "Not a soul, as far as I know. But—"

"Then we've nothing to worry about. It's our secret to keep." Eve petted Copper's messy hair, almost smiling.

"That'd be true," Copper said. "Excepting for Master Lorcan's candle order's scattered all over the street. And the fact that nobody else orders the gray ones he favors."

"He's right, Eve," Tommin said, wishing the room would quit spinning. "I'm doomed."

"Tell me where it happened," Eve said.

"You can't go over there," Tommin said. "If someone were to see you, they'd think—"

"You needn't worry about that," Eve said. "I'll be careful."

"Drachma Street, near the old well," Copper said.

"Make Tommin some tea with honey before he faints," Eve said as she headed for the door. "And if Lorcan comes back before me, tell him I went to get his mint leaves from the shop."

And then she was gone.

"Me, I don't know if she's brave or mad, our Eve," Copper said. He hung the kettle over the fire and flopped into a chair across from Tommin.

"A little of both," Tommin said. "But mostly brave."

He wouldn't say it out loud and make Copper cry again, but Tommin thought it would be some kind of miracle if Eve didn't get caught retrieving the candles.

Faintly, his palms began to itch. Master Rafferty would have said Tommin had all the luck of a three-legged black cat walking under a ladder on Friday the thirteenth, and Tommin would have had to agree.

He could only hope that Eve's luck was a far sight better than his own.

# Chapter Twenty-Six

## *An Teachtaireacht*

## (The Errand)

Eve slipped into the shadows between two buildings and covered herself with Glamour, impersonating the hefty, long-bearded night watchman. After the Second Cup, her skills in Glamour and Charm had become so great that she'd been able to go about town disguised as Lorcan, Copper, and Schoolmaster O'Ferrell on numerous occasions without ever being caught.

It shouldn't have been possible; the Leps always saw through each other's Glamours. But her magic was different. Better. She half wondered if, with practice, she might be able to make herself invisible. That was something she'd try later, once they were free. Now, she ran from street to street as the night watchman, albeit faster than the out-of-shape fellow could ever dream of running.

She darted into Drachma Street. The candles lay scattered on the ground beside an overturned wooden box. She gathered them quickly and set the box in the shadow of a lamppost.

Next, she looked for the Faerie cat. She found it lying lifeless, just where Copper had said it would be. Its dull eyes seemed to accuse her, but she didn't hesitate to lift its stiff body. She carried it a few feet and then set it down on the ground beside a rectangular grate. Straining and grunting, she lifted the iron grate that covered the stream of ever-flowing dirty wastewater. With one hand, she stretched back and grabbed the animal. And then she dropped it into the reeking stream.

"Hey there," a voice called out from the corner. "Is there a problem, Watchman O'Mooney? Trolls coming up through the pipes, are there? Ha-ha!"

Eve dropped the grate and maintained her Glamour. She stood and looked toward the other watchman, a short, bald fellow with bushy eyebrows. "Just checking the drainage here," she said in O'Mooney's voice.

The other watchman scratched his neck and said, "Well then. Full crocks and bright rainbows to you. See you around, mate."

Eve waved farewell. Once the other watchman left, she hurried to grab the box of candles and ran all the way back to Lorcan's house.

Safely tucked in her bed that night, Eve couldn't stop thinking of Tommin. How he'd put his life on the line for Copper's sake. How in a moment of crisis, he'd obeyed his heart and saved the boy. His human heart. No self-respecting Leprechaun would have dared to fight the king's clowder to help a slave—not even a prized Faerie-bat slave. And the way he'd looked at her when she'd safely returned with the candles! Like her return was a gift, not just a relief.

Blood rushed to her face. She had no experience in such matters, but she suspected she might be falling in love with Tommin.

It would be so unwise, so utterly ridiculous, and possibly dangerous. No, she couldn't allow it.

She rolled onto her side and pulled the covers over her shoulder. Better to spend her time thinking of how to escape or how to get the information she needed to free Copper and Tommin from their enchantments.

But when she closed her eyes, all she saw was a boy standing beside a workbench in a shoe shop in Loughgillan.

# Chapter Twenty-Seven

## An Leabhar Dearg

## (The Red Book)

After breakfast, Lorcan left for a meeting, having charged Copper with polishing the silverware, Tommin with fetching mushroom bread from the bakery, and Eve with visiting the tailor. She'd have the so-called honor of bringing home the sacred red coats she and Tommin would don after the drinking of the Third Cup, after they'd taken the final step to conversion.

Eve walked beside Tommin to the center of Neathgillan. They didn't speak, since Newlings were forbidden to converse on the street—and any passing full-blooded Lep had the authority to beat chatty Newlings into repentance. She tried not to look at him at all, not even when she knew his eyes were on her. Especially not then. Nevertheless, she did meet his gaze when they stopped at the corner of Fortune Lane and Abundance Street. They nodded farewell to one another, and the hint of a smile he offered made her heart beat much faster than she wanted it to.

She took Abundance Street, and she focused her thoughts on more important matters than her silly infatuation. Before she called on the tailor, she planned to visit Schoolmaster O'Ferrell—but not as herself. No, she'd wear the guise of the high officiant, the very Lep the other

Leps feared most (due to his short temper and the fact that as the king's seventh gold-son, he'd gotten away with murder at least a dozen times).

When she was certain no one was watching, Eve crouched behind a monument to a long-gone Leprechaun king. She closed her eyes and pictured the high officiant, imagined his features settling over her own, and felt her magic move to embrace her from head to toe.

She arrived at O'Ferrell's house a few minutes later. The schoolmaster's slave boy paled and shook when he opened the door and saw the officiant standing there. Eve felt sorry for the boy, but she couldn't drop the Glamour now.

"The l-l-library," the boy said. "Master's in th-there. D'you know . . . d'you know the way, sir?"

Eve nodded. She couldn't help patting the boy on the head and saying regally, "Well done, my fine fellow," as she passed by.

"High Officiant," O'Ferrell said, scrambling to his feet and bowing. "You honor me. I wasn't expecting—"

"I'm not here for tea and conversation. I need a book, and I've heard your library holds the rarest tomes in all the Neathlands." Eve surveyed the floor-to-ceiling bookshelves and did not doubt the truth of what she'd heard when in the pub, Glamoured as Lorcan. She'd had to buy a shocking number of drinks and use a fair measure of her unique form of Charm to get the timekeeper and the town crier to admit they'd even heard rumors of ways to reverse the gold-son-making curse. In fact, the timekeeper had blacked out right after mentioning O'Ferrell's forbidden collection, so even now, she was guessing.

O'Ferrell bowed low again. "My books are at your disposal, sir. Might I assist you in finding—"

"A book on Leprechaun curses and blessings, specifically their doing and undoing. And not that watered-down blather you teach the Newlings. What I require is *The Scarlet Tome of King Gulden the Eighth*." Eve ran her fingers along the spines of the books, searching for the title.

"Surely you know that book is forbidden," O'Ferrell said with false repugnance.

"And I also know you possess it," Eve said forcefully, bluffing and adding a measure of persuasive Charm. By the stars, she hoped her hunch was right and he truly did have the book. She pointed her officiant finger at the schoolmaster's nose. "You have it, and you'll share it with me this minute."

"Oh! Of course," O'Ferrell said with a nervous chuckle. "You mean *that Scarlet Tome*. Yes, it's in the cabinet over here. Locked up, kept safe. I was planning to send it to the Great Himself as a gift . . ." He fumbled with his keys and opened the cabinet door. The blood-red book he pulled out was no bigger than his hand. "Take it. With my compliments, sir."

"You'll forget this visit, won't you, O'Ferrell?" Eve said as she pocketed the book in the real jacket she wore beneath her Glamoured robes.

"The moment you're gone," O'Ferrell said. "Sooner, if you like."

Without saying good-bye, Eve turned on her heel and left. She hurried to the monument, hid again, and dropped the Glamour, more full of hope than she'd been in her life. Her pocket might contain the keys to freedom for herself and Tommin, and perhaps even Copper.

If the streets had been empty, she would have danced her way to the tailor's shop.

# Chapter Twenty-Eight

## *Rudaí Briste*

## (Broken Things)

Sated by a recent Take, Tommin sat at the kitchen table, stitching a silk slipper while Copper prepared their meal. His thoughts revolved around returning to life Above, feeling sunlight or clean raindrops on his skin, breathing air that didn't smell of mold and mud, eating anything besides mushrooms.

At the sound of Eve's footsteps, he looked up.

"You look peaceful," she said as she pulled out a chair and sat.

"That last Take did it, sorry to say." Guilt warmed his cheeks. "And shoemaking always soothes me."

Eve leaned toward him and folded her hands on the table. "I have things to tell you. Important things. Yesterday, I found this book—"

Lorcan Reilly threw open the kitchen door, rushed into the room, and slammed the door behind him. He hung his hat on a peg. Grinning and puffing out his chest with pride, he said, "Town crier's made the announcement, lads. All Newlings who are qualified to take the Third Cup are to report to the palace grounds six days hence. The ceremony will take place during Lá Samhna. A most auspicious time for conversion."

Copper lost his grip on the tureen, and it landed on the table with a clatter. Soup sloshed onto the tablecloth in front of Eve, but he made no move to wipe it up. He crossed his arms over his chest and said, "That means we have to leave in *three days*! It's all well and good for you. I'm the one having to pack everything and remember all your odd bits and bobs, and all the while doing everything else around here. Cooking, cleaning, running here and there at all hours . . ." His lower lip quivered.

Swaying slightly and stinking of *poitín*, Lorcan raised Gladys and pointed at Copper. "Enough of your blather, or Gladys will have a bite of your backside. Now, go make my mint tea."

"Yes, Master," Copper said glumly. He left the table and made the tea, rattling and banging dishes and tins as he did so.

Lorcan leaned Gladys against the wall and sat between Tommin and Eve. He reached out to rest one hand on Eve's cheek and the other on Tommin's. The scent of strong drink hung about him like a foul cloud. "Oh, my Newlings. What a proud day it will be, the day you drink your Third Cup! It shall be only the beginning of the wondrous future we'll share. Once you've fully converted, once I've brought all seven of my gold-sons into the fold, no one on or below the earth will be able to prevent me from doing whatever I please. I'll cut down the old king and set myself in his place, and I'll have more gold, silver, treasure, and tribute than any other Leprechaun alive. Every Faerie tribe will have to obey me and worship my greatness. Ah, it will be grand! And won't you be blessed to see it all and to know you're my offspring?"

Tommin glanced at Eve. She looked every bit as uncomfortable as he felt. Of course she did. They were sitting at a table with a madman—a madman who hungered for power and had planned to use them to get it ever since they'd been infants.

Copper set the teapot in front of Lorcan and hurried away without pouring it.

Lorcan stood and hurled the teapot at Copper's head. Copper moved just in time to avoid the flying crockery. It smashed against the wall, splashing tea from ceiling to floor.

"I have every right to kill you," Lorcan said calmly. If he'd shouted, he might have been less frightening. "And perhaps I will after you clean that up. Or perhaps I'll wait until we return from the palace. You see, I won't need you much longer, you worthless brat. Before long, I'll have better servants than you groveling at my feet night and day. You'll be food for cats when I'm finished with you, lad."

"Go ahead," Copper said, hands on hips. "Kill me. Doesn't matter to me."

"Hush, Copper," Eve said. "You don't mean that."

"I do," Copper said. "I've had enough, haven't I?"

Laughter erupted from Lorcan's mouth. He gripped the edge of the table, his entire body shaking in the throes of wicked delight. Tommin and Eve sat still, like mice in plain view of an owl. Copper sobbed as he cleaned up shards of pottery.

Finally, Lorcan quieted. He ate, tearing into his food like a wild beast. He gestured to Tommin and Eve, demanding that they eat, too. Tommin and Eve exchanged uneasy glances as they forced themselves to nibble mushroom biscuits. Finally, Lorcan belched and said, "Go to bed, Newlings."

This was one time Tommin was glad to obey.

He found Copper in their room, curled up like an injured animal, crying into his blanket. He sat beside the boy and laid a hand on his shoulder.

"Soon, we'll be free," Tommin said. "Everything will be better. I promise."

"I'll never be free," Copper said without looking at Tommin. "Leave me alone and go to sleep before the master hears you gabbing. I'm in enough trouble without you adding to it."

With a sigh, Tommin lay down on his lumpy mat and pulled his scratchy blanket up to his chest. He listened until Copper's sobs gave way to gentle snoring, and then he closed his eyes and tried to sleep.

When the first bell of the new day sounded, Tommin was still wide awake.

# Chapter Twenty-Nine

## *An Bóthar Ríoga*

## (The Royal Road)

Three days later, at the sounding of the second bell of the morning, in the central square of Neathgillan, Eve and Tommin joined the other four Newlings who'd qualified to finish their conversions. Forbidden to speak, they stood in a semicircle and sized up one another's clothes, shoes, and travel sacks. All looked serious, except for Alby. Alby smiled like a child who'd just been given every toy he'd ever wanted—and a big cake, too.

Eve watched Lorcan saunter up to the other three gold-fathers. They shook hands and lit pipes and started to tell tales about the size of their Takes and the superiority of their gold-sons.

Frowning, Copper stood with a few other servant boys. Each gloomy-faced lad waited beside a pushcart full of boxes and bags bursting with food, drink, shoes, clothing (the Leps' finest as well as their ceremonial garb), coins to pay the innkeepers they'd lodge with, and innumerable gifts of gold and silver for the king. One boy (so thin he made scrawny Copper look fat) scratched under the collar of his obviously new shirt. Another shifted his weight from foot to foot in a nervous dance. Copper kept perfectly still, rebellion glinting in his eyes.

Tommin waited, eyes closed, standing a little apart from the other Newlings. Was he thinking? Praying? Wishing? He rubbed one arm, a boyish gesture of unease that made Eve want to offer him comfort. To tell him not to give up hope.

Lorcan had run them all ragged in the days leading up to their departure, barking orders and waving Gladys about at all hours, even stealing most of the time they should have been asleep. Which had left little time for Eve to delve into the forbidden red book, and no time for her to share it with Tommin.

But she'd had enough time.

Enough time to find the pages with the cure for the Leprechaun's curse, and enough time to sneak out and Glamour and Charm the herbalist into giving her some of the things she needed to save Tommin.

Just as Eve was about to move closer to Tommin, the air started to vibrate with a low rumbling sound. Eve turned to see what was making the strange noise. After a few moments, a parade of purring cats marched into the square, followed by a Leprechaun wearing a robe made of multicolored silk squares and a tall peaked hat studded with gems.

"That's him," Alby whispered, poking Eve in the ribs with his elbow. "The Keeper of the Cats. One of the Great Himself's favorites, he is."

"Shut your gob, Alby!" his gold-father shouted, following the reprimand with, "Thanks be to gold that he'll not live under my roof again after the ceremony. Boy never shuts up for two minutes together."

The green-robed high officiant (whose book Eve wore tucked into her tightly wrapped chest bindings) arrived, followed by a group of Leprechauns carrying ornate brass lanterns on long poles. The officiant blew a single, lengthy note on a curled silver horn. "Line up," he called. "Cats and Keeper, then household servants, gold-fathers, and Newlings. Lantern bearers, take your assigned places at front, sides, and rear. When I sound the horn again, we will begin our solemn march to the palace of the Great Himself. 'March' being a fine word used in place of 'walk,' which is more of what we'll be doing. But solemn we will be. And silent, as our laws decree, save for the sacred songs I'll lead you in at the appointed times. So, if you must speak, speak now. I shall sound the horn again in precisely one minute."

"Eevar, are you as excited as I am?" Alby asked, leaning close. "Do you think the king has a menagerie? With gryphons and unicorns and such? I've always wanted to see a unicorn."

"Perhaps," Eve said.

The horn sounded. Alby whined. Eve inwardly rejoiced. Silence had been her language for so many years that sometimes it felt like an old friend. She knew silence was often a very good thing indeed, especially when one needed to think and to plan, as she did now. Of her own ability to escape, she had no doubt. With her great Charm and Glamour abilities, she could get away whenever she chose, and no one could stop her. Effecting Tommin's cure and getting safely away would be tricky, but she believed she could accomplish it. But as far as freeing Copper and returning him to his tribe . . . that was a problem for which she still had no solution.

On her toes, Eve stretched to look for signs of movement. She could see a pair of lanterns swaying just above the heads of the crowd, and then the lights began to move, and the purring of the cats grew louder and deeper.

Alby opened his mouth to speak, but Eve gave him a sour look that sent him skittering to his proper place in the lineup. She moved to Tommin's side, and he smiled faintly at her as together, they took their first footsteps toward the palace.

His smile. It stirred those feelings she'd been denying, the flutter in her stomach and the sweet ache in her rib cage.

Foolishness and weakness. Not at all what she needed.

Quickly, she pushed her mind in the opposite direction—toward her false uncle. She wondered which face she should wear when she destroyed Lorcan Reilly, which face would shock him most. Copper's? Her own? In the right pocket of her green tailcoat, she fingered the vial of dried salamander ears and ruttyweed leaf she'd taken from the herbalist.

Applied to a silver blade and administered within the hour through the skin, the ingredients were guaranteed to kill any Leprechaun under five hundred years old—or so said the forbidden book. She'd waited a long time to see Lorcan dead. She'd wished for it daily, year after year. Even now, when she could get away without bloodshed, she hadn't changed her mind about wanting him dead.

But to deliver Tommin from the Leprechaun's curse, she'd have to orchestrate Lorcan's death by poison perfectly. She'd need to collect a bit of Lorcan's blood before striking him with the lethal blade. According to the book, if she mixed three drops of Lorcan's life with the ingredients of the second vial she carried, and if Tommin renounced his Leprechaun rights and then drank the remedy, Tommin's days as a gold-son would be over. The book made no promises, of course. Magic sometimes did what it pleased.

Inside her fine coat, between the lining and the velvet, another secret rustled—a map she'd "borrowed" from Lorcan's neighbor Eddie McGowan. The map showed an old route linking tunnels in the palace gardens to a Faerie circle not far from Dublin. She meant to slip the folded parchment to Tommin as soon as she could—for she had no need of it. She'd committed it to memory the day she'd laid hands on it. Now, to find a moment to pass the thing when keen Leprechaun eyes wouldn't spot the exchange . . .

Behind her, Alby laughed like a donkey braying. Eve didn't trust him any more than she trusted Lorcan. His sloppy ways didn't fool her; she knew from their school days that he possessed a quick and shrewd mind, and that his code of ethics matched the textbook Leprechaun's—which meant he would have sold his own mother for a few shiny coins. She looked over her shoulder at him and scowled.

"Oops," he whispered. "Forgot to keep quiet."

The officiant's voice rose in song as they approached a wrought-iron gate that almost touched the ceiling of dirt high above them. He sang slowly, shaping each word, caressing every note. The language, strange to Eve's ears, dispersed magic all around them—little specks of airborne silver dust. Like stars had come loose from the sky and were dancing for joy, Eve thought. Tommin grabbed for one, closing his fingers around its brightness, but when he opened his hand to offer it to Eve, nothing remained.

The song ended, and the air grew warm. They moved through the gate and into a tunnel carved through white rock. The cats' purrs reverberated about them. The lantern bearer beside Eve walked close enough for her to smell the beer on his breath and the beeswax of the candle he carried. She had no choice but to inch closer to Tommin until her shoulder brushed his. At her side, their hands collided for an instant. Her cheeks burned, and she was glad he kept his gaze directed forward.

Eve interlaced her fingers over her stomach as she walked, trying to gain better control of her limbs as well as her thoughts and emotions. She'd never expected to find friendship with anyone, let alone to fall in love. She'd never had the least desire for either, believing both were just games humans played at, socially accepted ways people used one another for their selfish gain. But that was the Leprechaun way of looking at things, wasn't it? The belief of a race who loved nothing but wealth. And apart from her talent for Glamour, she was human.

She was human, and he was two-thirds Leprechaun.

"Eevar?" Tommin whispered.

She shook her head and clasped her hands more tightly. "Quiet," she said to him—and to herself.

# Chapter Thirty

## *An Pálás is Leor Cait*

## (The Palace of Many Cats)

Tommin heard the palace bells tolling before the palace came into view. They roused him from his drowsily walking state like a bucket of cold water to the head. His heart pounded with excitement. Finally, after long days of being herded along on blistered feet and long nights spent sharing overcrowded inn rooms with penny-pinching Leprechauns, he'd come to the end of his journey.

Tomorrow morning, he'd drink the elixir again. The wonderful, glorious, fizzy elixir.

He breathed deeply, attempting to calm himself. He glanced at Eve, wishing he could ask her to remind him of the hundred reasons he truly did *not* want to be a Leprechaun; he was having a hard time remembering more than two. If only he could get his hands on a few coins, he'd feel better and think better.

But no, that wasn't the way he wanted to live. Was it?

He was so tired. And hungry. The dried mushrooms they'd eaten while traveling had only left him hungrier than before he ate them.

Ahead, a pair of glittering gates swung open. Trumpets blasted. The Faerie cats howled in unison, a sound that made Tommin's skin crawl. He still had nightmares about killing the cat, in spite of Eve's assurance that she'd completely disposed of the evidence.

The procession passed through the gates and stopped in front of a raised platform built of red stone. On the platform, a Leprechaun clad in a bright-green velvet suit and a plumed hat raised his arms. "Welcome, citizens of Neathgillan, on behalf of the Great Himself, long may he reign and prosper! Your rooms have been prepared in King's Capital Hall behind me, and you will find a schedule of events posted on your door. You may walk in the royal sculpture gardens up until thirteenth bell tonight. The Feast of the Newlings begins at fifteenth bell. Breakfast will be served at second bell tomorrow, with the Ceremony of the Third Cup and the Sacred Conversion to follow. And as always, you are reminded not to interfere with the king's clowder in any way. That is all."

Lorcan stepped between Tommin and Eve, put his arms around their shoulders, and steered them toward King's Capital Hall. The three-story building had been carved into the solid stone wall of the huge cavern that housed the royal compound, its doorways and window openings framed by engravings of vines and flowers, lifelike except for their solemn gray coloring. Hundreds of strings of bright lanterns stretched between the buildings, giving the place as much light as a cloudy day above ground. Pure-white, fine gravel crunched beneath their feet as they walked.

"Come, my gold-sons," Lorcan said jovially. "We must cleanse ourselves from the dirt of the road and clothe ourselves in our finery. In a few hours, we shall be in the presence of the Great Himself. Although I daresay you will find *he* is not a tidy character. But the king may do as he pleases, yes?"

Copper stood in front of King's Capital Hall with the other gold-fathers' slave boys and their pushcarts of luggage and sundries. He tapped one foot and rolled his eyes. He'd get a beating for it later, Tommin knew. "The apartment we got is way up on the third floor. It'd be nice if somebody else could carry some of this junk up all them steps," Copper said.

Gladys smacked against Copper's hip with a thwack. The boy cringed only for a second, although Tommin imagined the pain warranted tears.

"We are Leprechauns, not slaves," Lorcan said. "Tommin and Eevar will never fetch and carry again after they've fully converted tomorrow morning. They might as well get accustomed to their roles now."

Tommin saw Eve give Copper a sympathetic shrug. The boy looked away quickly and started to unload the cart, swearing under his breath. The other slaves giggled until he called them the foulest of names.

"Come, Newlings," Lorcan said. He gestured for Eve and Tommin to follow him up a narrow set of walled-in steps. Tommin climbed behind Eve. After they crossed the second-floor landing, she stopped, and he almost collided with her. He hardly had time to be surprised when she reached back and slipped a square of folded paper into the space between his shirt and coat.

"Map. We'll talk tonight," she whispered.

"What was that you said, Eevar?" Lorcan asked, looking over his shoulder.

"Tonight," Eve repeated. "The feast will be grand, won't it? And seeing the Great Himself. Imagine!"

Lorcan pushed the wooden door open and ushered them into the apartment. "Well, you've seen greater," he said. "You were raised by greater, and soon all will know it. Tonight, after the feast, Eevar, I have arranged a meeting for you with the Faerie sorceress Oak-Apple. She's skilled in assessing hidden magical potential and will tell us how best to employ whatever talents you've been blessed with." Leaning against the door, he took a silver flask from his coat pocket and drank deeply. He offered the flask to Tommin, but he refused it with a shake of his head.

"I hate to disappoint you, Uncle, but I'm fairly certain I have no hidden talents," Eve said, perching on the arm of a yellow horsehair sofa. "I can manage a little Charm and Glamour, but there's nothing special about that. Any second-level Leprechaun can do that much."

"Ah, but you're wrong. There's more to you. More *in* you. How else could you—a *female*—have survived drinking two Cups of Fortune? It's never been done! There's a tale of a girl trying it once, you know. It's said that as soon as she swallowed one mouthful of the First Cup, a blue fire consumed her where she stood. And yet here *you* are, healthy and bright as a new penny." He moved to her side, lifted her chin with his fingers, and looked into her eyes. "I see untapped power in you. At my side, and with my aid, you might well become the first queen our People have ever known."

Lorcan patted Eve's cheek before walking away from her. As he crossed the room, he twirled Gladys between his fingers.

The look on Eve's face told Tommin she'd rather die a hundred deaths than be Lorcan Reilly's queen. Did the fellow actually mean to take her as his wife, this young woman he'd raised as his niece—to flout the morals of both Leps and men? Was there no end to his depravity?

Tommin thought he'd be sick on the carpet at the thought of Lorcan kissing Eve.

A frantic knocking at the door did not prevent Lorcan from plopping into a fat armchair and propping his dusty shoes on a plump velvet ottoman.

"Let me in!" Copper shouted from outside.

Tommin opened the door. Copper fell into the room, landing on the bags and boxes he'd lugged upstairs. The boy swore and struggled to his feet.

"Stupid child," Lorcan said. "You brought too much at once. Always overestimating yourself."

Murder gleamed in Copper's eyes.

Murder Tommin thought he might commit himself before he'd let Lorcan Reilly marry Eve.

# Chapter Thirty-One

## *An Féasta na Leipreacháin*

## (The Feast of the Leprechauns)

Inside the great hall of the palace, Tommin counted no less than one hundred Leprechauns dressed in scarlet coats and shiny-buckled shoes. The Newlings, on this last night of their part-human lives, wore their green coats. Tomorrow, the Great Himself would hand them their own sacred red coats after they drank the Third Cup of Fortune and fully converted into Leprechauns.

Tommin stood below a window, wishing for a draft, beads of sweat rolling down his forehead. A fire danced in the enormous fireplace, blazing torches adorned the walls, lanterns hung from the high ceiling, and every table held an assortment of candleholders and oil lamps. The light was lovely, but the heat made Tommin feel like a roasting chicken. He unbuttoned his collar. Lorcan would scold him if he noticed, but Tommin was too hot to care.

Eve returned from the punch bowl with Alby at her heels. A trio of musicians began to play nearby.

"Slow down, Eevar," Alby said. "I've spilled half my drink chasing after you."

She handed a cup to Tommin and leaned close. "I can't seem to lose him," she said. "And we need to talk."

"What did you say?" Alby shouted above the music of fiddle, flute, and drum.

"I said the punch is good," Eve said. "You should get more before it's gone."

Alby smiled. "I should." He turned around and left them.

Tommin raised an eyebrow. "How did you . . . ?"

Eve smiled and lifted her cup. "A bit of the Leprechaun Charm."

"You can't Charm other Leprechauns," Tommin said.

"*You* can't, but I can. I'm what they call an aberration." She drank her cup dry and set it on the windowsill. "Close your mouth and stop looking like I've turned into a frog, will you? You'll attract attention."

Tommin tried not to look astonished. "Better?"

She laughed. "Not by much. Listen, Lorcan is coming this way. We're going tonight. Running. Meet me in the sculpture garden, by the statue of King Silverpenny VIII. After last bell, as soon as you can make it. When Lorcan takes me to meet his Faerie friend . . . well, I'll just say he won't be troubling you again. I've told Copper he—"

Tommin's hands trembled with shock and excitement. Punch sloshed onto his green coat.

"Ah, my Newlings!" Lorcan said. "Enjoying yourselves, are you?"

"Yes, Uncle," Eve said. "This is indeed a glorious night."

Lorcan pointed at the stain spreading across Tommin's lapel. "And what's this, Tommin? Thank gold you're not such a bumbler when you're on a Take!" He pulled a silk handkerchief from his pocket and slapped it into Tommin's hand.

Just in time, Tommin remembered that Leprechauns never apologize and rarely say thank you. He dabbed at the spot and hoped he didn't look guilty. He glanced at Eve. Her freckled face gave away nothing, and she stood as confidently as any full-blooded Leprechaun in the room.

Lorcan moved closer and glowered. "Don't think I haven't seen you two making eyes at each other. It's against the law, and besides, are you not siblings, my children? Fortunately, after the Third Cup, all your base human desires will be gone forever. Gold and silver, silver and gold will satisfy you more completely than any human love ever could."

"You're wrong," Eve said. She gave Tommin a convincing look of disdain, although Tommin would have sworn her cheeks had turned rosy.

"Perhaps I am wrong," Lorcan said. "Let me refill your cups, Newlings." Like Alby had, Lorcan turned and left them, walking slowly through the crowd.

"Did you do it again?" Tommin asked.

Eve nodded.

"Well done."

A look of sheer mischief bloomed on her face, and his part-human heart tripped like a gangly new colt. There was something else there, too, something that made him wonder if Lorcan had indeed seen her "making eyes" at him.

By the saints, the room was hot.

He stepped closer to her and laid a hand on her sleeve. "Eve?"

A gong sounded from a balcony above them. A herald called out, "Find your places at the tables. The Great Himself approaches in all his majesty. Long may he live and prosper!"

"Long may he live and prosper!" the crowd replied.

"I'll meet you after last bell," Tommin whispered in Eve's ear. The scent of her hair intoxicated him like a handful of pennies. Two handfuls, perhaps.

She smiled at him, and then moved into the crowd of seat seekers.

At the Newlings' table, Alby and Marcas sat between Tommin and Eve. Alby chattered about the stylish cut of his new red coat and the number of secret pockets it had. Marcas nodded and picked at the tablecloth.

Trumpets blared. Everyone stood as a pair of bejeweled brass doors swung open. A grizzled, wild-haired Leprechaun stepped into the room.

He wore layer upon layer of red coats, and several dingy cravats sagged in bows on his chest. His big toes stuck out the fronts of his scuffed shoes, and one shoe lacked a buckle. Upon his grimy head, he wore a towering golden crown. When he smiled, he revealed a set of crooked teeth almost as green as his skin. "Welcome, one and all," he said. "I'm trusting you brought me tribute, else I'll send the lot of you to the Trolls before supper." He paused for a moment, and then laughed heartily. "Fooling with you, I am." His face darkened. "Or am I?"

A few Leprechauns chuckled. The king limped to his gilded throne, scratching himself and muttering. He turned three times, counterclockwise, and kissed his own fingers before he sat. "Sit, you blasted band of robbers!" he shouted.

"Let the feasting begin!" the herald declared.

Two doors at the end of the hall flew open, and serving boys scurried forth like lines of ants. They carried trays and platters heaped high with food, brimful pitchers and bowls, and all kinds and colors of bottles and tureens. They filled the tables quickly and retreated to the kitchens. The Leprechauns fell upon the meal like wild beasts upon a carcass, grabbing and tearing, grunting and snapping.

Alby reached out to snatch a chicken leg from the steaming platter before him. "When Master Owen told me there were no manners in the king's dining hall, I thought he was joking."

"The king does as he pleases, and the court follows his lead," Marcas said timidly. "That's what the *Great Book of the Leprechaun People* says."

Tommin filled his plate with roast beef and potatoes, thick-sliced bread, honeyed carrots, and buttered dumplings, and then found he was too excited by Eve's plan to eat more than half of it. Nevertheless, it wasn't long before the rich food in his belly and the hot room made him drowsy. He leaned on his hand and watched a pair of serving boys carry in a many-tiered cake dusted with gold and silver sparkles. The musicians played as more desserts arrived on the tables: rainbow-colored jellies, pies full of strange fruits, little cat-shaped biscuits. The Leprechauns kept eating and talking, laughing and arguing, and in spite of his best efforts and his nervous anticipation, Tommin's eyes drifted shut.

A bell sounded.

Tommin opened his eyes.

The bell rang out again and again, like an alarm. Like they'd tolled the church bell in Loughgillan when there was a fire. He stood and looked toward Eve. She was on her feet, too, eyes wide, hands still clutching her fork and knife.

An arrow flew past Tommin's ear so close that its fletching grazed his skin. Heart pounding with terror, he ducked down behind the table and then peered over the edge at the Great Himself. The king stood on his throne, bellowing orders as an arrow pierced his broad chest, another lodged in his temple, and a third struck his thigh.

"Assassins!" shouted the herald. Frantic Leprechauns and servants stampeded toward the doors, upsetting tables and chairs and tripping over one another. Cats hissed and howled and scrambled between legs and out the narrow windows. Arrows zipped through the room like angry bees. An army of huge, gray-skinned, muscular monsters, naked save for loincloths and quivers full of black arrows, marched through the main doors, shaking the floors with the pounding of their rocklike feet. The stench of their never-washed bodies saturated the air.

"Eve!" Tommin shouted as he dove under the table. "Get down!"

"Troll attack!" Alby cried, joining Tommin on the floor. Eve and Marcas crouched down beside them. "They've broken the treaty, the brutes," Alby said. "Blasted Trolls. Can't trust them far as you could throw them."

"Follow me," Eve said. "There's a passageway under the floor that leads to the barns. Stay low, and don't stop moving. Their arrows are poisoned; they kill almost instantly."

"What about Flanagan and Osheen?" Marcas asked, voice trembling with fear. "And Daniel and Joseph?"

"Wait for them if you like," Eve said. "I prefer to live." On hands and knees, she crawled quickly through the narrow space between the tables and the wall, and Tommin kept close behind her. When she reached the corner, she dug her fingers under the edge of one of the gray stone floor tiles and pulled at it, groaning with effort.

"I'll help," Tommin said, squeezing past her and then digging under another edge. His fingertips burned and his nails cracked as he worked at the stubborn square of marble. He looked up once as he worked, but couldn't see anything past the curtain of tablecloth. It was just as well; hearing the Leps' screams and the Trolls' grunts and bellows chilled his blood enough. Finally, the tile broke free, revealing a hole just big enough for a person to drop through into the dark passage below. "Let me go first," he said. "To see if it's safe."

Alby shoved Eve aside and then pushed Tommin. "I'll go first," he said. "Looks like Marcas decided to stay, the fool. Oh well." He jumped into the hole. Tommin heard a thud as Alby hit the floor below. Tommin followed him, landing on his feet and then moving to make way for Eve. She dropped down next to him.

In the dark, Tommin's hand met hers. He didn't know if she'd reached for him or if their hands had accidentally collided, and he didn't care.

A light flared. Tommin released Eve's hand like it had caught fire.

"Never leave home without a light," Alby said, holding up a candle. "Master Owen gave me a set of these magical candles as a Third Cup present. Nice, eh?"

"Go that way," Eve said, pointing. "And hurry. The sooner we get away from here, the better."

They scrambled through the narrow passage, accompanied by faint echoes of the fight going on above in the great hall: the Leprechauns' death cries, the Trolls' victory chants, the yowling of the cats, the sound of furniture being smashed.

The tunnel ended at a wall where a crude ladder had been carved into the stone. Alby climbed up and pressed a panel above his head. It sprang open, and he heaved himself out. "All clear up here," he called down to Tommin and Eve.

"Good," Tommin said. "Go ahead, Eve."

She put her hands on the ladder, then hesitated. She looked back at Tommin. "We have to lose Alby," she whispered. "I don't trust him."

"Neither do I."

"Once we're well away from the Trolls, I'll Charm him into wanting to go off on his own. But first things first. Do you have the map, in case we get separated?"

Tommin nodded. "And what about Copper?"

"He knows to meet us." Eve began to climb. Halfway up, she paused and looked down. "Tommin? If anything should happen . . ."

"We'll have nothing but good luck from this day forward," Tommin said. He only half believed it until she gave him the priceless gift of her smile. With that, his faith in the future multiplied tenfold. He watched her scale the ladder to the top, and then he followed, trying to ignore the growing itching sensation in his palms and the pernicious thoughts of treasure seeping into his brain.

# Chapter Thirty-Two

## *An Bealach Amach*

## (The Way Out)

After the ambush, no bells rang to mark the passing hours.

Tommin had been sitting with Eve and Alby in the unused barn for what seemed like half a day or more, keeping still and quiet, listening for rampaging Trolls. His hands itched and burned, his heart beat erratically, and his head throbbed. He'd never left his cravings unsatisfied for this long, and he knew ignoring the need might soon lead to disaster. He knew that soon, his skin would break out in the multicolored hives called rainbow pox, and after that, he'd drift into the gold-deficiency coma. The coma could last days, weeks, or years. Centuries, even.

He shivered at the thought, or maybe it was from the fever that came with the pox. He rolled up his sleeves and checked his arms. No spots yet.

Alby's head nodded, and he fell asleep with his back to the wall.

"Are you all right?" Eve whispered. She plucked the candle from Alby's fist and brought the light close to Tommin's face. Concern was etched on her brow. "You look terrible."

"Gold deficiency," Tommin said. "It's coming on quick, I'm afraid."

"No," Eve said. "You have to fight it. Get on your feet. It's as good a time as any to look for Copper in the statue garden—before this one wakes up." She helped Tommin to his feet.

His knees trembled. He held Eve's arm to steady himself.

"If I could find a few of those little gold pills, or even take the buckles off someone's shoes . . ."

"Why not his?" Eve pointed to Alby's feet. "He's asleep, so it would be stealing. It should help a little."

"But if I wake him?" Tommin's teeth chattered. He stared at Alby's buckles and breathed deep to absorb the scent of their silvery goodness.

"I'll Charm you out of trouble or something. Go on. You'll never make it to freedom in the state you're in now, and I surely can't carry you."

Tommin knelt at Alby's feet. Very cautiously, he undid the strap of one shoe and slid the buckle free. Bliss filled him as he worked at the other shoe. In for a penny, in for a pound, as the Leps liked to say. With both pieces of bright silver in hand, he stood.

He felt new again. "Let's go."

Outside the barn door, they stopped to listen and look. The dim light of a few lamps on posts showed them no one, and Tommin heard nothing but his own breathing and strong, steady heartbeat.

Eve extinguished the magic candle and pocketed it. She took off running, and he followed her, zigzagging through deserted lanes, stopping now and then to check for the presence of Trolls or Leps. A hint of smoke drifted through the air, as well as a stench Tommin feared came from burning bodies.

They darted through a gate and past statues of beasts, men, and Faerie folk. Eve never slowed until they reached a statue of a Leprechaun king. There, she stopped, panting and bending to rest her hands on her knees.

"Oh no," she said. "Copper. He isn't here."

From far off came the steady chant of marauding Trolls.

"We need to go," Tommin said. The Take of the silver didn't keep his heart from sinking at the thought of leaving Copper behind. "I know we promised to take him, and I hate to say it, but he might already be dead. If we stay here, *we'll* be dead for certain."

"I'll find him. Just give me half an hour. If I don't come back by then, promise you'll go ahead without me. I'll catch up. The passage starts under the dancing-cat statue. There's a removable panel in the plinth, and steps beneath. Here." She handed Tommin one of Alby's magical candles. "Stole it like a Leprechaun," she said, smiling.

"No. I'll go with you." He never wanted to be separated from her again. They needed each other. He wanted to tell her that, but there simply wasn't time. The chanting was growing louder, and the earth trembled from the heavy marching of huge Troll feet.

"No, Tommin. Wait here. I can use my Charm and Glamour to get past the Trolls. Yours isn't strong enough."

"But . . ."

She leaned closer, took his face in her hands, and kissed him. "I swear I'll return to you, Tommin. Trust me."

She turned and ran before he could recover enough sense to speak. Being kissed by Eve, he thought, felt very much like a good-sized Take.

He crouched behind the base of the king statue, squinting into the distance, his heart thumping wildly with fear and hope. The roars of the Trolls and cries of the Leprechauns echoed through the statuary; the ground beneath him shook harder and harder, forecasting their imminent arrival.

Every second of Eve's absence was an eternity.

And then he saw her, and Copper tripping alongside her on his short legs, gripping her hand. He thanked the saints and the angels and stood up straight, ready to greet them.

Eve saw him and smiled. And then the arrows struck her, one after another, sticking into her chest and arms like pins in a pincushion. She fell. Copper screamed.

Tommin took one step forward, and then he saw the Troll. Ten feet tall, filthy, fat, and swinging a mighty club. The thing bellowed and lunged to grab Tommin's shoulder, but he dodged just in time.

"Run!" Copper shouted. And he had no choice, not if he wanted to stay alive.

In his mind, he promised Copper he'd come back for him. He promised Eve he'd carry out her wish.

Her final wish.

And then his feet moved without his permission, carrying him swiftly to the cat statue. With blurred vision and trembling hands, he somehow managed to open the plinth and shut it behind himself. He stumbled down the steps into the darkness.

He sat still on the ground, very still, vaguely aware of the coolness of the damp earth under his palms, the wetness seeping through the seat of his breeches. The darkness swirled about him, moved through him. He breathed it, tasted it on his tongue, and absorbed it as the reality of what had just happened penetrated his soul.

Eve was gone.

No, not merely gone. Not just off on some errand or taking a sea voyage.

Dead.

The strongest of Leprechauns could not have survived even *one* of the Trolls' poisoned arrows, and Leps healed better than any other Faerie tribe. Eve, nowhere near fully Leprechaun, must have died as soon as her body took the first arrow of so, so many.

The tears started silently seeping out of his unseeing eyes. He fumbled in his pocket for Lorcan's handkerchief, and his fingers brushed against Alby's magical candle. He didn't want to beckon its flame. If anything was right in the world, it was the heavy darkness. Eve had been his light since he'd lost Granny, the one person left who'd still believed he could be better than a thieving magpie. The one person who—and he felt sure of it, remembering her hasty kiss—had loved him. With her gone . . . well, even if the sun shone on him with all its might, he'd still feel cloaked in cold blackness.

He wanted to go back. To take her in his arms and kiss her once more. To tell her he loved her, even if she couldn't hear him.

Maybe she'd known.

He hoped she'd known.

# Chapter Thirty-Three

## Saighead agus Sprioc

## (Arrow and Target)

Eve closed her eyes and lay still. She heard Copper cry out; she heard his footsteps as he left her side.

Her heartbeat slowed.

Battle raged all around her. Rioting Trolls and fleeing Leprechauns tripped over her body, trampling her legs and arms, but she barely felt it. Perhaps the poison had numbed her.

So, this was what dying felt like. Like disappearing bit by bit, like she was nothing but a drop of dew slipping downhill into a slow-moving stream.

For a few fleeting moments, she considered what her life had been: years of misery at Lorcan's hand, years of plotting revenge against him, simmering in hatred.

And then—the miracle. She'd found friends in Copper and Tommin. She'd loved them both. Copper as the little brother she'd never had, and Tommin . . . well, now she'd never know what they might have become to one another. As consciousness faded, she regretted only one thing: that she'd not opened her heart to Tommin sooner. She should not have fought her feelings for so long. But she'd been an infant when Lorcan took her; she had no true memory of being loved or seeing love, other than in passing (couples holding hands in marketplaces, kissing in alleyways, exchanging fond looks across crowded rooms).

She'd thought falling in love with Tommin was a mistake, when the real mistake was denying love's power.

The sounds of fighting faded. A picture of Tommin's face flickered in her mind, and then everything disappeared.

# Chapter Thirty-Four

## *Bóthar Fada Dorcha*

## (A Long, Dark Road)

From above came the sound of the plinth door opening and closing, and then footsteps descending. Tommin held his breath and slid his body back into the corner. Perhaps whoever it was would pass by without noticing him.

With a crackle, a flame burst to life and illuminated Alby's face.

"Shame about Eevar," Alby said coolly. "And Master Lorcan's slave. Copper, was it? He almost made it, didn't he? By gold, it was gruesome, what that Troll did to him. Be glad you didn't see that."

"Shut up," Tommin said. So Copper was dead, too? It was too much for his mind to grasp. Too much for his heart to bear.

"You stole my shoe buckles, and two of my three candles, and then abandoned me," Alby said. "If anyone has reason to be upset, it's me."

Tommin stood and balled his fists. The urge to murder rose up within him like a prodded bear.

"Hold on, Tommin," Alby said, raising his hands in surrender. "No need for violence. After all, we're going to be traveling companions. From what I remember reading in one of Master Owen's diaries, this tunnel leads to a Leprechaun settlement near Dublin. Third Cup, here we come, eh?"

"Wonderful," Tommin said dully. His throat hurt. His eyes stung. His heart felt like a huge shard of glass lodged under his rib cage. Eve and Copper had deserved better. He should have done something differently, something that would have prevented their deaths.

Alby reached into Tommin's pocket and fished out the magical candle. He shook it three times, and a flame appeared on its wick. Alby shoved the candle into Tommin's hand. "Let's go. I hear Dublin's quite a city. Lots of treasure there. Of course, the Neathdublin Leprechauns have territories set up. It's all complicated. But if no one catches you, no harm done, right?"

Tommin followed Alby because he did not know what else to do, and because Eve had told him to take this path. He could not think beyond that. He'd walk this dark road to Dublin with a Leprechaun Newling he despised and distrusted, and when he got there—*if* he got there—he'd figure out what to do next.

Alby talked and talked, and Tommin said nothing. He simply set one foot in front of the other and silently cradled his grief.

# Chapter Thirty-Five

## Faoi Thalamh agus Os Cionn

## (Underground and Above)

Hour after hour, Tommin and Alby trudged through the underground tunnels: dirt above, dirt below, and dirt at arm's length to their sides. Sometimes tangles of tree roots hung down from the dirt ceiling, and sometimes walls of spiderwebs blocked their way until Alby set them aflame with his candle. The damp air clung to Tommin's clothes and hair. The scent of soil stuck in his nostrils. His stomach had long since given up its growling declarations of hunger—not that he cared if he ever ate again.

The tunnel twisted and turned, rose and fell, and then lay flat and straight for miles. Alby talked and sang until his voice weakened to a raspy whisper. Tommin ignored him, caught in a circle of thoughts that began and ended with his failure to help Eve and Copper.

"See that?" Alby lifted his candle so it shone on a symbol carved into the wall. "I reckon that means we're almost there. Left turn ahead, and we should set foot in Neathdublin within another hour or two. Thanks be to gold, I say. I'm itching for a Take, aren't you?"

"As always," Tommin said. Being agreeable seemed the best course of action as they neared the end of their journey. He didn't want Alby to suspect that he had no intention of taking the Third Cup in Neathdublin, nor did he want the talkative fellow to find out that while he'd been napping, Tommin had been plotting his own path to freedom using Eve's map.

The tunnel split. "To the left," Alby said. Tommin followed him.

"I bet you a silver coin you can't recite all thirty-seven sacred principles of Leprechaun life in order," Tommin said. Quietly, he shed his shoes and abandoned them. His unshod feet would make less sound on the ground when his chance to run came. He slowed his pace, letting the space between them expand.

Alby walked briskly, as if invigorated by the challenge. "Ha! I could do it in my sleep! Number one: a Leprechaun must pursue wealth, being humbly obedient to the gold lust in his heart and the needs of his green flesh. Number two: all full crocks of gold must be buried Above according to the ancient traditions, with the recitation of the sealing words and the application of blood, in order that the rainbow . . ."

Tommin turned and sprinted back the way they'd come, as silently as a Neathgillan cat on the prowl. Where the tunnel split, he veered onto the path Alby had not chosen. He ran until his legs burned and his chest ached for want of air, and he kept running. The tunnel rose steeply, and finally, he saw light ahead. A gust of sweet, fresh air swept over him.

He ran out into the eye-shocking sunlight and fell into a bed of soft ferns in the center of a circle of spotted toadstools. He rolled onto his back with no intention of sleeping, but fall asleep he did.

He dreamed Eve lay beside him there, basking in the sunshine and their freedom. She cupped her hand at his ear and whispered the cure he needed. He kissed her cheeks, her hair, her mouth.

He woke up alone.

# Chapter Thirty-Six

## *An Foghlaí*

## (The Trespasser)

In all his life, Tommin had never seen such a perfect moon. It sailed high above the streets of Dublin, a white ship skimming through a sea of stars. He never wanted to go underground again. If he could not live in the light of the sun and moon, he'd prefer not to live at all.

Hunger dogged him as he walked into the city: for food, for drink, for gold, and for a long night's sleep in a clean bed. A pair of shoes would also be nice. Which need to fill first, that was the question.

Glamoured as a blacksmith of average height, he wandered the dim streets, crossing to the other side when anyone approached. In this neighborhood, the buildings he passed were shabby, just as dirty as Neathgillan's dwellings. After a while, they gave way to nicer houses and shops. The scent of gold beckoned and beguiled him, and he hurried after it. He crossed the street, drawn forward by the heavenly aroma.

**H. Kennedy's Jewelers**, said the fancy sign that hung over the sidewalk. In the window, gold necklaces and rings lay on velvet cushions, reflecting bits of moonlight. Enthralled, Tommin forgot to breathe. He touched his nose to the glass. Such a thin separation held him apart from what he needed.

"You!" a man shouted. "Get away home with you! Stupid drunkard."

Tommin ducked into an alley. His body demanded that jewelry, no matter what moral arguments his part-human mind conjured. By the time he found the shop's back door, his temperature had climbed to high fever.

The door swung open on silent hinges. He stepped inside, pulse racing, and tiptoed toward his goal. He hurried into the next room and collided with someone.

He stepped back. The young woman before him wore a shift and nightcap. She squinted at him. "Robert? Is that you?"

*Her eyesight must be terrible,* Tommin thought, although the room *was* very dark. He put on a more handsome Glamour and a good measure of Charm, trying to make her see just what she expected to see.

She smiled. "I knew you'd come."

"Go and get dressed," Tommin said. "We'll take a stroll in the moonlight."

"I'd like that," she said. "Father should sleep till Tuesday, he was that exhausted when he got home today from India with his diamonds."

"Good," Tommin said. The strong gold scent sent a shiver up his spine. He scratched his hand. "Hurry and dress anyway, my love."

She kissed his cheek and rushed off. "Anything you say, Robert. I'll just slip upstairs a moment." She giggled as she scurried off.

Before the girl had a chance to return, he pocketed enough good gold from the jewelry shop to keep a full-blooded Leprechaun sated for a month. He exited quickly, forgetting to shut the door as euphoria exploded inside him.

Tommin ran. He ran fast. He was a shooting star, a beam of infinite light, a hot bright streak of perfect Bliss careening past shops and houses.

He tripped.

No matter. Nothing hurt. No pain could dim pleasure as strong as his. He stood, brushed the dust off his knees, and walked on.

Tommin wandered the streets until the sky began to lighten, marveling at the ceaseless activity of city folk: delivery men driving horses and carts, painted women calling out from dim doorways, boys slopping water on shop windows, glassy-eyed drunks meandering home.

Ahead, he spied a shoe-shaped sign hanging over the sidewalk. He hurried to the window, keen to examine the quality and style of the shop's wares. A man stepped out of the shop and paused to light his pipe. But no, this was no man. Tommin saw right through the light layer of Glamour the fellow wore: green-tinted skin and a dark-red jacket.

"Fresh one, are you? So new you've forgotten to wear your red coat, eh?" The Leprechaun scowled and blew streams of smoke out his nostrils like a storybook dragon. "Fresh from the Take, too, if my eyes and nose do not deceive me." He set his pipe on the window ledge and took a step toward Tommin.

"I'm only looking at the shoes," Tommin said. He decided it would be a good time to run, but before he had a chance to lift his foot, the tall Leprechaun snatched him by the shirtfront and tugged him onto his toes. He drew Tommin close, and Tommin turned his head. The fellow's breath reeked like a drainage ditch.

"You've been stealing. And if you've been stealing on this street, you've been stealing from me."

"It wasn't here," Tommin said, praying some passerby would come to his rescue. He glanced about but saw not a soul.

"Liar." The Leprechaun jerked Tommin hard and pressed his back against the window frame. "This is my territory, lad. And according to Lep law, I can kill you if I want. I've got the stuff to do it in my pocket, so I do. Poisoned knife made by Trooping Faeries, sharper than Satan's toenails."

"I didn't know this was your territory," Tommin said. "I'm new, like you said. Just got to town a few hours ago." The idea of fighting back flitted through his mind. With the strength he'd gained from the Take, he might be able to beat the fellow.

Before Tommin could make up his mind, the Leprechaun had drawn a knife and set the blade at his throat. "I half feel sorry for you—though I shouldn't. So here's my offer, Newling. Hand over your Take and I'll let you live."

"Fine," Tommin said. "But I can't reach into my pockets unless you let go of me."

The Leprechaun released him and stepped back, still brandishing the knife. Tommin fumbled for the treasure, sickened by the thought of parting with it. The instant he placed the jewelry in the Leprechaun's open hands, Tommin began to tremble and itch. His stomach clenched, and his muscles twitched.

The Leprechaun laughed as the twice-stolen goods gave him all the joy and nourishment they'd just revoked from Tommin.

"Look at the sorry state of you!" the Leprechaun said. He gazed at Tommin pityingly. "Well, you'd best come with me before you pass out altogether. I'll show you what we Dublin Leps call the Grand Commons, where anyone's free to pick a few pockets. Steal a couple coins and you'll be healthy as the Great Himself on tax day."

This one was as fickle as Lorcan and the rest, Tommin thought.

"Don't just stand there. Don't you know returning a Take will send you into the coma faster than anything? Time's against you, Newling. Come on." The Leprechaun grinned and pointed. "It's just a block or two this way."

*Never trust a Leprechaun,* Master Rafferty's voice said inside Tommin's head. And so Tommin took off running.

He heard the pounding of the Leprechaun's shoes on the cobblestones close behind him. His heart fluttered in his chest like a one-winged butterfly. Forget the coma, he was simply going to die. Soon. Any second now.

He turned down a dark alley. A door stood open, and he threw himself inside. He rolled down a flight of stone steps, every painful scrape and bump magnified by his gold-bereft condition. Finally, he lay still and waited to be found by the Leprechaun, death, or the gold-deficiency coma.

# Chapter Thirty-Seven

## *Íoslach nó Tuama*

## (Cellar or Tomb)

Tommin opened his eyes. Above his head, a few thin bars of sunlight held spinning motes of dust. Every inch of him hurt, and dying seemed like a pleasant idea—especially if it meant he'd be reunited with Eve in some leafy, bright paradise. The possibility brought a feeble smile to his parched lips.

Still lying on the floor, Tommin lifted his head, searching for something he could drink. If he was going to die, he'd rather not be thirsty while he did it. In the corner, another little room branched off the cellar, and he thought he saw bottles on shelves there. He rolled over and began to crawl a few inches at a time. One tear dripped from his eye and hit the dirt floor. Just one. It was probably the last his body could squeeze out, so racked with thirst it was.

After what felt like a week, he crept over the threshold. He shoved the heavy door shut with his shoulder and reached up to slide the bolt into place. He was too tired to wonder why someone had put a lock there. He stretched out his arm and grabbed a bottle. With what remained of his strength, he smacked its neck against the shelf until it broke, and then he drank the old, rich red wine until not a drop remained.

Blood dripped from his lip onto his chest. Drinking from broken bottles was dangerous business. The warmth in his belly gave him a little comfort, in spite of his itching rainbow pox and hammering headache.

He closed his eyes and pictured Eve. He remembered her mouth on his—that one perfect moment in his life. And for that one moment of his complicated, cursed existence, he was grateful.

For Eve, he would have suffered it all again.

Slowly, he slipped into oblivion.

# Part Two

# Chapter One

## *Pléaráca Deireadh Fómhair*

## (October Revelry)

It was the end of the world. The instruments of doom blared and shrieked, darkness had swallowed all light, and an earthquake shook creation like a dog with a rat in its teeth.

Flat on his back, Tommin sucked in lungfuls of stale, dusty air. His limbs tingled unpleasantly, as if he'd lain in one position for too long. If the apocalypse was raging outside, perhaps he'd stay put and let it come to him—wherever he was, whoever he was. Apart from his name, large pieces of his memory seemed to be missing.

And what was that on his forehead? He swiped at it, finding it cool and metallic. He picked it up between his finger and thumb, and it made a faint, peculiar buzzing start inside his chest. He squinted at the thing; it was definitely a coin of some sort. Perhaps it had fallen through the little crack between the wood slats above his head, the crack he could see the tiniest bit of light leaking through. Maybe the coin had landed on his face and awoken him. It didn't quite make sense, but then why should anything make sense when the world was at its end?

The horrid music ceased, and the quaking lessened. Tommin thought he heard laughter and conversation coming from above him. Who would throw a party at such a bleak hour? Wouldn't weeping and prayer be more fitting? Or were the revelers Satan's own, rejoicing over the fate of the damned?

The party went on and on. Tommin sat up, tired of waiting for his doom. He decided he wanted to see the sky one last time, even if it blazed with falling stars and a blood-bathed moon. Also, he needed something to drink, and he had an odd longing to get his hands on a few more coins. Odd to think of money during the apocalypse, but he did.

He ran his fingers over a wall and then shelves. He felt the smooth curves of a bottle and picked it up. The liquid inside sloshed, mocking his thirst, so he cracked the bottle open with a whack. He dimly remembered doing the same thing in the past, or maybe he'd read about it in a book. In any case, the wine tasted terrible. Vinegary. He drank it anyway, tossing the bottle aside after he emptied it.

Turning his body to the left, he resumed his nearly blind exploration of the room. His fingers found a crusty bolt, and he pried and pounded until it gave way. With a tug and a grunt, he forced the door open. Stepping forward, he hit a wall. *Perhaps,* he thought, *I missed the apocalypse. It may well be that I'm already in hell, and this is part of my eternal torture. Door after door, wall after wall forever, with nothing to drink but nasty sour wine, and nothing to eat but cobwebs and dust.*

Well, the partygoers above him sounded merry enough. Surely they had something better to eat. And maybe they had gold or silver in their pockets, just waiting there for him to snatch it out. Inspired, he kicked the wall. His foot smashed through the plaster. He kicked again and again until he'd made a hole big enough to climb through.

On the other side of the jagged opening, Tommin discovered a room lit by several small, pear-shaped, glowing glass lanterns. Stacks of brown boxes and shelves of strangely wrapped items took up most of the floor space. He followed a narrow pathway, stopping briefly to pluck a large potato from a bin; he might roast it later if he came upon a bit of hellfire suitable for cooking purposes. From a bright-yellow crate, he lifted an amber-colored bottle and stuck it in his pocket. If this was to be his last meal, he'd make a picnic of it.

Without pausing to entertain his dread of what bedlam lay ahead, Tommin scaled a flight of wooden steps to another door and forced himself to turn the metal doorknob. He stepped into a corridor, came face-to-face with a young woman and gasped. A strange face she had, all painted with bright colors. And her dress! Tommin stared at her exposed knees. So this must be what a harlot looked like. He vaguely recalled hearing that Hell would be well stocked with such women.

"Hey, is this the way to the jacks?" she asked. Her eyelashes moved like hairy spiders when she blinked. "You know, the loo? The toilet?"

Speechless, Tommin shrugged and brushed past her into a big room packed with dancing, squirming, outrageously dressed revelers. Humans and Faerie-looking beings, as well as strange creatures with flesh and hair of impossible shades, wings, horns, tails, bloody fangs, shimmering skin. Pulsating demonic music blared from unseen instruments. Colorful signs glowed on the walls.

Hell smelled like spilled beer, sweaty bodies, fried potatoes, and rotting flowers.

But above those scents, Tommin smelled gold and silver. Inside him, a fierce hunger made urgent demands.

He slipped past a few ladies, his hands deftly unhooking one woman's necklace and sliding a bracelet off another without anyone's notice. Bliss and strength surged through his veins, and he remembered clearly what he was: the gold-son of Lorcan Reilly, a green-blooded Leprechaun from the Neathlands. Born to Take, and blessed by the Cup of Fortune with Glamour and Charm. Knowing that, he thought, was enough. Even if the rest of his history remained forever forgotten.

A man with an orange beard and a brass-buttoned emerald jacket slapped Tommin on the back. "Nice costume, man," he said. "Ghost of George Washington, is it? The cobwebs are a great touch. Me, I hate these fancy-dress things. My girlfriend made me come. See that smoking Little Red over there? She wanted me to be the wolf, but the rental place ran out of wolves. Hence, the lame Leprechaun getup. I'm not even Irish. I'm from Oregon, you know? Grandparents were French and Sioux." He lifted his glass. "*Sláinte* and all that, George."

Little Red came over and grabbed the man's arm. "They're playing our song, Theo." He winked at Tommin and then followed her like a puppy after its master.

Tommin watched the couple wrap their arms around each other as an invisible singer wailed about true love. They danced so close together that had he not known better, he might have mistaken them for a single many-limbed monster. That, Tommin knew instinctually, was no way for a Leprechaun to behave with a human, wherever the fellow had come from.

"Punch?" A young blonde in a pink sparkly gown offered him a glass of unnaturally red liquid. A pair of translucent rose-colored wings stuck out from her back. "Hot in here, isn't it?" She glanced down at his feet. "Is that why you've taken off your shoes? Brilliant idea."

Tommin accepted the punch and drank it in one gulp. Icy cold and too sweet, it was no Cup of Fortune.

The girl swayed with the music; her wings fluttered and twinkled. *Was* she one of the Faerie folk? He had to ask. Perhaps she could help him find his way back to the Leprechauns' lands. Trying to be discreet, he leaned close and spoke into her ear. "Are you a Faerie?"

She laughed. Shouting to be heard above the clamor, she said, "I know. The costume's kind of juvenile. But it was half price, and to tell you the truth, I always wanted to be a Faerie."

"Costume? So you're not a real Faerie?"

She eyed him from head to toe, her expression somewhere between disappointment and disgust. "Either you're totally sloshed or you suck at flirting. Well, anyway, happy Halloween." She stepped away, disappearing behind a giant yellow bird man as another floor-shaking song commenced.

Frenzied dancing broke out among the partygoers. Tommin was jostled and bumped again and again as he slowly worked his way into a vacant corner. In spite of his Takes, he felt rather ill. The longer he spent at the party, the smaller and hotter the room seemed to become. He could barely breathe, and his ears rang painfully from the noise.

Across the room, a crowned, velvet-robed king and queen entered, and Tommin caught a glimpse of the rainy street behind them. Whatever lay beyond this place must not be *so* terrible, since they were smiling and appeared unscathed. If there was any chance fresh air and silence existed beyond the vibrating walls of this part of hell, he was willing to risk venturing out. He brushed past monsters and prostitutes and wove his way between tables, chairs, and highly scented bodies. And finally, after what he considered a minor battle of sorts, he gave the door a mighty shove and escaped into the street.

Tall streetlamps glowed pinkish gold above the smooth, black-surfaced road. A few leaves skittered across Tommin's path as he wandered away from the nightmarish party. He looked back over his shoulder at the place, reading the sign over the door: **The Crooked Farthing Public House.** Well, that was a name for hell he'd never heard before. If he could help it, he'd never enter such a place again. *Could* he help it? That remained to be seen. Who knew what the rest of this world was like? What if the Crooked Farthing was the best place in all of wherever he was?

Heaven forbid.

Dead leaves stuck to his damp stockings. He pulled his green coat close against the chilly breeze. He walked fast, taking in everything he saw: impossibly tall buildings, shops with window displays of odd clothes, colorful dishes, fruits and vegetables, and things he couldn't identify. When he neared another thumping, brightly lit pub, he crossed the street to avoid the throng of merry mischief makers spilling out its door.

He heard *it* coming then, a beast that growled and grumbled louder and louder as it approached. Its eyes shone forth like two suns. He dove behind a metal box to hide from the demonic creature, certain it would sniff him out and eat him within the next minute. Instead, the sleek black thing rushed past, spraying him with cold puddle water as it rushed down the street faster than anything he'd ever seen. Its gleaming rear-end eyes glowed at him before it disappeared around a corner with a terrifying squeal.

He crouched behind the box, expecting the beast to return for him.

When someone tapped his shoulder, Tommin sprang to his feet.

"You all right?" asked an elderly gentleman dressed like a priest.

"Did you see that?" Tommin asked, pointing down the street. "That thing?"

"Too much to drink at your party, eh? You need a taxi, lad? This is no neighborhood to be wandering alone in at two in the morning."

"Isn't this the end of the world, Father?" Tommin asked. Puddle water dripped from his hair into his eye. His wet shirt clung to his chest. "And what are you doing here among the hell folk, anyway?"

The priest chuckled. "I ask myself those same questions every day, lad. Come on. I've one bed left in the shelter. You'll shiver yourself to death if you don't get inside and dry."

A gust of wind swept through, and Tommin's teeth began to chatter. He trusted the old man, even if he was a hell priest. Besides, the offer of a bed and rest was suddenly more than he could resist.

"Thank you, Father," Tommin said, as if he were human and mannerly instead of a thieving, thankless Leprechaun.

# Chapter Two

## *Dearthóireacha na Fola Glas*

## (Brothers of the Green Blood)

After breakfast, the priest gave Tommin an orange plaid coat, tan ankle-length trousers, and a pair of hideous, ill-fitting cloth shoes and assigned him the task of sweeping the sidewalks in front of the shelter in exchange for his stay.

The sun shone weakly through a smattering of clouds as Tommin brushed the brown leaves into a pile. He hadn't had the chance to ask the priest anything about the events of the night before, but it seemed to him that the world might have decided not to end after all—whatever strange world this was.

It certainly was not the world he'd known before waking up in the cellar of the Crooked Farthing. Yet he still remembered nothing more than his gold-father's name and that he was a Leprechaun.

He set the broom against the wall and walked away from the shelter, done with pretending to be a human.

After two nights of freezing on park benches, Tommin felt awful. When his palms started itching, he welcomed the invitation to steal. A bit of gold would warm his blood and maybe heal him of his cough.

He left the park and walked to the busy shopping district. A pair of mothers pulled their children closer as he passed, reminding him to put some Glamour over his worn clothes and dirty body.

A blonde stood on the corner with a metallic rectangle pressed to her ear, talking aloud to herself like a madwoman (like so many humans he'd seen since ending up in this nightmare). He smelled the gold in her earrings and coming from one of the bags dangling at her wrist.

Without breaking his stride, he walked past her, dipping a hand into a rectangular blue bag, fishing out a velvet-covered box, and pocketing it before blending into a queue of rowdy teenagers.

His lungs cleared, his blood rushed, and he smiled.

One of the rolling beasts roared past, bellowing one of the terrible demon songs he'd heard at the party. He flattened himself against the wall. Although he'd seen many of the monsters since his first night in the city, they still scared the life out of him.

"What's wrong with you, mister?" a boy asked, peering up at him. "Seen a ghost, have you?"

"Don't talk to strangers, Billy," said the teenage girl beside him, ushering him toward a set of shiny glass doors.

Tommin walked back toward the park. He fingered the gold chain in his pocket, enjoying its texture and goodness, until a feeling of unease slowly eclipsed his happiness. He glanced over his shoulder. A brown-haired man in a long black coat, his eyes covered by dark rectangular spectacles, appeared to be following him. There was something familiar about the man, something intangible and disturbing.

"Hey," the man said. "Wait. We need to talk."

Tommin took off running.

"Hey!" the stranger shouted again.

Hearing the man's shoes slapping the pavement close behind him, Tommin ran faster. He darted in and out of dark alleys and squeezed between buildings. He dared to scramble over a few metal beasts—thankful these were quiet, still, and dead eyed. He ran through a garden and a churchyard, lungs burning and legs cramping. Through crowds and over a bridge, past statues and fountains. Some landmarks he passed twice, three times, as he fled.

After half an eternity of running, he had to rest or he was going to pass out. He slowed down and stole a backward glance, but saw no one. Just ahead, a wooden bench offered him respite. He stumbled toward it.

The stranger leapt into his path. "Gotcha!" he said, grabbing Tommin by the back of his coat. "You're coming with me."

"No! Let go! What do you want, anyway?" Tommin tried to wriggle away, but the fellow had a mighty grip.

"Gold. Same as you, brother." With his free hand, the man removed his spectacles. His irises bore the gold flecks of a century-old Leprechaun. And now that Tommin had a chance to notice, the fellow's skin held a hint of green.

"Saints above," Tommin said. With his stunted memory, he wasn't sure whether to be glad or terrified. "Am I in trouble?"

"You should be, trespassing on my territory and Taking with all the grace of a one-eyed Troll. But I'll let it slide, seeing as you just came out of the coma. I'm right, aren't I? I can smell a coma victim a mile off. I'd wager you skipped a couple hundred years from the look of you." The stranger smirked and put his spectacles back on. "We need to have a little chat in private, you and I, if you plan on staying alive. Now, will you come along with me nicely, or will I need to get nasty? I'm only trying to help, mind. I've a soft spot for coma cases—but my patience is thin as a banknote tonight."

Tommin's bones felt like jelly. His heart stopped for a moment before taking off in a mad gallop. *A couple hundred years?* He grabbed for the stranger's arm to keep from collapsing into a heap.

"It isn't *so* bad. You'll get accustomed to the twenty-first century in no time at all." The Leprechaun let go of Tommin's coat, put an arm around him, and guided him down the street. "You slept through some fine times, though, lad. Nowadays it's flimsy paper money and cheap metal coins, electronic banking . . . *and* most of the jewelry's fake rubbish. You'll have to learn new tricks to feed your habit here. It's a fat lot of work, but the rainbow! Now that's what we live for, eh? Same as it always was, pure Bliss that lasts a week if you do it up properly."

Tommin tried to smile but failed. His nerves were in a tangle, the running had exhausted him, and he didn't quite trust this Leprechaun. "Where are we?"

"Dublin. Where did you think you were?"

"Oh." Memories returned in flashes: the jewelry store with the breathtaking display, Charming the girl who lived there, his blood running hot with the pleasure of an enormous Take, being caught by the angry Leprechaun and forced to return his plunder, falling into the cellar, dying . . .

Not dying, after all. Only succumbing to a centuries-long coma.

"Did you hear me, brother?" the Leprechaun almost shouted.

"No."

"Eh, well. Never mind. Here we are. Up these steps and we'll see you fed and to bed. And tomorrow, explanations and lessons, and a nice Take if you behave yourself."

Tommin followed the Leprechaun up a flight of black metal steps to a balcony set with a wooden table and chairs. He watched as the Leprechaun jiggled the door handle and spoke gibberish to it until it gave way.

"Did you Charm that into opening?" Tommin asked.

"Haven't got a key, but have got a bit of magic. Traded a Faerie a pair of shoes for it a few years back. Come in, and be quick about it. Don't want to get caught. I've only been here two days, for gold's sake, and the owners are out of town till Tuesday next."

Tommin hurried into the dark room, and the Leprechaun shut the door behind him. At the sound of a faint click, a row of lights appeared in the ceiling.

"How did you . . . ?" Tommin pointed up.

"Electricity this time, not magic. And don't bother asking me to explain *that*." The Leprechaun went to a tall silver box and opened its door. From its brightly lit white interior, he took out two brown bottles. He uncapped them, handed one to Tommin, and gestured for him to sit on a plump leather chair.

The cold glass stung Tommin's fingers, but the liquid inside tasted heavenly.

*"Sláinte,"* the Leprechaun said. He draped himself over another plump chair and tossed his spectacles onto a small table.

Tommin watched him drink. In this light, the Leprechaun's beard and hair were reddish brown. He had tiny wrinkles around his eyes, and his skin held the slightest hint of green—so that anyone who wasn't looking for it would have overlooked it or thought it a trick of the light.

"Go on and stare. I am a handsome devil," the Leprechaun said, grinning. "Quite a favorite with the ladies before I converted. But what's a woman compared with gold and silver, eh? Nothing but nagging and work, and never half as thrilling as a big Take that fills your crock to overflowing."

With that, Tommin's hands started to itch. He sat on them and prayed he could hold out till morning.

"My name's Riksdaler at the moment, if you're wondering. A money name. Chose it myself," the Leprechaun said. "Can't remember the name I was born with." He set his bottle on the floor and looked Tommin in the eye. "The past is best forgotten, brother. Especially your human past, if you haven't already figured that out. But from the color of you, I reckon you were little more than a Newling when you fell comatose. Probably barely digested the Third Cup before you got yourself deep into mischief. Am I right?"

Tommin nodded. He wanted to scratch his hands, his arms, his neck. Sitting still was excruciating. A shiver shook him.

Riksdaler groaned and swore. "Itching already, are you? And I thought we were in for the night."

"Sorry," Tommin said.

"None of that," Riksdaler snapped. "Leprechauns never apologize. Best to get you sated before the sun comes up."

"I could go on my own," Tommin said.

"And I *could* let you, but when you wandered into some other Lep's territory, I'd be blamed for it as much as you were—because heaven knows you'd rat me out in under a minute when they gave you the stick. Myself, I don't fancy being sent off to the Neathlands prisons or being banished to some goldforsaken hick town in America. So it's the pair of us going after the Take, like it or not." Riksdaler stood and stretched like one of the Great Himself's cats (another memory that burst into Tommin's mind)—and then he disappeared into the next room.

Questions and anxieties spun circles inside Tommin's brain. Prison or banishment to America for trespassing? Living in humans' homes and drinking their beer?

Should he run? He felt like he should.

Eyes on the exit, he stood.

A leather coat bundled with a pair of long blue breeches and a thin shirt flew at Tommin and hit his chest with a thwack.

"Put those on while I find you shoes. My gold, brother, I can't stand the stink of you much longer. You'll have to shower when we get back," Riksdaler said from the doorway to the next room. "You weren't thinking of bolting, were you? I'd hate to lose my temper on you."

Tommin offered a wobbly smile. "Stretching my legs," he said.

"A bad liar, aren't you now? I reckon you're going to cause me a world of trouble. So that's what I'll call you: Trouble. A new name for your new life. Right. Shoes, then." Riksdaler disappeared back into the other room.

Tommin didn't care what anyone called him. All he knew was that he needed something shiny to put an end to his escalating pain. He stepped into the strange long breeches and pulled them up. They clung to his legs and behind. The one-piece, short-sleeved, stretchy gray shirt hugged his chest and abdomen. *Saints, I must be a sight,* he thought. *I should be called Ridiculous, not Trouble.*

*Magpie,* a sweet voice said inside his mind. His name, long ago—he knew it with certainty, for his heart testified to it by skipping a beat.

Riksdaler returned with a pair of brown boots. "These'll have to do, unless you fancy flowered sandals." He tossed them to Tommin.

Catching the boots, Tommin said, "Magpie. I'm called Magpie."

"Yeah, whatever, brother. Hurry with the coat and let's go. The sun will be up in an hour, and I burn easy." Riksdaler ran his fingers through Tommin's hair and then stood back to look him over. "Better," he said. "Less Rip Van Winkle and more unwashed rock star." He grabbed a pair of black spectacles and handed them to Tommin before heading for the door. "You needn't look at them like they're from another planet. They're just shades. Sunglasses?"

"But my eyes aren't weak. And it's still dark outside."

"Wear them anyway. Now, just stay close and keep quiet," Riksdaler said as he ushered Tommin onto the balcony. "Magpie."

Descending the stairs, Tommin filled his lungs with cool autumn air. Gold beckoned from nearby, singing his name and teasing him like a loose-moraled woman. He followed Riksdaler down the steps and onto the street.

As they walked, Tommin's gold lust mingled with guilt. That was perplexing. What kind of Leprechaun was he, anyway, to feel bad about doing the thing he was meant to do—what his blood made him do?

Is that why he fell into the coma, because he'd resisted feeding his blood with treasure? If only he could remember more of his previous life . . .

"There," Riksdaler said, pointing to a tall brick building with a rotating glass door. "Glamour up. Charm the security guard, and take the stairs to the second-floor condo. I've been there before. Lady's a compulsive shopper, always buying rings and watches. Leaves her door unlocked. Go on, then."

The scent forecast a good Take, and Tommin let it lead him. Desire squashed the twinge of guilt. His whole body trembled with anticipation as he entered the building, hastened past the conveniently dozing guard, and scaled the steps two at a time toward the splendid prizes Riksdaler had promised.

# Chapter Three

## *Ribín Airgid agus Óir Réalta*

## (Silver Ribbon and Gold Star)

The bedside clock said 12:18 a.m. Tommin stared at the ceiling and wished he could either fall asleep or find himself magically transported into morning. He'd spent too many nights awake since he'd come out of the coma almost two months ago. Maybe his body had had enough rest during his years in the cellar, and he'd never have a full night of sleep again.

By the saints, that was a bleak and disturbing thought. Didn't his mind deserve some nightly time off after all he'd had to learn and adapt to lately?

The twenty-first century still astounded Tommin. Cars and phones, computers and fast food, stores selling produce grown on the other side of the earth, the strange clothes, the poor manners. Worst of all, the paper and plastic money and—of all the horrors—electronic funds. What satisfaction could humans derive from *imaginary* money? Gold was magic, silver sorcery. Those things you could touch and hold, treasure and bury.

Rainbows would never spring from a crock full of credit cards or computer printouts.

Riksdaler had taught him to survive. How to work his way through a crowd on the train, stripping passengers of rings, earrings, watches, and bracelets without slowing his gait from one end of the car to the other. How to avoid security cameras on streets and in shops. Where to exchange flimsy paper notes and cheap metal coins for real gold, and where to bury his crocks to get the best rainbows and the greatest amount of Bliss. How to keep peace with other Leprechauns by respecting their territorial boundaries.

Sometimes, for a few hours or days, Tommin liked Dublin life. Or he thought he did. It might have been the gold Bliss working on him. Usually, though, he felt unsettled and unsure, as if he'd lost something valuable and intangible—or some*one*. Which unsettled him all the more, since he knew he should not have felt attached to anything he couldn't put in a crock and bury.

When he *could* sleep, he had vivid dreams, and some he regarded as memories. He dwelled on them, replaying them in his mind as he lay awake in borrowed apartments, tangled in strangers' sheets, his head pressed into their pillows while they vacationed or worked abroad. His dreams restored to him the old woman he'd called Granny—how she'd called him Magpie, mended his clothes, and cooked his meals—and how she'd loved him when he hadn't deserved it.

He dreamed of the Elixir of Fortune, of its blue, fizzling perfection bathing his taste buds with ecstasy.

He dreamed of making shoes for an old man called Rafferty and heard the shoemaker call him by his true name: Tommin Kelly. One day, he promised himself, he would make shoes again. He'd find a set of the old tools and fashion them in the old way, cutting leather by hand, tapping each wooden peg into place just so. To look at modern shoes made him half-sick. Ugly, rubbery, glued-together, factory-made abominations.

And sometimes, he thought of *the girl*. Truth be told, he thought about her a lot. Of course, he never mentioned this to Riksdaler; Riksdaler's temper was something to avoid, and such talk would surely spark it. No, Tommin didn't fancy having his ears boxed again or sitting through another scathing lecture on proper Leprechaun behavior.

The girl's name never came to him, but her fair, freckled face appeared often in his dreams. As surely as he knew the scent of silver, he knew the exact shade of her red hair and the single crease that formed on her forehead when she worried. He knew the timbre of her voice and the shape of her hands. She was as real to him, and as untouchable, as the stars in the sky.

Once, he'd dreamed that she'd kissed him. If he'd ever felt like a terrible excuse for a Leprechaun, it was then. That night, he'd finally admitted to himself that he loved her, the girl with no name. *Had loved* her . . . because she was surely long dead.

Only if she'd had Faerie blood could she have outlived his two-century-long coma. And deep down, he knew she'd been human.

It should not have mattered to him. *She* should not have mattered to him. And yet . . .

Between his un-Leprechaunish pining for the girl and bouts of un-Leprechaunish guilt about stealing, Tommin arrived at the conclusion that he was somehow defective. The black sheep of the tribe, perhaps, or the child who'd been dropped on his head too often. Perhaps he'd misspoken when swearing one of the Leprechaun oaths or spilled some of the elixir during a Cup ceremony.

Unless he wanted to risk being executed by the Leprechaun High Council or Faerie Courts for being a dangerous anomaly, he had no choice but to keep his misgivings and bewilderment to himself. He'd have to cope with being alone in the world. With feeling like a teenager and an impossibly old man, with being alternately greed driven and penitent, coldhearted and in love with a ghost.

Wider awake than ever, Tommin climbed out of bed, wrapped himself in a blanket, and went to the window. From the penthouse he shared with Riksdaler, late-night Dublin spread out before him, bedecked for Christmas with tiny, twinkling lights. They sparkled like something he'd seen long ago, before the coma . . .

A memory sprang to life then, a clear image of glittering silver bits of magic floating through the air. Shiny flecks conjured by the Leprechauns' song on the road to the Ceremony of the Third Cup.

*The Third Cup.*

*I never drank the Third Cup.*

He saw the Trolls, the zipping arrows, tables overturned, Leprechauns fleeing and falling . . .

A chill swept over Tommin. His teeth chattered as he gripped the windowsill.

*I never drank the Third Cup,* he thought. *I'm not a full Leprechaun. That's why I think of the girl, why I feel guilty for Takes, and why my times of Bliss fizzle out fast instead of keeping me content for a week or more.*

"You're up, too, eh?" Riksdaler's voice startled him. Tommin turned to find the Leprechaun leaning on the doorjamb, dressed in a silk robe. "Fancy going on a Take? In the spirit of Saint Nick's nocturnal visits?"

Tommin spun to face the window again. He fixed his eyes on a pair of clouds drifting like veils over the face of the nearly full moon. He felt sick all over, as if he'd caught every fever and flu known to mankind, but he managed to spit out the question he knew he shouldn't ask but couldn't keep from asking. "Did you know there was something wrong with me all this time? That I never finished converting?"

"What? Yeah, I had my suspicions from early on. But what's the difference? This isn't the old days; we don't *all* make shoes and live underground dressed up like Christmas Elves anymore. So you're not a hundred percent Lep. Whatever, brother. Live and let live, as the humans say. As long as you don't bother anybody and stay off other Leps' territories, nobody's going to call you on it. Besides, we're kind of an endangered species now, since the Trolls destroyed the last of the elixir in the Great Neathlands War last century."

"Wait. There's no more elixir?" Tommin felt the universe unraveling. He was nothing. He had nothing. No past, no future, no hope.

"Nah. It's a shame, right?" Riksdaler made a sound between a sigh and a groan. "Croesus, those Cups! Never tasted anything better. Never felt more like a god. A hundred rainbows' worth of liquid Bliss, weren't they?"

*No more elixir. Never another Cup of Fortune.*

So Tommin would be stuck in this in-between state forever—or for as long as a two-thirds Leprechaun might live. He pictured hundreds of years of inner struggle laid out before him like an unending cloverleaf motorway, loop after loop: stealing steering him into guilt, human longings circling around into Leprechaun hunger. Around and around he'd go, unable to stop or choose another road.

Riksdaler said, "Well, I'm going. You sure you don't want to treat yourself to a little Christmas gift? Warm your *partially* green blood this wintry night?"

"No. You go on."

"Suit yourself."

A few minutes later, Tommin heard the lift hum as it carried Riksdaler down to the lobby.

Intense thirst mingled with his nausea. He shuffled into the kitchen. As he gripped the refrigerator door handle, a fierce, terrible itching possessed his entire body like a fiery demon. With it came gold lust strong enough to steal his breath. Never before had it come on with such sudden urgency. He grabbed his leather coat from the wardrobe and ran, terrified he'd fall into another coma before he could find a Take. The way his heart skipped and faltered, he half expected to find the Angel of Death waiting for him when the lift doors opened.

He made it to the street and followed his nose to a flat on the next block. Under a tall fir tree trimmed with silvery ribbons and golden stars, he tore into several packages of high-end jewelry. He crammed the gifts into his pocket, his blood rejoicing but still asking for more.

Hours later, when the sun began to rise above the city, Tommin stumbled home with every pocket stuffed. Slung over his shoulder, he wore a Santa sack bulging with plunder: silver candlesticks and teapots, gold necklaces and bracelets, coin collections and a gem-studded idol of some Eastern goddess.

The night's Takes blurred together in his memory. Each one had thrilled him, and each had driven him to seek another. The Bliss had reached heights he'd never dreamed possible. He'd been gluttonous and greedy, intoxicated by his debauchery. He'd broken rules. And he wasn't sorry.

Not yet.

His blood hummed. His body buzzed. He felt so, so good.

When Tommin stepped off the lift, Riksdaler stood waiting. Without a word, he slammed his fist into Tommin's gut. Tommin fell to his knees. His bag of loot crashed to the floor.

"You must be the biggest eejit ever born," Riksdaler said.

# Chapter Four

## *An Litir*

## (The Letter)

"What were you thinking?" Riksdaler asked. He paced behind the sofa where Tommin sat with his head in his hands, still pulsing with Bliss.

"I wasn't thinking, obviously."

Riksdaler smacked him across the back of the head. "Eejit! You know, you were seen trespassing by at *least* three other Leps. I got vicious texts from Florin and Stater, and a brutal call from Hekte. One of them's bound to report you."

Tommin rubbed his scalp where Riksdaler's signet ring had scraped the skin. His fingers found blood.

"You'd better hope the Faerie authorities don't call you in for questioning. Not everyone's as tolerant as I am, you know. Two minutes with you and they'd figure out you're not a full convert. Then it would be death by poisoned blade at midnight for you, brother. Or worse." Riksdaler swore. "My gold, how'd I ever talk myself into helping the likes of you? If you get brought up on charges and name me . . ."

"I wouldn't. I won't. Look, I don't know what happened. I lost my mind. I couldn't stop Taking . . ."

"Not my problem. I'm done with you. I knew you were trouble, didn't I?" Riksdaler took a brown bottle from the refrigerator and headed toward his bedroom. "I'm off to Thailand, or maybe Denmark. Maybe Australia. Wherever you're not."

The intercom buzzed. Tommin went to the kitchen wall and pressed a button. "Yes?" he said into the unit.

"Mr. Leary? Letter down here for somebody called Tommin Kelly," the doorman's voice replied.

Tommin coated his voice in Charm so the doorman wouldn't notice he wasn't the penthouse owner, Leary. "Ah, yes. Kelly's a guest of mine. I'll send him down for it. Thanks."

"What was that, now?" Riksdaler shouted from his room.

"Doorman has a letter for me."

"That's it, then. You're done for. Can't say I didn't warn you." Riksdaler emerged carrying a backpack and a suitcase, his leather jacket zipped to his throat. He brushed past Tommin and pressed the lift button. "See you in another life, brother."

The doors slid open. Riksdaler stepped in, tugging his wheeled suitcase behind him.

"Riksdaler?" Tommin said. "I'm sorry."

Riksdaler donned his sunglasses and shook his head. "You'll never learn, will you? A Leprechaun never apologizes, Tommin. Never."

The doors shut.

⁂

Tommin tore open the fat cardboard envelope and dumped its contents onto his bed.

An Irish passport with his photo and the name Thomas Ryan O'Kelly. An airline ticket for a flight to Baltimore, leaving in four hours, and a bus ticket from Baltimore to Kentwood, Pennsylvania. Eight hundred and twenty-seven American dollars. A Dublin postcard, upon which someone had scribbled *LEAVE IRELAND IMMEDIATELY OR ELSE*...

The note bore neither seal nor signature, but he made up his mind to take its writer's advice. Rumor was that modern-day America had little magic and few Faeries. Perhaps he could live a normal life there. Perhaps his blood would settle, lose some of its magicality, and not require so many Takes.

He stuffed a few clothes and toiletries into a duffel bag. He grabbed a stack of euros from the dresser and tucked them into his coat's inside pockets along with the passport, American cash, and tickets. As he left the bedroom, he glimpsed the overstuffed Santa sack in the corner, wishing he had time to bury the Take properly.

"Sorry," he said to the pile of riches. Abandoning an enormous Take seemed to Tommin the sort of thing a Leprechaun *ought* to apologize for—no matter what Riksdaler said. Such a waste it was, leaving treasure behind and never honoring it with the rainbow it deserved.

He shouldered the duffel bag and exited the flat through the back window, scampering down the fire escape and jumping the last few feet to land in the alley.

"Tell your future?" a gravelly voice said from the shadows.

Tommin looked over his shoulder. Between a rubbish bin and a broken wooden crate, a wild-haired old man sat with his back against the wall. He was dressed in layers of filthy coats and shawls and had a sprig of holly tucked behind one ear. He raised a paper-wrapped bottle in salute.

"Cat got your tongue?" the old man said. "But I reckon you don't like cats, do you?"

"Sorry," Tommin said. "I have to go. I have a flight to catch."

"Hurry and scurry. Run, run, run. It's all you've done lately, eh? Running again now, and you won't stop for a long while, neither." The man extended a gloved hand, palm up.

Tommin had heard enough. He hastily pulled a few euros from his pocket and dropped them into the beggar's hand. He hefted the duffel bag and started down the alley.

"Wait! Don't you want to know the rest?" the man called after him.

"No. Thanks, anyway."

"Suit yourself, lad. Just remember, things are rarely what they seem!"

"I'll remember."

What Tommin *did* remember as he left the alley and hailed a cab was this: another grizzled old man dressed in many red coats—the Great Himself, king of the Leprechauns, lord of a thousand cats.

And then, a name. The *girl's* name.

*Eve.*

Her name echoed in his mind as the taxi carried him to the airport; it comforted him as the jet bore him away from his homeland. Knowing it made him happy and sad at the same time. Knowing it changed nothing and everything. The girl Eve was long gone, true—but he was somehow certain she had loved him, and he had loved her. If he never did another right thing in his life, he had *that*. He tucked the knowledge into his heart, burying it deep like a crock of pure gold, to keep it safe and hidden.

# Chapter Five

## *Ag Tosú Arís*

## (Beginning Again)

Through the streaky bus window, Tommin watched scenes flow one into another: fields of brown stubble, banks of dirty snow, abandoned motels, long icicles clinging to jagged rock faces, boys in black suits and straw hats on bicycles, signs advertising lottery tickets and fast food. He eavesdropped on conversations about sick dogs and new grandchildren.

He slept and dreamed of mushroom tea and a cranky, red-haired servant boy.

The bus brakes screeched, shocking him awake. "Kentwood," the driver said. "Everybody off."

With his sleeve, Tommin wiped window condensation from his cheek and the side of his head. He stood and grabbed his duffel bag from the seat. He was glad he didn't require Glamour to appear average height among the humans, having not properly converted. If he'd had to keep even a light Glamour going since Dublin, it might have drained him straight into another coma.

The other passengers filed toward the door. A whiff of silver tickled his nose as a woman dressed in bright silk shimmied past his seat. Bracelets tinkled on both her arms, beckoning him to follow.

He didn't need to Take. He'd stolen a few items while in the queue at the airport's coffee shop early that morning, and the watch and necklace had been of such quality that he still felt fine, but who knew when he'd have another chance? The shabby-looking bus station outside the windows did not portend riches aplenty.

It was easy, putting on the slightest bit of Charm, making the woman feel content and unwary, and then sliding the bangles off her left arm as her right arm struggled with her baggage. He slipped his prize into his pocket, enjoying the bracelets' musical clinking and the sweet sensation of Bliss they imparted.

Once he'd disembarked, he watched the other passengers embracing friends or climbing into taxis. He was in no hurry. He had nowhere to go, no one to meet. Fat clumps of snow began to fall around him. He gazed skyward, enjoying nature's strange magic, letting snowflakes melt on his forehead and cheeks.

"Are you Thomas O'Kelly?" a man's voice asked from behind him.

Tommin turned, heart pounding, ready to run. Again.

A black-haired young man with shiny steel piercings in his lip, eyebrows, ears, and nose smiled at him. "I'm Duke. A guy paid me to give you a ride to your apartment. He didn't tell you?"

"A guy?"

"Yeah. Billy *something*. Or was it Todd? Can't for the life of me remember what he looked like now, either. Man, that's freaky. Must be my allergy meds. Anyway, I'm parked over there." Duke pointed to a part-blue, part-white dented van across the street.

Tommin hesitated.

"I'm not a serial killer or anything. I swear." Duke twirled his key chain on his finger. "Oh. Hey, I have mail for you. Jeez, my memory's toast." He pulled a folded-over, smashed tan envelope from the back pocket of his jeans and handed it to Tommin.

Tommin peered inside at a plastic Pennsylvania driver's license, some official-looking documents, and a note scribbled in blue ink. He recognized the handwriting; it matched the writing on the note he'd received telling him to leave Dublin or die.

*ENJOY YOUR NEW PLACE. BE CAREFUL. YOU WILL BE WATCHED.*

"Everything cool?" Duke asked.

He wanted to say, *No, not at all*, but Tommin nodded. "Yeah," he said, imitating Riksdaler's streetwise voice. "Cool. Let's go."

What remained of the Bliss melted away and was replaced by unease. Were the notes from friend or foe? Was it better to obey the mysterious sender or to run and try to start anew somewhere else? Or would whoever it was find him no matter where he tried to hide?

Saints! Would the trouble *never* end?

His stomach growled like a wild beast as he tossed his bag into the back of the van.

Duke laughed and slammed the hatch shut. "I can relate to that, man. You want to get a burger? My aunt's diner is just up the street."

"Why not," Tommin said.

"Yeah?"

"Yeah."

Half an hour later, Tommin sat across from Duke in a restaurant booth. Duke mopped up a smear of ketchup with his last French fry; Tommin sipped a thick chocolate milkshake through a striped straw. Duke had said little during the meal, having kept his mouth busy chomping off big bites of burger and chewing handfuls of fries.

Plate cleaned, Duke patted his trim stomach and leaned back. "So. Your accent. You Scottish or something?"

"Irish."

"Oh. Like Leprechauns and four-leaf clovers, right?"

Tommin choked on the milkshake.

"You all right?"

Eyes watering, Tommin drank deeply from his water glass. He coughed a few times before he could speak. "Do I look like a Leprechaun to you?" he asked, his insides churning.

Duke laughed. "Nah. Too tall. And too young. You're only, like, maybe seventeen or eighteen?" He pointed at Tommin's plate. "Done?"

Tommin *was* done. Done with long plane rides, done with long bus rides, and done with getting the life scared out of him by a man who resembled a pincushion. And done with a multitude of other things as well—just too tired to list them at the moment.

Instead of using Charm to get out of paying the check (a trick Riksdaler loved to play on waitresses), Tommin pulled a twenty-dollar bill from his pocket and laid it on the table.

"You put that away now, honey," said the plump old lady standing behind the counter. "Your dinner's on me, as long as you promise to come back again real soon."

"Thanks, Aunt Gert," Duke said. He went to the counter, leaned across, and planted a kiss on her cheek.

"Yeah, thanks," Tommin said. The woman reminded him of Granny; the smile he offered her was genuine. "You're a fine cook."

Gert snapped a dish towel toward them. "Get out, the two of you," she said, grinning. "And stay out of mischief."

Duke gave Tommin a gentle shove out the door. "You flirting with Aunt Gert? You got game, boy. I see lots of free pie in your future."

Tommin smiled because he thought he should. And because he'd kept hold of twenty dollars. Paper money didn't satisfy him much, but it *was* money.

"You look ready to crash," Duke said when they arrived at his van. "Good thing your place is close. Hop in."

Before Duke pulled the van out of the parking space, Tommin had fallen into a black, dreamless sleep. Next thing he knew, someone was gripping his shoulder and shaking him gently.

"Dude? Rise and shine. This is it. Twenty-two Pine Street." Duke pulled the keys from the ignition, grinning. "Jet lag's a beast, right? I'll get your gear."

A few minutes later, as he followed Duke up a flight of wooden steps, Tommin caught a whiff of gold. The skin of his palms grew warm and tingly. "Saints, no," he muttered. "Already?"

Electronic music blared from Duke's jeans. He set Tommin's bag by the door and pulled a cell phone from his back pocket. He squinted at the lit screen. "Shoot. Gotta take this. See you around, eh?" He jogged down the steps, talking animatedly, and then turned to toss a key ring up to Tommin.

The key ring landed at Tommin's feet. He picked it up, unlocked the door, shoved the duffel bag inside, and relocked the door—a little frustrated that the gold scent was luring him away from his new home before he'd even had a chance to cross the threshold.

He blamed the nagging need on jet lag. He *had* meant to be better in America, to somehow wean himself down to a few Takes a month, and here he was, failing already. Multiple times. He was nothing but a pitiful, deported, part-Leprechaun, part-human thief.

And he was alone.

Alone except for whoever was spying on him, sending him tickets, and finding him places to live.

He jogged down the steps and across a patch of dead grass. He looked both ways before crossing the street, for traffic *and* for spies, but saw nothing but a scraggly squirrel. Honestly, did he expect a Faerie police officer or Leprechaun bounty hunter to wave from the shrubbery?

Saints above, he was tired. One Take, and after that, he planned to hide in bed for a long, long time.

# Chapter Six

## An Faireoir

## (The Watcher)

There was an old saying: good things come to those who wait. If this was true, someone owed her more good things than could be counted.

She had been waiting for ages. Literally.

In that time, she'd been called many names. Nora, Fiona, Deidre, Mary, Maeve, Sarah—even Hephzibah. Sometimes she'd gone years with no name at all. Shadows do not need names.

But her *first* name, and the one she kept in her heart as her own, was Eve. The name Tommin would know her by when she found him again.

She was old, but only in her soul. One of the gifts the Leprechauns' elixir had given her was everlasting physical youth. Only her eyes had changed, her irises darkening to a deep blue gray encircled with silver as the centuries wore on. As she waited, and as she searched the world for any sign of Tommin.

She knew he still lived. Somehow, she knew and never doubted—not even as the years bled into decades and then centuries.

Finally, on Christmas Day, she'd heard a rumor from a troop of Forest Faeries who lived in (and under) a Dublin park: in the hours between midnight and dawn, a rogue Leprechaun had gone on a stealing spree of epic magnitude, ransacking houses and shops, breaking rules as if possessed. He'd been seen by many (thin, pale skinned, with chestnut-brown hair), and woe betide the fellow when the Faerie Council got hold of him, they'd said grimly.

It was him. Her Tommin. At last, his present had aligned with hers. Whatever had hidden him from her, whatever strong enchantment, gold-deficiency coma, or magic-walled prison, no longer held him. Soon—and that word meant much to a girl who'd waited over two hundred years—she would see him again. Kiss him, hold him close, touch his face, tell him everything . . .

But first things first, for Tommin was not the only one for whom she'd watched and waited.

Lorcan Reilly had been a hard one to track, sometimes untraceable for years at a time. But he was no match for her. Over the course of several human generations, she'd mapped his movements from one end of Ireland to the other, throughout the Neathlands and the land Above. She knew his ways, his habits, his never-waning longing for the throne. Sometimes she'd watched him herself; other times, she'd learned of his doings through the Agency of Faerie Guardians—a secret organization she'd joined in the second decade of the Great Neathlands War.

By war's end, she'd helped bring to justice the Unseelie Faerie general responsible for unleashing the curse of hunger on all of Ireland. In years since, she'd captured a number of juvenile, lawbreaking Pookas; returned a kidnapped Merrow to the sea; trapped a Troll or two; and even recovered a lost unicorn from the deepest, most enchanted forest in the world. But always, her true heart's desire remained: to find Tommin and to offer him the cure for the curse—the cure that required the fresh blood of Lorcan Reilly.

Finally, things were falling into place.

She was ready.

# Chapter Seven

## *An Post Nua*

## (The New Job)

Duke found Tommin a job at his cousin's smoothie stand in the mall. Tommin took it because he didn't know what else to do. Sitting around his two-room apartment had made him more restless and depressed than ever—no matter how many little Takes he'd managed in a day.

Five days a week, Tommin made Banana Breezes, Mango Sunsets, and Super-Antioxidant Green Tornadoes. He mopped the floor, wiped the counters, and took out the rubbish.

He refused to man the cash register.

"Allergies," he told Renee, the gum-snapping blonde manager. "Money gives me a rash. I could go into shock and drop dead on the spot."

She believed him—and he hadn't even used a bit of Charm.

Tommin's life became (from what he'd seen on television and observed in the mall) very much like the normal life of a suburban human teenager. Duke taught him to ride a motorbike and to play video games. Girls brought him cupcakes and wrote their phone numbers on Smoothie Paradise receipts. Old ladies offered him gumdrops and mints and left generous tips. He and Duke snuck into cinemas, hiked in the woods, and ate at the Kentwood Diner for free. They talked about music and films and Duke's latest crush.

On the evenings Tommin spent alone, he crafted shoes using tools and leather he bought online. Fine brogues, dainty slippers, and heavy boots. He dropped them into the charity boxes behind the church near his apartment building and imagined bright-eyed children and toothless old men aahing with contentment as they slipped their feet inside their new, lovingly crafted footwear.

If it hadn't been for his compulsion to steal and bury, Tommin might have forgotten he was part Leprechaun. But the urge to Take never left him alone for long. On his breaks at the mall, he picked pockets and pilfered jewelry from shoppers. He moved with grace and ease, wearing a light Glamour and avoiding the security cameras. Like Fred Astaire in the old films, he was all fluid motion with no mistakes, no missteps.

Most of the time, he didn't dwell on the ensuing guilt. What was the point? He did only what his body demanded, what it required to stay healthy and strong. With no cure on the horizon and no one in all of cyberspace selling the little gold pills, why torture himself by abstaining from thievery?

Unfortunately, his need for silver and gold grew greater with each passing week. Soon simple shoplifting and pickpocketing would not sustain him. What then? Full-on jewelry-store heists? Hollywood-mansion robberies? And when *that* wasn't enough . . . ?

Behind the counter at the smoothie stand, he retied his yellow apron. His palms itched as he tossed a handful of sliced strawberries into the blender. Wanda, the pink-haired girl from the Pierce Me Boutique, leaned on the counter and eyed him like a tigress staring at a side of beef.

"When are you gonna let me pierce your ears, Tommy?" she said when he handed her the smoothie. "You know, you could come to my place some night after work, and I'd do it for free."

"I'll think about it," he said. Being polite took effort when the itching and headaches started. No wonder books and films portrayed

Leprechauns as churlish and moody. There was truth behind it. Truth *and* relentless hunger. He cast a glance at the clock. Twenty minutes until his break and his next chance to Take. He might be able to make it . . .

Across the hall, a female mall security guard stood eyeing him, muscular brown arms crossed over her midsection. *Gloria*, that was her name. She'd introduced herself the first day he'd worked there—and by the saints, she always seemed to be within shouting distance. Surely she should have caught him thieving by now. Perhaps she needed more training or a pair of spectacles.

"This is the best smoothie ever," Wanda said, swirling the straw through the pink liquid. "You're an artist. A smoothie artist."

Tommin said, "Thanks," and made the mistake of meeting Wanda's worshipful gaze for a moment. He hoped she'd not take it as encouragement. When he looked to see if Gloria was still watching, she'd disappeared. "Thank heaven for that."

Wanda raised an eyebrow. "Jeez, you're a strange one, Tommy. Cute, but strange."

The man in line behind Wanda cleared his throat and drew Tommin's attention. Of medium height, with neat brown hair and serious blue eyes, dressed in a well-made suit and silk tie, he looked like an ordinary banker or real estate agent—but there was also *something* about him . . .

Wanda turned to face the man and said, "Oops. Sorry, mister. Didn't know you were waiting there." She stepped away from the counter. "Call me, Tommy."

"Sure," Tommin said distractedly.

Wanda sauntered off, hips swaying like a water buffalo's.

"What would you like, sir?" Tommin asked. "The Strawberry Spectacular is the pick of the week."

"Chocolate Bliss," he said with a Dublin accent and a sly smile. "With extra Bliss."

Tommin opened his mouth to tell the man they had no such drink, but he changed his mind. There were gold flecks in the man's eyes. The air around him trembled like heat waves above pavement. *With Glamour.*

Mind racing, Tommin turned and grabbed a pitcher. His hands shook as he filled it with chocolate chips, mocha syrup, and a scoop of chocolate frozen yogurt. A cold lump of panic formed in his throat, obstructing his breath.

"Worked here long, brother?" the man asked. Tommin felt his gaze on the back of his head, like ants crawling in his hair.

"A few months." Tommin splashed almond milk into the pitcher, onto the counter, and down the front of his yellow apron. He attached the pitcher to the blender base and pushed the "Turbo" button. His heart pounded so hard against his ribs he thought they might crack.

Should he run for the back door? Play dumb? Play along?

"I'm starting a new business in the mall here. I think you'd be a brilliant partner, so I do."

"Um . . ." Tommin poured the drink into a plastic cup and pressed the lid on. He turned to face the Leprechaun. "Thanks, but . . ."

"I won't take no for an answer. We're going to have the grandest of times," he said, pulling the cup out of Tommin's tight grip. He leaned over the counter and whispered, "Gold-brother."

"That's on the house," Renee, the manager, said from her stool at the register.

"Thanks, love." The Leprechaun stranger winked at Renee, reached into his vest pocket, and pulled out a card. He looked Tommin in the eye, grinned wickedly, and set the card on the counter with a snap. "Meet me at the diner at seven tonight. We have a lot to discuss, partner." He took a few elegant steps, then turned and said, "Now, don't you be late, Tommin Kelly."

"He'll be on time," Renee said. "Come back soon!" She fanned herself with an inventory sheet. "What a hottie. You should totally go work for him."

"I doubt I have a choice," Tommin said. He ran into the back room and threw up into a bucket.

Just when he'd finally started to build a life of his own—*this* had to happen. Anger, fear, and confusion took turns punching him in the gut. *And* his hands itched. He sat on the cold concrete floor and wished it would open up and swallow him.

"You okay, Tommy?" Renee called from out front.

"Fine." He stood and brushed the dust off the seat of his jeans. "I'm taking my break now." *And somebody's watch. And possibly a few rings.*

"Have fun."

Fun had little to do with it.

He tossed his apron into a bin and went out the delivery door to get some fresh air. He stood beside the dumpsters (where the air was less than fresh) and looked up at the clouds. For the love of heaven, why did that Leprechaun have to show up at the Cherry Grove Mall? Were there no boundaries in America, no territories maintained by the Faerie authorities like in Ireland?

If he'd had a number for the Faerie cops (who might or might not have existed), he would have called them.

As it was, he knew not a soul he could ask for help.

# Chapter Eight

## *Lorg agus Folaigh*

## (Seek and Hide)

Eve sat on the edge of the wishing fountain and watched the skinny boy working at the smoothie place.

She'd done it every day for two weeks, this watching. This hiding behind a Glamour so strong and special that there wasn't a Faerie being in the world who could see through it or detect its presence.

Today, Tommin had put on a yellow apron embroidered with pineapples and oranges. He wore his hair long in front, so it hung into his eyes, just as it had two hundred years ago. He still slouched a little. He still tripped over his own feet when he wasn't playing the Charming Leprechaun.

In her lonely travels, she'd seen many wonders. Great whales rolling and splashing in the sea, the aurora borealis shimmering against a curtain of stars, a thousand phosphorescent blossoms floating above a maze of mirrors in the Faerie queen's night garden, clouds of butterflies settling onto a forest like winged fire. But nothing in all the world had ever made her heart sing the way the sight of Tommin did.

She wanted to run to him, leap over the counter, and pull him into her embrace. Or to approach him slowly, to watch his face change when he recognized her, to see him overcome by joy—and then to watch him run to her, like the hero of some romantic film.

No. Giving herself away to Tommin would be too risky. Dropping her Glamour anywhere, for any length of time, or even whispering her true name to Tommin would be too risky. If she'd learned anything as an agent, it was that someone was always watching. Always listening.

That "anyone" could be Lorcan or one of his spies. If Lorcan were to capture and contain her, she'd be unable to rescue Tommin when he needed her. Unable to save him from being converted, and unable to offer him the remedy.

And then there was the troublesome matter of her own fugitive status. When she'd run off to find Tommin this time, she'd gone AWOL. She'd broken her contract with Celestine Greymoss, the head of the Guardians and the only being in the world who knew her true name and history. Madame Greymoss had been generous once, letting Eve live when the law demanded the execution of anomalies such as she—in return for Eve's eternal service to the agency and the use of her unique gifts. But Madame Greymoss never gave second chances. Eve didn't doubt that every Faerie agent and bounty hunter on and under the earth was vigilantly waiting for her to slip up and reveal her un-Glamoured face. If she were to also unwittingly lead them to Tommin, those same agents would gladly turn him in, too—and no good could come of that. Faerie law, millennia old and as fixed as the moon in its orbit, was quite clear on such matters. If the responsible gold-father did not come forward to claim his wayward part-human gold-son within three days of the Faerie Court's worldwide summons, the unconverted and/or insane gold-son would be put to death.

In either case, conversion or execution, the human boy Tommin would be lost.

So she sat still, and she watched. Sooner or later, Lorcan would come to claim Tommin, and then everything she'd planned and waited for could come to pass. Meanwhile, she took notes in a little leather-bound journal.

*Day Three: Blue T-shirt, black jeans. Spilled a Cherry Monsoon and cut his finger slicing watermelon. Stole earrings from Macy's and a bracelet from one of the mall hairdressers. Seems healthy and in good spirits. No sign of the enemy.*

*Day Twelve: Black T-shirt, blue jeans. Must have cut chin shaving—tiny red line there. Flirted with old lady until she smiled and blushed. Went to lunch with Duke. Uses lots of ketchup. I don't know how much longer I can hide from him. It pains me not to speak to him when I'm so close. Must be patient. No sign of the enemy.*

Today, day fourteen, was the day everything changed. The day the stranger in a business suit showed up at the smoothie stand, wearing a thin veil of Glamour.

As soon as she saw him, Eve sprang to her feet. Holding her Glamour steady, she tucked her journal into her bag and moved to stand behind the Leprechaun. She listened to his invitation.

She would have bet every dollar on earth that Lorcan Reilly had sent this fellow to do his dirty work. A hundred years ago, there had been rumors that in his ceaseless quest for power and the throne, he'd taken on another gold-son to replace her, using the last precious ounce of the Elixir of Fortune to convert him. This suit-wearing Lep might be her own gold-brother.

If this was Lorcan's lackey, it was possible that Lorcan himself lurked nearby, although as far as she knew, he'd never left Ireland once in the last two centuries.

The familiar urge to end Lorcan Reilly's misery-causing life rose up in her like a tide of black water. Until recently, she'd resisted because she'd believed he'd lead her to Tommin—but instead, some Forest Faeries and a few hours of Internet searches had finished that job. In truth, if it weren't for the fact that she needed fresh blood from Lorcan as part of Tommin's remedy, she would have killed him already. She'd had opportunities. Not five weeks ago, she'd stood behind him, cloaked in heavy Glamour, poisoned knife in hand, trembling with hatred.

For Tommin's sake, she had granted Lorcan a stay of execution.

Ten or twenty times.

The unfamiliar Leprechaun set a card on the smoothie-stand counter and walked away. When he disappeared into the bookstore, Eve remembered to breathe.

And then she realized no one stood between her and Tommin. He was only a few feet away, so close she thought she could smell him—a cleaner version of him than she'd known long ago, but *him* nonetheless. Like the forest after rain, only better.

She stepped closer, careful not to drop the Glamour. Behind the mask of magic, tears streamed down her face. She had not been this close to Tommin—close enough to reach out and touch him—since she'd kissed him in the gardens of the Great Himself, before the arrows struck her.

If she'd been a true Leprechaun, she would have died that day.

But she was not a Leprechaun. She was something different, stronger—and her strength had brought her to this place and this boy after two hundred long years.

Tommin dropped the man's card into his apron pocket, taking no notice of her; in her emotional state, she'd put on so much Glamour that she'd gone invisible. For a moment, he looked right through her, and then he covered his mouth and fled into the storeroom.

The temptation to run after him, to comfort him, to drop the Glamour and tell him everything, almost overwhelmed her. It took every ounce of determination she could muster to walk away from the smoothie stand and to keep walking, past the pet shop, past the Gymboree and the Colonial Candle store. Each step she put between her and Tommin pierced her as painfully as the Trolls' arrows.

An automatic door opened, and she stepped into the late-afternoon sunlight. Her eyes searched the parking area. The well-dressed Leprechaun was nowhere to be seen, but she had every confidence that she'd see him again soon—and Lorcan, too.

With a screech of brakes, a bus stopped a few yards away from where Eve stood. Several mall employees boarded. She followed them, unnoticed by the driver, and took a seat beside a smudged window. She peered out. Still no sign of the businessman Leprechaun or Lorcan.

More waiting, more watching. This was her life.

For now.

# Chapter Nine

## *Moladh agus Pancóga*

## (Proposal and Pancakes)

"Look at the state of you," the suit-clad Leprechaun said, dumping a third sugar packet into his cup of coffee. "You're ill, man. You ought to *take* better care of yourself."

Tommin's sweaty palms were sticking to the red vinyl bench of the diner booth. "I'm fine," he said. The smell of his own coffee turned his stomach. The sight of the Leprechaun across the table made him want to run until his legs fell off.

Duke's aunt set plates of steaming pancakes and bacon in front of Tommin and the Leprechaun. "Anything else I can get for you, boys?" she asked. She patted Tommin's shoulder. "I did the bacon nice and crispy, just how you like it."

"Thanks, Gert," Tommin said.

"We're grand," the Leprechaun said, waving her away.

Tommin pushed his plate aside and crossed his arms over his chest. "Just tell me what you want. Or better—how I can get you to leave town."

The Leprechaun grinned. "Oh, I'm not going away. I was *sent*, you see. Sent to help you. You needn't be so wary of me. This is for your good, Tommin. All for your good."

"Who sent you?"

"Higher-ups."

"And you are?"

"Jimmy Callahan, so says my driver's license." He poured syrup over his pancakes and bacon and then sliced them into neat squares. "I'm co-owner of the Shamrock Gold Exchange, a clever little enterprise that's going to make you and me rich as the gods."

"What if I refuse?"

Jimmy pointed his fork at Tommin. "That would be a terrible shame, now wouldn't it? With all the trouble you've caused, the higher-ups would likely get an execute order on you, and then . . ." He made a cutting motion at his throat. "A poisoned blade in the alley or a poisoned bullet in the car park would end you so quick you'd not have time to beg for mercy. Or not so quick, depending on who writes the order and picks the poison. They say the slow poison gives you weeks of hellish pain before it finishes you off."

Tommin stared at his plate. No way he'd get a single bite down, maybe not ever again.

"Your problem is you're so undernourished you aren't thinking straight. I want to help you with that, to teach you how to do it up right in this century. Give me a chance, yeah?"

"I don't know."

"Look at me," Jimmy said. "Come on. In the eye, now. I was like you. Gold coma brought me from the eighteen fifties into the nineteen nineties. I fumbled about, messed up, got sick as a dog . . . until I met another Lep who taught me the game. Now, it's all good. I've buried crocks all over America, seen the sights, climbed the mountains, swum the rivers—even kissed a girl or two. Waste of time, that was, besides being against the rules. Anyway, what I'm saying is this: we're brothers, and I want to help you. You should let me help you."

"Leprechauns don't help people." Tommin held his water glass in a death grip. Cold drops of condensation rolled over his skin.

"In the old days, that was true. And some Leps are dirty players. But most of us help our kin when we can. We're a dying breed, you know. Less than a hundred of us left in the world."

Jimmy signaled the waitress. He gave Tommin a too-friendly smile. "Fancy some pie?"

Tommin shook his head.

"Hey, I know you're skeptical. I was, too, when I met my mentor. But he saved my life, and now I want to pay it forward. Just give me a chance, yeah? Just work one week with me at the mall. You won't regret it, I promise."

Tommin shoved his plate farther away and leaned back in his seat. "Fine," he said. "One week." What difference would it make? What harm could it do? Jimmy was right; he was undernourished. The thought of another coma and having to adjust to another time lapse sent a shiver through him.

"Look at you, scratching your hands," Jimmy said. "It's no way to live, brother, starving in the midst of a feast."

Tommin hadn't noticed he was scratching. Maybe because he was almost always scratching.

Aunt Gert approached, order pad poised. "Dessert, boys?"

Tommin shook his head. Jimmy ordered a whole coconut cream pie.

After eating every last crumb, Jimmy leaned back and put his hands behind his head. "It's a grand life, this. No famine, no bare feet and aching bones. Don't even have to get dirty unless you want to. You'll never have to make another smoothie, either. Although I must admit you do make a great Chocolate Bliss." He stood. "Let's get a little something; then we'll go back to your place, and I'll tell you how the cash-for-gold business works, eh?"

As soon as they stepped out into the cool spring night air, the scent of gold tickled Tommin's nose. He wondered if he should tell Jimmy that he'd never drunk the Third Cup—or if he already knew.

"Smell that?" Jimmy asked. "Enough for both of us, I reckon."

He decided to take the risk, to go along with Jimmy's scheme for now. He had no family, no real home, only one friend, and a scrap of self-respect that did nothing but add to his misery. What did he have to lose, truly?

Tommin nodded, and Jimmy patted him on the back. They exchanged a look, and Jimmy's face lit up with a wicked smile.

"Race you!" he said, taking off and looking ridiculous running in his fancy suit.

Tommin chased after him, driven by gold lust and a sudden, surprising, giddy camaraderie. Maybe this would be good after all, this mentoring thing. Maybe Jimmy was the answer to prayers he hadn't dared pray.

# Chapter Ten

## *Seasamh Nó Teitheadh*

## (To Stand or Run)

Cloaked in heavy Glamour, Eve stood on the sidewalk outside the diner. She watched Tommin sprint down the street after the suit-wearing Leprechaun named Jimmy. She heard him laugh as he splashed through a puddle.

This was going to be tricky, keeping Tommin safe while staying hidden from him. Look at him, running after trouble and laughing.

The words of Tommin and Jimmy's conversation echoed in her mind. She knew a lie when she heard one, and Jimmy's story was full of them.

Tommin was headed straight into a trap.

# Chapter Eleven

## *Airgead ar Mhalartú ar Ór*

## (Cash for Gold)

In the center court of the Cherry Grove Mall, Shamrock Gold Exchange set up business at a rented kiosk built to resemble an old-fashioned market cart—with modern track lights, a computerized cash register, and lots of hidden drawers and cabinets.

Jimmy placed advertisements in the local newspapers and appeared in an over-the-top television commercial (with an Irish jig as background music and Jimmy dressed in a cartoonish Leprechaun costume). On opening day, the queue of customers waiting to "have a gab with Jimmy the Leprechaun and get a crock o' cash for your old stash" stretched halfway down the Macy's wing of the mall.

The premise was simple: people brought old jewelry and coins to the Shamrock Gold Exchange, and Jimmy and Tommin gave them paper money in return. Sure, it stung a little to give up the cash, but the Bliss that came from giving customers far less than what they were owed made up for it. That was the *Take* part of the business—the subtle, legal thievery that greened the blood and gladdened the Leprechauns' hearts. Easy as pie, it was. A bit of Charm, a bright smile, and a few clever words (working the Irish accent always helped with the ladies), and the Leps ended up with handfuls of gold and silver.

Crocks full by week's end.

Tommin walked around in a daze, permanently elated. Saints, he'd never felt so strong and fulfilled. He forgot to feel guilty for Taking. He forgot to think about Eve and Granny. He forgot he'd ever wanted to break the curse to live a normal human life.

The rainbows they sent up blazed like multicolored fire. The ensuing Bliss knocked Tommin off his feet. He rolled in the grass like a happy puppy while Jimmy laughed and said, "Didn't I tell you, Tommy lad? Nothing's better than this!"

Looking back, Tommin saw how silly he'd been to doubt Jimmy. How stupid he'd been not to embrace his Leprechaun nature sooner.

Jimmy was his hero. They were both heroes. The kings of mammon. The gods of gold.

Leprechaun brothers.

# Chapter Twelve

## *An Cailín Díolacháin*

## (The Salesgirl)

The owner of Euro-Spa Delights Bath and Beauty Emporium hired Eve on the spot. Eve used only a little Charm, and enough Glamour to give her the appearance of a teenaged Audrey Hepburn—all big eyes and sweet allure.

"Three rules," said the mostly bald, possibly Greek, potbellied owner. "You speak with an exotic accent, you dress nice, and you give hand massages with the lotions like everyone you meet is a movie star or royalty. Hot, sexy royalty, yes? You woo the customer, and then they buy. Works like magic, yes?"

"I'll do my best," Eve said, trying out an accent similar to the boss's. "Like this?"

"Good! Good! Be here at nine tomorrow, and my niece Grazi will train you. Dress nice, yes?"

"I will. Thanks." Eve turned to walk away from the lotion and bath products stand. She caught a glimpse of Tommin at the neighboring kiosk. He wore a new dark-green business suit and shiny black shoes, and he was examining a ring while a fluffy-haired old woman eyed him worshipfully. He'd Charmed her well; the look on her face and the slight shimmer in the air around Tommin's body told Eve as much.

Eve couldn't blame the woman for falling for Tommin—whether he'd used Charm or not. Hadn't she fallen hard for him in spite of her vows to care for no one but herself?

He laughed at something the old lady said. Eve fell for him a little more. It shouldn't have been possible, but stars above, how she'd missed him. One century was a long time, and two . . . well, she'd make sure she never lost track of him again.

Something made him look her way. For a moment, he met her gaze and held it. Her Glamour faltered, but she caught it just in time. There was no way he'd seen her true face—and yet he blushed and smiled at her before returning to business.

"Steady now," she whispered to herself as she made for the mall exit.

Maybe taking a job next door to Tommin was not such a good idea. But how else could she keep an eye on him without wearing the exhausting, heavy invisibility Glamour? Working at Euro-Spa Delights would require only a little Glamour and Charm and wouldn't deplete her energy in a few hours. Lately, she'd found herself tiring more easily, and she needed to stay strong and alert in case Lorcan showed up.

"Hey!" a familiar voice shouted behind her. "You dropped something."

*Keep walking,* she told herself. *Don't you dare stop.*

"Miss?" Tommin called. "Could you stop for a moment, miss?"

She stopped. She held on to the Glamour with all her strength—a taxing task when he drew close. He smelled like summer and new shoes.

"You dropped this." He handed her the card her boss had written her work schedule on. "Looks like we're going to be neighbors." He smiled, and she laughed. A silly, fake, humiliating laugh.

Blood rushed to her cheeks and ears. Thank heaven there was no way he could see it through the Glamour.

"Great. Thank you for bringing this," she said quickly, surprised she remembered to use her fake accent. "I have bus to catch. Good night." She practically ran toward the doors.

"I'm Tommin. I mean, Tommy. Thomas. Thomas O'Kelly from Shamrock Gold Exchange," he called after her. "Nice to meet you."

She waved without turning around.

Once outside, she leaned against the wall and covered her face with her hands. "Fool," she murmured.

"You okay, honey?" a woman's voice asked.

With a start, Eve uncovered her face. She should have sensed someone standing right in front of her. Maybe she needed to sleep more, or maybe spending so much time mooning over Tommin had dulled her wits.

The middle-aged black woman before her wore a navy-blue security-guard uniform with a name tag that said Gloria Glass. Her short blue-black hair was streaked with red. Eve had seen her around the mall plenty of times, come to think of it, just never this close up.

"I'll be fine," Eve said.

"You sure? Was that boy bothering you? I can have a word with him—"

"No, no. I'm fine." The bus pulled up, and an old couple got off. "I have to go," Eve said. "But thanks."

"Not a problem," Gloria said. "Take care."

*I should,* Eve thought as she boarded the bus. *I should take more care than I ever have in my life. Otherwise, I'll ruin everything I've waited for.*

The bus stopped in front of Tommin's apartment building. She got off and went around the back to unlock the door of the tiny downstairs efficiency she'd rented. As soon as she stepped inside, she dropped her purse and almost all her Glamour. Never for a moment did she forget that someone might be watching her, especially in this age of hidden cameras no bigger than a poppy seed.

Sometime after midnight, Eve awoke and sat straight up in bed. In her mind was a crystal-clear image of Gloria Glass. One detail stood out as if in a spotlight, one thing she'd not consciously noticed earlier. On the collar of her uniform, Gloria wore an almost undetectable diamond-shaped emblem. A symbol only a fellow agent of the Faerie Guardians would recognize.

# Chapter Thirteen

## *An Mháirt ag an Ionad*

## (Tuesday at the Mall)

Jimmy took the day off to go to Philadelphia to trade some of the Shamrock's paper currency and less valuable jewelry Takes for high-quality gold coins. The purer the gold in the crock, the better the rainbow, the stronger the Bliss.

At nine o'clock, Tommin switched on the kiosk's lights and computer. He straightened the stacks of brochures and business cards. And then the lotion girls arrived next door.

Grazi was short but shapely, with olive skin and black ringlets of hair hanging halfway down her back. She had a different red dress for every day of the week, each low cut and curve hugging. He'd never seen a man succeed in passing her by without falling prey to her smooth sales pitch and practically indecent hand massages. The new girl stood beside her, a demure violet beside a hothouse rose.

With a serious demeanor, Grazi started to train the girl, explaining pricing and stocking procedures, but after half an hour, Grazi's all-business tone vanished as she moved on to teenage-girl chatter. Through a bit of furtive eavesdropping, Tommin learned about all the best places for lunch and how best to avoid the mall's creepy custodian.

He realized he'd been staring when Grazi waved at him. He looked away fast, fumbling with the brochures. A pile slipped to the floor, and he scrambled to pick them up, trying to summon the Glamour of someone who hadn't just embarrassed himself twice in under a minute. After that, he switched on the computer and attempted to work on the sales figures spreadsheet. His fingers kept hitting the wrong keys, and he accidentally deleted Jimmy's entries for the month.

Before long, he peeked around the end of the kiosk again to get another glimpse of the new girl. Shiny dark-brown ponytail, big brown eyes, skin like cream. A black-and-white dress that grazed her knees. Saints, she was pretty. Pretty and . . . what was it? Magnetic? No, something gentler. All he knew was he could spend all day watching her dust and restock shelves or listening to her rehearse her sales pitch with Grazi.

By noon, Tommin knew he was in trouble.

Three Takes (with a good amount of Bliss) and he still wanted nothing but the chance to get closer to the lotion girl. He wanted to talk to her, to buy her ice cream, to run away to Bermuda with her.

How had it happened? How had he fallen in love with a human when he'd just gotten so good at being a Leprechaun?

It was dangerous, forbidden by Leprechaun law—and just plain stupid, besides.

Jimmy would kill him if he found out.

Tommin dabbed his perspiring forehead with his silk pocket square. Perhaps tomorrow he'd not be so affected by the girl. Maybe he'd caught the flu or needed to bury a crock to build up his blood.

"Yoo-hoo! Young man?"

Tommin turned and conjured up some Charm for the blue-haired, grandmotherly customer. "Good morning, me darling," he said, playing up his accent. "How can I help you this fine day?"

He wished he could say the same thing to the lotion girl.

He was in serious trouble.

# Chapter Fourteen

## *An Buachaill Béal Dorais*

## (The Boy Next Door)

Eve had to admit she was strangely jealous of the way Tommin stared at the Glamour-clad version of her while she worked. How he stuttered when trying to make small talk as he passed by the lotion kiosk. How he blushed (and tried to veil it with Glamour) when she caught him gawking at the her-who-wasn't-quite-her twenty times a day.

Tommin did seem to rein himself in when Jimmy showed up to work at the Shamrock. Which meant he stared only when he thought Jimmy was too distracted to notice.

One Wednesday when Jimmy was absent, Tommin strode over to Euro-Spa Delights, wearing a light sheen of Charm Eve found rather endearing. He straightened his green silk tie and grinned. "I want to try some lotion," he blurted. "I mean. Could I try some? Please?"

"Doesn't your boss care that you leave your shop unattended?" Eve asked in her Greek-Russian-French-hybrid accent.

"I'm my own boss," Tommin said.

"Okay then, Mr. Boss. This is the special." Eve grabbed a big basket full of lotions, creams, gels, and sponges. "Only fifty dollars today. Your girlfriend will love it, yes?"

"No. I mean, I don't have a girlfriend." He shifted his weight from foot to foot like a little boy caught in mischief. "Um . . . Aren't you going to put the lotion on my hands like you usually do for customers?"

She hugged the basket tightly, panicking inside. She wanted nothing more than to touch him, and it threatened to undo her magic and her resolve. "Well, I really think you should hurry back to your work, yes? Be responsible employee?"

He tilted his head to the side. His eyes sparkled as he poured on more Charm. "If I'm going to spend fifty dollars . . ."

She gave up trying to resist. She'd just do her best to get it over with quickly. "Well, okay." She reached out, palms up. "Give me your hands."

The instant his skin met hers, an electric shock passed between them. She jerked her hands away.

"Sorry," he said. "Static. Because of your shoes, probably. Try again?"

Eve grabbed his wrists and turned his hands over. Her knees went wobbly as she squirted lemon-sage-scented lotion into his palms and began to knead and rub his skin. The effort required to keep the Glamour steady made her head throb.

Perhaps some small talk would help her stop thinking about pulling him into her arms. "You do a lot of business over there," she said. "You like stealing from elderly?"

"It's an *exchange*," Tommin said. She noticed him cranking up the Charm another notch. "They bring us old stuff they don't want, and we give them money to pay the power bill and the dentist. How is that a bad thing?"

"It's bad because I think you deal unfairly. Give less than what the jewelry is worth." She rubbed his hands harder, hoping he'd find it uncomfortable—because touching him was driving her mad. She glanced at his lips. It would be so easy to lean in and kiss him.

"You're just as bad," he said with a wry smile. "Scamming people into buying overpriced lotion with your accent and your fine speeches and your hand rubbing. Right now, I'd do just about anything you asked me."

Eve dropped his hands. Sustaining the Glamour had become too painful. "Then give me fifty dollars and go back to your kiosk, Tommin."

"After you tell me your name." He pulled a fifty from his pocket and held it between his fingers.

"Penelope," she said.

"Penny." Tommin handed her the money and lifted the gift basket. "A grand name for a pretty lass."

"It's *Penelope*," she insisted as he walked away. She opened the cash drawer and slid the bill into place. Worry made a lump in her throat, worry for Tommin and herself. This flirting couldn't continue. It wasn't . . . useful. Or safe.

The security guard Gloria stopped next to Eve. "That boy bothering you again, honey? I think he's got a crush on you, maybe."

"I think you're right."

"He is kind of cute, in an Irishy sort of way. Has he got a chance?"

"Maybe," Eve said. "It depends . . ." When had she become such a terrible liar? Anyway, what was a Faerie Guardian doing suggesting romantic involvement with a Leprechaun? Maybe she'd been wrong to assume Gloria had been assigned to keep an eye on Tommin. Maybe she was keeping track of another Faerie-blooded mall worker, one Eve had yet to meet.

"Mmm-hmm. I thought so. You're all lit up like a Christmas tree. I think you've got it just as bad as Shamrock boy." Smirking, Gloria grabbed the sample tube of rosewater-scented cream and rubbed a dab into the back of her hand. "That's nice."

"The lotion?"

"The lotion *and* the love. I like a mall romance. Keep me posted, honey."

A bottle of bubble bath fell to the floor. Eve followed it until it rolled to a stop. She placed it back on the shelf.

"I'd like to ask you about something, in private," Eve said, turning to face Gloria. But the security guard was already gone, and halfway down the corridor besides, talking with a delivery man.

"Never mind, then," Eve muttered as she perched on the stool beside the cash register. "It was probably a bad idea, anyway." She snuck a glance at Tommin, a little embarrassed that she'd been talking to herself in the middle of the mall. When their eyes met, he grinned like he'd won the lottery.

She ought to have asked Gloria to arrest him for something. Or maybe she should have turned herself in for some imaginary crime. One of them needed to be locked up before things got any more out of hand. Before word got back to the Faerie authorities that a Lep wasn't behaving like a Lep and Tommin got hauled in for examination and provided a not-quite-green-enough blood sample.

Of course, there was no law against a Lep being friends with a human. She'd simply have to convince Tommin, and herself, that friendship was their only option.

Heaven knew it wouldn't be easy.

# Chapter Fifteen

## *Líomóid agus Sáiste*

## (Lemon and Sage)

On the far side of the Shamrock kiosk, Tommin lifted his hand and inhaled the aroma of the lemon-sage lotion Penny had massaged into his skin. It smelled almost as good as gold.

He closed his eyes and replayed their encounter. She'd tried to insult him, but saints above, she'd looked adorable while she'd been at it. The knit brow, the scowl—as endearing as a box of kittens!

And she'd called him *Tommin*, so she must have been paying attention the day they first met, when he'd run after her to give her the schedule. When he'd slipped and forgotten to call himself Thomas or Tommy.

The cherry on the sundae: he'd just caught her looking at him. Bold as brass.

If he'd been a betting man (and no one with Leprechaun blood would consider indulging in such foolishness), he would have wagered big money that she liked him.

He couldn't stop smiling all afternoon.

Saints and angels! He was a terrible excuse for a Leprechaun.

In the back of his brain, an alarm sounded faintly. A reminder that he needed to mind his manners and not get too carried away by his human feelings, because if Jimmy found out he wasn't a full

Leprechaun, he might tell the higher-ups. And if the higher-ups found out, he'd be doomed. Dead.

Near closing time, he was watching Penny unpack a box of fancy candles when something tugged his sleeve.

"Mister?" a small voice said. "Scuse me?"

Tommin looked down into an elfin face framed by two blonde braids. The child blinked her sky-blue eyes and lifted a clear plastic bag full of tangled plastic jewelry. "I saw your TV ad with the green man. Can you help me like he said? Will you give me a lot of money for this?" she asked.

Tommin squatted next to her. He took the bag and held it up to the light, pretending to admire it. "Well," he said, "this is quite a lovely collection of things. You don't really mean to sell your treasures, do you?"

The girl nodded. "Hercules is sick, and Mom says the vet costs a lot." Her eyes brimmed with tears. "He might die, and he's just a puppy. Rose Hunter's dog died last week."

Tommin pulled his handkerchief from his vest pocket and wiped the girl's tears. "Well, we don't want that to happen." He stood, opened the bag, and emptied it onto one of the Shamrock's black plastic trays. He set the tray on the electronic scale. "You're in luck," he said. He punched a code into the computer, and the cash drawer slid open. He took out four twenties and handed them to the girl. A stabbing pain shot through his chest, and his stomach threatened to expel his dinner.

"Thank you! Thank you!" Glowing with joy, the girl skipped away.

He had to sit down, or he would have fallen down. He gripped the edges of the stool with both hands. His green blood burned in his veins, punishing him for the crime of generosity.

He shut his eyes to stave off the dizziness. Dealing in cash didn't usually have such an effect on him. Maybe he was dehydrated or coming down with a virus.

"Hey." Penny's voice startled him. He almost fell off the stool.

"Sorry. I was . . . I just . . ." She handed him a Smoothie Paradise cup and said quickly, "I saw what you did for that girl. That was really nice. And I wanted to apologize for being mean before. And also, I noticed you're looking a little under the weather, so I got you a Pineapple Pep-Up. Friends?"

"Of course. Yes. Thanks," he said. He held up the cup. "This might help. I'm sure it will help."

"I've got to get back to work." She turned and practically sprinted to the lotion stand, the plastic bottoms of her flat shoes slapping the tiled floor.

He'd never felt so simultaneously sick and happy. As he slowly sipped the smoothie, he vowed to make her a pair of shoes more worthy of her dainty feet.

A few minutes later, he felt steady enough to close up shop. He locked the drawers and turned off the lights while mentally choosing the type and color of leather he'd use when he made Penny's gift.

"Sir?" a woman said behind him.

He turned. The little girl he'd helped stood beside a taller, angry-faced version of herself.

The woman held out a pile of twenties. "I believe this belongs to you."

The little girl's lower lip quivered as she stared at the floor. "Sorry," she said.

"What kind of creeper are you, giving all that money to my daughter?" the woman said, nostrils flaring. "You can bet I'm going to report this to the police."

For a moment, Tommin panicked. And then he put on a good amount of Charm and his brightest smile. He poured on the exaggerated Irish accent. "What kind of creep would I have been if I hadn't wanted to help your poor wee child's sick doggy? Now, don't worry your head about it, miss. You go on home and take care of your pet. Everything's grand between us. No debts, no offenses."

The mother's expression transformed from furious to embarrassed. "Oh," she said. "Forgive me. I must have been confused. Um . . . Well, thank you. You're very kind." She tucked the money into her handbag. "Would you like to join us for dinner tonight?"

"I'm afraid I can't. Another time, perhaps?"

The mother and daughter walked away hand in hand. He'd had no idea being charitable could be so dangerous. Perhaps acting like a Leprechaun was safer than playing the Good Samaritan. Tommin grabbed the smoothie and downed the rest of it in a few huge gulps.

Well, in spite of the pain and panic, he would have done it all again. That one good deed had somehow made him feel more like himself than he had in ages. And as a bonus, it had earned him a bit of respect from Penny.

And there it was again, the confusion, popping up like a stubborn weed. Whenever he thought he'd rooted it out, it sprouted anew. Being Leprechauns with Jimmy brought him Bliss, but what was that compared to sharing love and life and hope with humans?

Gold was sweet, but it was a cold companion.

Why did he have to choose one or the other?

He picked up his phone to text Duke. It had been ages since they'd gone out for a burger. Jimmy didn't like Duke; he said Duke was riffraff and a nuisance and told Tommin not to associate with him anymore, as it might damage Tommin's public image—whatever that meant. But Jimmy wouldn't return to Kentwood till the wee hours of the morning. That left plenty of time for an evening out with Duke.

He was feeling much better now.

Penny switched off the lights at the lotion stand and then waved good-bye as she shouldered her bag. Tommin watched her until she disappeared around the corner, and then he headed off to meet Duke at the diner.

Maybe it was wrong to walk the fence between Leprechaun and human, and maybe he couldn't get away with it forever, but for the moment, it was a fine thing indeed.

# Chapter Sixteen

## *Mí Iúil i Meiriceá*

## (July in America)

"It's July," Tommin said. He picked up a red, white, and blue bottle of lotion. Penny dusted a shelf with a rag and seemed to be attempting to ignore him. "Strawberry-Blueberry-Vanilla Freedom," he read. "Funny how patriotic Americans get for one day a year."

"Don't you have customers?" Penny glared at him adorably. She'd gone back to her usual semigrumpy neighbor routine the day after she brought him the smoothie for being nice. He didn't mind much. Whatever she said or did made him happy as a Leprechaun with a full crock.

He put his hands in his pockets. "It's Wednesday. Senior Citizen Day is Tuesday, so Wednesday's slow. Surely you've noticed."

"Right. Well, if you're bored, you could go to the stockroom with me and help me carry boxes." Her accent sounded different today. Maybe he was imagining it.

"My pleasure. Give me two seconds to lock up the Shamrock. Jimmy's out of town again."

As Tommin shut down the computer and locked the cabinets, he sang along with the mall's piped-in soft rock music. His hands itched faintly—but he could ignore that for another hour or two without causing himself any lasting harm.

He followed Penny down the narrow corridor, admiring the back of her—the way her hips swayed ever so gently as she walked, how proudly she held her head, the pale-blue veins behind her knees. "That's a pretty dress you're wearing," he blurted as she fumbled with keys at the stockroom door.

"Thanks," she said. "Thrift store. Boxes are over there." She pointed to the right.

He trailed behind her obediently, like she was queen of the mall. When they stopped walking, he straightened his necktie and gathered his courage. "Penny?"

She picked up a box and placed it in his arms. *"Penelope."*

"Penelope. There's a carnival in the park this weekend."

She piled another box on top of the first. Her face was serious, as usual. Like a mask. A pretty mask, but one he believed she was hiding behind. He always had this odd feeling around her, like she was a secret agent or a disguised princess on the run. Maybe he'd watched too many films with Duke.

"Will you go with me?" he asked, without any false Charm, feeling like the teenager his body suggested he was—no matter that he'd been alive for centuries.

"I don't think so." She picked up the last box and headed for the door. "Thanks, though."

"Please," Tommin said. He bumped into the doorframe. One of the boxes banged into his cheekbone, and he exclaimed in pain.

"Be careful," she said, turning to face him.

"Too late," he said.

She set her box down. She ran her fingers over the hurt spot under his eye. "That's going to be an impressive bruise."

He wished he had more injuries. "I'll be fine."

She retrieved her box and moved along the corridor. "Your old-lady friends will love it. They'll fuss over you more than ever. They'll bring you dinners for a week." Penny laughed—a sound as exquisite as angels singing.

"Don't you feel sorry for me?"

"A little."

"Sorry enough to go to the carnival with me Friday night?" Desperate for a yes, he piled on a lot of Charm. Way more than the customers got. He'd tried to avoid it. He wanted her to go because she liked him, not because he'd tricked her.

They stopped at the lotion stand. "Well . . ." She looked straight into his eyes in a way she'd rarely done. "Well, I guess I could go with you. As friends."

"Friends." He'd take it. He'd take whatever she offered. His face broke into an enormous grin. He knew he looked like an idiot, but he was too happy to care.

"You have a customer," Penny said. "You should go."

"Yeah." Tommin waved to the velour-jumpsuit-clad woman waiting at the Shamrock kiosk. "I'll be right over, me darling," he said in his exaggerated accent.

"You're awful," Penny said as he walked away. But there was a smile in her voice, he was certain of it.

# Chapter Seventeen

## *Fiontar agus Luach*

## (Risk and Reward)

Eve smacked herself in the forehead once Tommin left the Euro-Spa stand.

*Silly girl,* she scolded herself as she pried open a box of lotions and began to arrange them on a shelf. *Stupid girl.*

She should have refused his invitation. Honestly, she never should have taken this job a few yards from his, or the apartment in his building. She should have stayed way in the background, completely invisible.

She should have kept her heart in check until she'd saved him from the curse.

It was too late now.

She was juggling with fire. The truth was, she liked a bit of danger. Maybe she'd become a little addicted to excitement in her time as an agent. But no thrill was worth Tommin's life. Or her own.

Next time they met, she'd have to remind him again, and firmly, that they could only be friends. But stars above, she didn't want to.

A bottle of lotion slipped from her grasp and fell back into the box. Her fingers went numb. Her vision blurred and then cleared. She reached for the edge of the shelf and breathed deeply, concentrating on not dropping the Glamour. She had to stay covered.

In the last two centuries, she'd never been ill. Not once. But in the last month, her body had started playing tricks on her. Tired one day, dizzy the next, dropping things . . . What on earth was wrong with her? What if it got worse?

As strange as it felt, she wished Lorcan would hurry and make his move.

# Chapter Eighteen

## *Uachtar Reoite agus Tinte Ealaíne*

## (Ice Cream and Fireworks)

Strings of white lights stretched from tree to tree throughout the park. A warm, gentle breeze spread the scents of French fries and hot sugar, sausages and popcorn—and carried along the sound of the high school band playing patriotic marches. Tommin marveled at the scene: children clutching plush animals while bright balloons bobbed from ribbons tied to their wrists, adults holding ice cream cones and cardboard trays overflowing with batter-covered mysteries.

A hint of gold tickled Tommin's nose, and a whiff of silver. His itchy palms irked him as he waited beside Penny in the queue for caramel-covered apples. Still, he'd never felt as lucky as he did at this moment, standing close to the prettiest girl in town.

"This is . . . ," Penny said, smiling.

"Magical?" Tommin offered.

"Yes."

"I knew you'd like it. Do they have carnivals in your country?"

She nodded. "Not like this, though. No lights. Plainer food. Lots of . . . goats."

Tommin laughed. "Goats?"

"Goats," Penny said with conviction. "In fancy clothes."

"You're joking."

"You check the Internet when you get home, then. Google 'carnival goats.'" She laughed. He didn't care if she'd made up the story or not.

They moved forward a step. Tommin gave in to the impulse to wrap his arm around her shoulders. She didn't shrug it off—which surprised and delighted him. To ensure that she wouldn't change her mind, he put on a tiny bit of Charm. "So, where are you from, anyway? Where is this magical land of carnival goats? I can't place your accent."

"A tiny island in Greece," she said. "Very small. Only a few families."

"And how did you end up here? If you don't mind my asking?"

"My father's cousins own the lotion business. We look after our own, yes?"

"That's good. Family's good." For some reason, he believed this story less than the one about the goats. His theory about her being a disguised runaway princess seemed more plausible. But he wouldn't pry into her private life. Let her tell him when she was ready. Didn't he have his own secrets? Saints in heaven, what would she say if he told her he was part Leprechaun?

He paid for the apples, trying not to wince as the money left his grasp. A voice boomed from a speaker above their heads, announcing that the fireworks show would begin in fifteen minutes.

"Duke says the best place to watch is near the lake," Tommin said, pressing a hand against the center of Penny's back and steering her onto the sidewalk. The thin cotton of her dress was soft to the touch, warmed by her skin.

Her apple tumbled to the ground and rolled into the grass. "Figs!" she said. "I'm sorry."

"Take mine." He handed his apple to her and bent to retrieve hers, grinning at her choice of swear words. "I'm not hungry, anyway."

"You're kind," she said. "A good friend, Tommy."

The way she said "friend" wasn't going to put him off. He tossed the grassy apple into the trash, and when he returned to her side, he put his hand on her back again.

The sidewalk steepened as they neared the lake. In the grass and on the pebbled beach, families and friends sat in groups or couples, on blankets and chairs, eating and talking, laughing and photographing each other. *I could live like that,* Tommin thought. *I could be a happy human—if only I could exorcise the Leprechaun.*

Tommin scratched his hands. He had to.

"Rash?" Penny asked. She took a very undainty bite of apple.

"Uh. Yes." Tommin pointed to a bench three teenagers were vacating. "Don't worry. I'm not contagious."

When they reached the bench, she sat close. Her knees peeked out from under the red-dotted fabric of her skirt. She smelled like vanilla and butter and caramel apple. If his hands hadn't been excruciatingly itchy, Tommin would have considered it the most perfect moment in history.

Penny leaned forward to set her core-on-a stick on the ground. "Let me see," Penny said. She took his hand and turned it over. "That looks bad."

"I'll live."

A silvery-blue streak of sparkling light soared up the sky above the lake and burst into a hundred bright fragments. Lucky for him, Penny seemed to have forgotten to quit holding his hand.

The fireworks flashed and twinkled, popped and thundered for half an hour. Sometimes, Penny gasped. Sometimes, Tommin cheered. They both applauded when the grand finale lit the sky with explosion after explosion of red, white, and blue.

After the last boom echoed into nothingness, almost everyone left the lakeside, but Tommin and Penny sat still. A few fireflies flickered in the grass and tree branches. Crickets played one-note songs on their wing violins.

Penny was still holding his hand. For some reason, the itching had faded to almost nothing.

He glanced at her out of the corner of his eye, afraid to disturb whatever happy spell hung in the night air. For a split second, something about her reminded him of Eve—the girl he'd loved long ago. But when she turned her face toward him and he met her gaze full-on, he saw only Penny. He saw in her eyes what he felt in his heart.

"I want to kiss you," he whispered.

"I want to be kissed," she said.

He took her face in his hands. Her eyes closed, but he didn't want to close his. It seemed too risky. What if she disappeared—the way a Leprechaun would if the human who caught him looked away?

Tommin kissed Penny with his eyes open.

He kissed her again and again, until they were both out of breath. She laid her head on his shoulder, and whispered, "Tommin, I have secrets."

"I know. Everyone has secrets, my darling." He kissed the top of her hair and settled his chin there.

"We can't do this again. I can't date you. It's too dangerous."

He sat up straight, feeling like he'd taken a solid punch to the gut. "What? Why?"

Her lovely face was awash with sadness. "I can't tell you now. But if you'll wait a while . . . I'll do everything I can to make things change so we can be together. I mean, if that's what you want."

"It's *all* I want." Tommin lifted her hand and kissed it. For the moment, it was true. If only it could stay true. If only the lust for gold would fade away like the sound of the fireworks had.

"So, after tonight, we'll have to be friends. Just friends. Until I work things out. Please? I wish I could tell you more, but I can't."

"Just friends after tonight," Tommin said. "It might kill me."

"I think you're stronger than that."

"If you kiss me again, I might believe you."

Penny laughed. "That makes no sense at all, Tommin."

She kissed him. Her mouth was warm and sweet. Her hands cradled the back of his neck. Rainbows swirled in his head, and something very like Bliss surged through his veins, as strong as if he'd buried two full crocks at once.

They watched the stars above the lake until the sun rose to erase them from sight, and then they walked home hand in hand. He didn't itch at all—but his heart ached a little at the thought of going back to being nothing but friends.

At her door, he tried to pull her into his arms again. She shook her head. "Go upstairs," she said. "We're only friends, remember?"

He stole one last kiss and then hurried away, hoping she hadn't seen the tears in his eyes.

Were they happy tears or sad? Or both at once? That was the question he pondered as he climbed the stairs and unlocked his door. He stepped inside and kicked off his shoes. His mouth still tasted like hers. He considered not brushing his teeth before heading to bed.

"Where have you been?" Jimmy asked from the shadows.

# Chapter Nineteen

## *Bréaga agus Aiféala*

## (Lies and Regret)

"Did you not hear me, brother? I asked where you've been."

Tommin flicked the light switch. Jimmy, who sat slouched on a leather recliner, shaded his eyes and swore.

"I went to the carnival. Did you forget you have your own place now?"

Jimmy held up a tin of cookies made by one of Tommin's elderly customers. "You have better snacks."

"Your flat is above a grocery store, for heaven's sake!" Tommin surprised himself. He was never this snippy with Jimmy, never so bold.

"Oh my gold! Look at the state of you!" Jimmy sat up straight. Cookie crumbs rolled off his shirt and onto the floor. "You've been up to mischief. I can see it all over you."

"That's ridiculous." Tommin's face flushed hot. He walked to the sink, filled a dirty glass with cold water from the tap, and drank it down quickly. His face stayed hot. Blast Jimmy for spoiling his splendid mood.

"I can tell from here your color's gone off. You look gold sick, and yet . . ."

"Get off it, Jimmy. I'm going to bed." He set the glass in the sink. He walked past Jimmy on his way to the bedroom, and Jimmy grabbed his sleeve.

"No. No, you're not. Not until you tell me what you've been up to."

"I told you. I went to the carnival."

Jimmy sprang to his feet and grabbed Tommin by the shoulders. "I'm not playing, Tommy boy."

"I was with the lotion girl. So what? You said *you* kissed girls. It's nothing. Let go of me."

"You can't do that! You're not fully converted."

"You knew?" Tommin felt as if he were drowning, as if Jimmy had tipped him out of the boat and then smacked him with an oar.

"Of course I knew. I've always known. Why do you think the higher-ups sent me to keep an eye on you? We've all been waiting for you to do something asinine like this. And now I'll have to rescue you."

"I don't need rescuing." Tommin took hold of Jimmy's wrists and tried to break his grasp. Jimmy only gripped his shoulders harder. He'd been a fool not to Take before coming in for the night. Of course, he hadn't anticipated needing extra strength when his plan was to head straight to bed.

"Ah, but you do. It screws up your metabolism, messing around with humans like that. You want to go into another coma? My gold, you're stupid." In spite of the fact that Tommin had quit fighting him for the moment, Jimmy shoved him hard against the wall. "So here's what's going down. I've got connections in the Old Country. I think I can score you enough elixir to finish the conversion and erase the damage you've done. It's gonna cost you, believe me. You'll owe me a cut of your Takes for the next century at least."

"There is no more elixir."

"Anything can be bought if you have enough to pay for it."

"I'll think about it," Tommin lied. He didn't have to think about it. He had no intention of converting. Not while Penny walked the earth. In fact, he'd been thinking of looking for a cure.

Jimmy took a step back and gave Tommin a parental scowl. "You let me do the thinking. You're not capable anymore—if you ever were. And like I said, you've screwed up your metabolism. Time is your enemy now. Your green blood is breaking down, and the coma you'll get this time might last forever. I've heard of Leps going mad from this kind of thing, foaming at the mouth and eating their own flesh. You want that, Tommy? Do you?"

Tommin shook his head.

"Then pack your bags. I'll order the tickets home."

"But I'm banned from Ireland. Besides, didn't you say you'd kissed girls? You seem fine to me."

Jimmy punched Tommin in the jaw so fast he didn't see it coming. "Quit the back talk, will you! That was different. My blood's not human-tainted like yours, you eejit. Now go and pack and let me take care of everything else."

Rubbing his aching jaw, Tommin slunk into his room. Madness, flesh eating, and permanent coma? All from a few kisses? It sounded like nonsense—but then, hadn't he felt a strange Bliss when he kissed Penny? Hadn't his rash disappeared after she'd held his hand? Maybe messing about with human romance *did* have consequences for a part Leprechaun. He certainly felt sick now.

He took the duffel bag from its hook in the closet and started packing. He didn't want to die or disappear into another century. Not now that he had someone to live for. Perhaps a trip to Ireland would be a good thing. Where else in the world would he stand a better chance of finding a way to end the curse? If he could do it in time to avoid actually going through with conversion . . .

"Hurry up," Jimmy shouted. "The flight leaves in six hours, and it's a long drive to the airport."

On his pillow, Tommin left the pair of lemon-yellow ballet flats he'd made for Penny. He wished he'd had the nerve to give them to her before the carnival.

A few hours ago under the stars, everything had been so right. And now nothing was right.

"Tommin! Don't make me come in there and drag you out! We're going for your own bloody good, for gold's sake!"

"Coming." He composed a quick text to Penny and pressed "Send." Perhaps later, he could sneak in a call from a restroom or something, if he ever managed to get out of Jimmy's earshot for two minutes.

Tommin shouldered his bag and then followed Jimmy outside. Jimmy pressed a button on the key fob in his hand, and the silver Porsche parked at the curb purred.

"This *was* meant to be yours. But I don't think you deserve it," Jimmy said as he opened the sleek door and ducked inside.

Saints, Tommin hated Leprechauns. Every last greedy, unpredictable, moody one of them.

Although she was likely asleep in her bed, he waved good-bye to Penny as they drove off.

"Eejit," Jimmy muttered.

# Chapter Twenty

## *Ar Iarraidh*

## (Missing)

When late afternoon arrived and no one had shown up to work at the Shamrock Gold Exchange, Eve panicked. She used the Euro-Spa kiosk's smartphone to call Gloria. She'd lost her own phone, probably at the carnival.

Gloria showed up five minutes later. "Where's the fire, honey?"

"The Shamrock's closed. I think something's wrong. No one has been there all day. They've never been closed before. Not even once."

"When was the last time you saw that boy of yours?"

"Last night. Well, early this morning." Her face grew hot beneath the Glamour. She didn't have time to explain the innocence of their night together. "He would have told me if he was taking time off. I'm sure of it. We were . . . friends."

"Dang," Gloria said, running a hand over her black-and-red hair. "Oh, dang. I'm in trouble this time."

"Look," Eve said. "I don't have time for games, so I'm going to tell you the truth. I know you're with the agency. I've worked for the AFG, too."

"Double dang. You're here to fire me, right? Yeah, I guess I deserve it, losing track of that boy. See, the other guy I've been assigned to watch,

Hansi—the Gardener Gnome who does the mall's landscaping—went all schizo, and let me tell you—"

"You messed up. I get it. Consider yourself off Tommin's case. I'll take it from here." Eve switched off the kiosk's computer and lights. She certainly wasn't going to just hang out at the mall all day, waiting for Tommin to return. She'd have to hunt him down herself.

"Hey, wait! There's a tracking device imbedded in his passport. If he left the country . . ." Gloria pulled her phone off her belt and poked the screen a few times. "Yep. Looks like he's over the Atlantic."

*Lorcan Reilly, you wily devil,* Eve thought, for surely he was behind this. She had no doubt this turn of events was part of Lorcan's perpetual scheme to convert Tommin and take the throne. Knowing that a gold-son had to take the Cup of his own free will, what had he—or his right-hand Lep Jimmy—said or done to finally convince Tommin to return to Ireland?

Jimmy was such a skilled liar. If he wasn't Lorcan's true gold-son, he was certainly qualified for the job.

Eve started to run, and then realized she'd not get far on foot. Her legs felt weak as dandelion stems, and her chest ached. She stopped and turned around. "Come on, Gloria," she shouted. "You've got a car, don't you?"

"That I do."

"You're temporarily back on the case, then." She leaned against the wall and waited for Gloria, struggling to catch her breath and wishing her body would stop betraying her.

"Anything you say, honey." Gloria adjusted her belt as they fast-walked toward the exit. "And I thought this day was gonna be boring."

Inside her apartment, Eve grabbed her passport from the drawer of her bedside table. Next, she pulled a silver-covered wooden chest out from under the bed. She knelt and measured the ingredients for Tommin's cure according to the recipe she'd memorized over two hundred years ago, dumping them into a single glass bottle. She jammed the cork in; no way would a bit of it spill on her upcoming journey. She also pocketed the carved stone vial of poison she planned to use on Lorcan. Lucky for her, she could Charm her way past airport security carrying the odd-looking mixtures.

She stood and grabbed a sweater from the closet. Inside the cardigan's pocket, her phone chimed, begging to be charged. She hadn't lost it after all. Any other time, she might have rejoiced; now a phone meant little to her. Unless . . . she checked her messages as she crossed the living room. Tommin hadn't left without a word after all.

The text, sent less than an hour after they'd parted, was sweet but cryptic.

Penny. Sorry. Unexpected trip. Left you gift on my bed. Key under flower pot. Back soon. Yours, T.

Making sure her Penny Glamour was in place, Eve rushed upstairs and let herself into Tommin's flat.

A minute later, she found the most exquisite pair of shoes she'd ever seen.

She kicked off her sandals and slid her feet into the buttery-soft leather. If her courage failed her, she'd look down at her feet and remember how much she loved the boy who'd made these shoes, the boy whose future lay in her hands—and in the bottles she'd hidden in her pockets.

# Chapter Twenty-One

## *An Fhaoistin*

## (The Confession)

Gloria coaxed the Volkswagen Beetle to ninety miles per hour. Eve shut her eyes, trying to convince herself not to throw up.

"You okay?" Gloria asked, fiddling with the radio controls.

"Fine," Eve said. She gripped the door handle. Every ounce of energy she could muster went to maintaining the Glamour.

"So, you're with the AFG? Would have never guessed. You one of those Channel Islands Faeries?"

"No," Eve said. She was definitely going to be sick. "Pull over, please. Please!"

With screeching brakes, Gloria veered into a truck stop. Eve got out of the car. She stumbled over to some hedges and threw up. And then everything went black.

---

Eve opened her eyes and looked up into Gloria's face.

"Well now," Gloria said. "Aren't you a surprise, girl?" Gloria squatted and scooped Eve into her arms. She carried her toward the car. "Wonders never cease. That's what the old folks say, and I'm inclined to believe it."

"Oh no," Eve murmured, realizing she was un-Glamoured. "No."

Gloria set Eve in the passenger seat and fastened her seat belt as if she were a child. "Hush," she said. "Don't get worked up. I'll drive and we'll talk. How's that sound?"

Eve shut her eyes. She considered trying to put her Glamour on again, but she was so tired. It might be best to save her strength. Besides, who would see her at the speed Gloria drove?

Back on the interstate, Gloria turned the air-conditioning on full blast. Was this some new sort of interrogation method? Eve wondered. Freeze the suspect into confessing to the crime? She huddled against the door and wrapped her arms around herself.

"I'm not sure what to do with you," Gloria said. "Never in my wildest dreams did I think I'd end up capturing one of the most wanted semi-Fae in the world. You do know you have a price on your head, don't you?"

"Of course," Eve said.

"Ten thousand Faerie guldens," Gloria said. "Imagine. I could buy an island with that. Maybe two islands."

"You could. Gloria, I've never been one for begging, but I'm begging you now—"

"Unless you can beg to the tune of eleven thousand guldens, I don't know if I'm much interested."

"What if I offered you Lorcan Reilly? He's worth twice that."

"Now you've got my attention."

"He's the one Jimmy's taking Tommin to. I can help you capture him. With my gifts."

"I've read about your gifts. Pretty impressive, when they work. But, girl, you're sick. You way overused the Glamour, didn't you? Kept it up for years, I'm guessing. You do it another couple times, and you'll go out like a candle in a hurricane. For good. Didn't anybody ever tell you Glamour costs you? The Leps, they feed it gold, and other Faeries feed it stardust or unicorn breath or baby-dragon-scale powder. But maybe you thought you were too special for all that."

"I didn't know," Eve said. "I'm only part Lep, remember? Anyway, I never needed anything before to stay healthy, not in two hundred years." It did explain a lot: her weariness, her recently acquired habit of dropping things, her lack of focus.

"Hey, I'm just telling you what I know. Warning you the next time you try Glamour, you might be done for." Gloria swerved to avoid hitting a squirrel. "Close one."

Eve decided it was as good a time as any to appeal to Gloria's merciful side. If she'd spare a squirrel, perhaps she'd have sympathy for a one-third human boy under a curse. "Gloria?" she said meekly. "I have to save Tommin."

"That weak little trickster? He's not worth dying over. That dang squirrel's more worth it than he is. Leps are a dime a dozen. I don't know what you see in him, honey. And don't say 'true love,' for goodness' sake. Have some self-respect. Some respect for Faerie law and tradition."

"I won't say it, then."

Gloria shook her head. "You are something else."

"Exactly. And that's why I have a price on my head. And also why I need your help. Look, Gloria, you'll do what you want in the end. You're smart; you've probably already half worked out a plan to claim the bounty for both Lorcan and me. But I'm begging you; help me free Tommin from the curse before you turn me in. It's all I want. All I've worked two hundred years for. I wasn't going to rat on you for losing track of Tommin, you know."

"I know. I know. You're a good girl. I've got a sense about folks. That's what's plaguing me about this whole deal. Dang it."

"So, Gloria, consider this: if Tommin becomes human, he won't need all the crocks he's buried. You could end up with quite an inheritance."

"I like the sound of that. Keep talking."

"Are we still headed to the airport?"

Glancing at the GPS screen, Gloria said, "We'll be there in thirty minutes."

"Enough time for us to make a few plans."

Gloria slapped her palm against the steering wheel. "Oh, all right, then," she said. She stepped hard on the gas and swerved into the passing lane. "Dang if I don't like you too much not to help you out. Although I'll tell you right now, there's no way I'm going to the dang Neathlands. I don't do caves, or underground, or any of that dark and cobwebby nonsense. My tribe, we're all about the nice, flat, dry land where the sun can hit you."

"Understood," Eve said. "Completely." She'd been trying not to think too much about her upcoming visit to the Neathlands herself. The devious Faerie cats, the damp air, the coldhearted Leps, one mushroom meal after the next . . . if there were a word for not missing a place in the least, she would have used it to describe how she felt about the world below.

"And believe me, I won't be letting you off the hook. That little Lep better pay up when he's human again."

"I promise he will," Eve said.

"Yeah. True love. Ugh." Gloria wriggled in her seat with fake revulsion.

"I thought you said you liked a mall romance."

"This isn't about the mall anymore. This is about Faerie justice."

"Exactly," Eve said. "Now, do you have any of that stardust with you? Or the dragon-scale stuff?"

"Almighty! You could talk a Troll into buying soap." Gloria chuckled. "In the glove box under the manual. Just go easy on it. Half a thimble's worth should do you."

Eve reached over and cupped Gloria's shoulder. "You're a good one, Gloria. Thanks."

"Shut up, I'm trying to drive," Gloria said. But Eve saw a tear in the corner of her eye. No wonder she'd been assigned to a shopping mall. She was more suited to be a benevolent Faerie Godmother than a hard-nosed agent. A Faerie Guardian who folded so easily and had a soft spot for bribes and love stories—well, she wasn't going to save the world from evil, was she?

Lorcan Reilly could have outwitted Gloria Glass in his sleep. Lucky for Eve, as long as the medicine worked, she wouldn't have to rely on Gloria's aid to defeat her old foe.

# Chapter Twenty-Two

## *An Tír Dhúchais*

## (The Homeland)

In the Dublin airport, Tommin stole two rings and a bracelet. The Bliss did not compare to the joy of kissing Penny, but it did ease his jet lag.

A black limousine waited for Jimmy and Tommin outside the terminal. When they got in, Jimmy said nothing to the chauffeur. The man just put the car into gear and drove.

"Here's the deal," Jimmy said, opening a bottle of mineral water and handing it to Tommin. "We're headed to Neathdublin. You don't speak unless spoken to. No questions, no comments, nothing."

"Fine," Tommin said, a little irritated by Jimmy's condescending tone. What happened to being "brothers"? Oh yeah. Tommin had kissed a girl—something Jimmy had done himself. Blasted Leprechauns and their twisted rules and backward ideals.

"We'll get the elixir. You'll sign the IOU. We'll do the ceremony with the official, and you take the oath and the Cup. And voilà, you're converted and you get to live."

Tommin set the bottle in a drink holder. "And then?"

"Then you go wherever the higher-ups tell you to go. It'll be Canada or Greenland, I'd wager."

"Grand."

"Croesus, Tommin! If someone offered me the Cup, I'd act a little more grateful and excited. It's *the Cup of Fortune*, for gold's sake."

"Well, I'm not you, am I?" Tommin looked out the window at the green scenery rolling past. *Home.* With a pang in his heart, he remembered his dear old granny, her kind eyes and gentle ways, how her belly shook when laughter overcame her, the soft lullabies she'd hummed to help him sleep. He remembered Master Rafferty tossing salt and quoting scripture to the sky, the sure touch of his callused hands as he taught a fatherless boy how to cut leather and file rough edges. He remembered climbing trees and stealing coins. Swimming in Lough Gillan. Wading in the stream and catching fish for dinner. So long ago.

He'd had a good human life. He'd been as good as his cursed blood would let him—until the day Lorcan Reilly came to the shoe shop.

He hated Leprechauns. He hated himself. Because he was one of them, wasn't he? Wanting one thing and then another? Greedy. Greedy to satisfy whatever longing he had at the time, whether it was for gold or for a lotion salesgirl.

Yes, he was a Leprechaun. Like it or not. Maybe he should quit fighting a war he'd never win. Maybe having the matter settled would be best.

Penny deserved better, anyway. He'd lied to her about who and what he truly was. And a lying, thieving Lep would never be worthy of a respectable, honest girl like her, no matter how many plastic baggies of fake jewelry he turned into cash for good causes.

"We should be there in half an hour," Jimmy said. "Make peace with it now, because it's happening."

"I'm ready," Tommin said. "I was wrecked at birth, wasn't I? I've never stood a chance of being anything but a Leprechaun. I might as well drink up and get on with it."

"Now you're talking sense," Jimmy said. "The higher-ups will be glad to hear you've seen the light."

It didn't seem like light to Tommin. It seemed like darkness. Darkness with a side of wickedness. A single tear slid down his cheek.

"Cheer up, Tommy boy. The blue drink will wash all your cares away."

He shut his eyes and tried not to think of Penny.

# Chapter Twenty-Three

## *An Fhíor Nochta*

## (Revealed Truth)

Eve stood in the cool, misting, sideways rain outside the Dublin airport, lightly Glamoured as a nondescript Irish girl. Gloria's medicine had strengthened her, but she still felt a little weak. The plan was for her to save her energy as much as possible. Once the driver arrived, she'd put on a strong Gloria-shaped Glamour, and the real Gloria would head back into the terminal to wait for her return.

The Faerie agent driver was taking forever to come. Next to Eve, Gloria shifted her weight from foot to foot like an impatient child.

"Is something wrong?" Eve asked.

"This whole thing's got my insides all stirred up like two tomcats stuck in a sack. Guess I'm more fit for the mall than this international intrigue stuff. I'll just go wait inside. You call and let me know when it's over. Bring Reilly to me, and we'll work things out from there. Here. You'll need these." Gloria dug deep in the pockets of her uniform trousers. With one hand, she pulled out the tracking device that linked them to Tommin, and with the other, she brought forth two little packets of stardust and dragon-scale powder. "Just take a little at a time. Be careful. Be blessed. I'm going." She pecked Eve on the cheek and dashed back into the terminal, almost colliding with an oncoming luggage cart pushed by a sour-faced stewardess.

Eve waited for the stewardess and a few Asian tourists to climb into taxis. And then, thankful for the oversized raincoat she'd bought in the airport shop, Eve pulled the hood over her head. She turned away from the security cameras and switched her Glamour to Gloria's appearance.

A red Mini Cooper pulled up beside Eve. A stunning blond Elf-tribe-looking man lowered the window and said, "Hop in and brace yourself. There was a mix-up with the cars, and I'm not great at the stick-shift thing, I'm afraid."

"That's fine. Just drive," Eve said, buckling her safety belt.

She set the tracking receiver in her lap. "South. They must be headed for Neathdublin portal three."

"I know it well," the man said. "We'll be there in twenty minutes." The car made a horrid scraping noise as he shifted gears. "Sorry."

"I could do no better," Eve said.

The man smiled. "So, rumor has it you're going to take down Lorcan Reilly."

Eve's eyes widened, although she shouldn't have been surprised. Even the best Faerie agents were famously terrible at keeping secrets, and Elves were the worst among them. "I've been waiting a long time for this."

"So has all of Faerie kind. He's the lowest of the low, that Leprechaun. Anyway, I wish you luck."

"Thanks."

"Do you know him, then? Personally?"

"Oh yes," Eve said. "I've known him far too long." *And he's about to pay for every scar and bruise he ever gave me.*

# Chapter Twenty-Four

## *An Rí Todhchaí*

## (The Future King)

At dusk, the limo rolled to a stop in the middle of a forest. Jimmy and Tommin got out, taking their bags with them, and the driver turned the car around and drove away.

Jimmy walked up to the trunk of a huge oak tree and pressed what looked like a knot in the bark. A door slid open. "Drop your luggage and come on," Jimmy said.

"Is that a lift? In a tree?"

"Beats all the tunnels and ladders we used to have, doesn't it? Now, no more talking until the ceremony."

The lift moved silently but fast enough to make Tommin's stomach flutter. Not that his whole digestive system hadn't already been churning and clenching ever since he'd discovered Jimmy in his apartment.

He had to remind himself to breathe. Again and again, he had to talk himself into believing that this would all be for the best. When he drank the Third Cup of Fortune, any damage he'd done to his blood by kissing Penny would be undone, he'd have more peace between Takes, bigger and better rainbows, and no more yearnings for anything but mammon.

The lift stopped. The door glided open. Jimmy put an arm around Tommin's shoulders and guided him down a marble-walled passageway.

Electric lights shone from dozens of Turkish-looking brass lanterns suspended from the high ceiling. Everything was clean and perfectly placed—nothing like the filthy underground land Tommin vaguely recalled living in.

Jimmy pressed his thumb against a little black pad on the wall, and another door whooshed open. They stepped onto a gravel path and followed it through a lush underground garden stocked with fruit trees and palm trees and flowering shrubs, and lit from above by long tubular lights that hummed like a thousand bees.

The path led to an open courtyard. In its center, a golden throne sat atop a black marble platform flanked by tall columns. Beside the throne, a gilded table held a familiar-looking crown.

"What is this place?" Tommin whispered.

Jimmy slammed his elbow into Tommin's ribs. "Shut up, eejit."

A Leprechaun officiant in flowing robes of red silk approached, his hands lifted in greeting. "Welcome. Come this way, brothers," he said. "All has been made ready for the sacred Ceremony of the Third Cup."

The officiant led Tommin and Jimmy into a grotto of vines lit by free-floating yellow-and-green-glowing orbs. Another Leprechaun waited there, his scarlet-coated back to them.

"I've brought him, Master Lorcan," Jimmy said. "Your seventh gold-son."

Lorcan Reilly turned, and his face twisted into a wicked smile. "What a grand day this is! My last two gold-sons come home to the Neathlands! Such a fine sight you are! Come, Tommin. It's been a long time. Too long. You must drink and be made complete, my lad."

Tommin stiffened with fear and anger. Bile burned his throat as he clenched his hands into fists. Jimmy gripped his upper arms from behind and said soothingly, "Go on, brother. You know it's for the best."

Tommin struggled against Jimmy's grasp. "This was all a trick? The Shamrock, the story about my body breaking down without the Third Cup?"

Lorcan gave him a pitying look. "You might call it tricks. I think of it as a plan to save you from yourself, lad. To steer you back onto the path of the true Leprechauns, where you've always belonged."

"I hate you," Tommin said.

"Of course you do," Lorcan said. "You've been sick with want for the elixir for over two hundred years. But it's not too late, lad. Your salvation is nigh."

"You're just a wee bit confused, Tommin," Jimmy said. "You've spent too much time with humans, and it's screwed up your brain. The Cup will cure you."

Tommin remembered everything then. Every lie Lorcan had told, every stroke of Gladys on his back. He remembered Lorcan's grand plan to take the throne and that Lorcan needed him to convert in order to become the Great Himself.

Every bit of suffering Tommin had known, he owed to Lorcan Reilly. Everything he'd stolen, everything he'd lost—all Lorcan's fault.

Tommin shook from head to toe with rage. Again, he strained against Jimmy's hold, but Jimmy's strength won out. "Let me go," Tommin said through clenched teeth. "I want no part of this. I won't help you become king. I'll die first."

"My poor boy," Lorcan said. "We mustn't make you wait any longer. Look how much you need that Cup! You look fit to faint, lad!" He nodded to the officiant.

"He cannot be given the Third Cup against his will, Lorcan Reilly," the officiant said. "You know our laws."

"Can you not see he's mad from the lack of it?" Lorcan said. "Get the Cup ready. Trust me, he'll change his tune soon enough."

The officiant left for a minute and returned with a gilded pitcher and gem-studded chalice. Immediately, Tommin smelled the elixir. Its vapors drifted into his nose, filled his lungs, slipped into his bloodstream, and grabbed hold of his soul.

He wanted it.

By Croesus, he wanted it.

All other thoughts ceased as lust for the Cup consumed him. Every cell in his body begged for it.

He would have run a thousand miles for the elixir. He would have swum through oceans and climbed the highest mountains to get to it. He would have slain a hundred men. He would have cut off his own arm. Anything to have it, to taste it, to swallow its blue liquid magic.

The ceremony began. The officiant chanted and sang the ancient words of the Leprechauns' sacred service of conversion. Tommin sobbed with longing. His tongue dried up, his bones cried out, his blood rushed and slowed, rushed and slowed.

At the sound of the elixir splashing into the Cup, Tommin fell to his knees.

# Chapter Twenty-Five

## *Caillte agus Tagtha*

## (Lost and Found)

As her driver turned onto the heavily forested road, every nerve in Eve's body felt like a tightly wound spring. "So, we're almost there," she said.

The driver reached over and patted her Gloria-Glamoured arm. "You sound nervous. Breathe slowly, and find your peace," he said in a soothing tone. Elfin voices were like that, as smooth and reassuring as tea with honey. "You can't afford to lose control when you're facing such an enemy."

Eve rubbed the index finger where she'd worn Lorcan's gold band long ago, falling back into her girlhood nervous habit. "I know, I know. But—"

"No. No 'buts' or 'what-ifs.' You focus on your mission and carry it out to completion. That's what we agents do."

She breathed in and out slowly, embracing the driver's tranquility. "You're right. I feel better. I'm glad the agency sent you. What did you say your name was?"

"Rannin, son of Tambling. One of the last of the East Erin Woodland Elves. And might I ask your name?"

"You might. But I'll have to ask you to wait to hear it until after I take down Lorcan."

"Understood."

The headlights shone on the wide tree trunk ahead. The end of the road. Rannin turned off the car. Eve shed the bulky raincoat. They both got out and stood in the shadow of the huge oak.

Smiling beatifically, Rannin handed Eve a silver ring with a single blue gem set into it. "Wear this. The stone is a button that activates a distress signal. Use it to call me should you need my aid. Unless you wish me to accompany you?"

"Thank you, but this is something I have to do alone."

"Then take this, too." He drew a sleek Faerie-made gun from the holster at his hip and gazed at it admiringly. "Loaded with number-eighteen tranquilizer darts, strong enough to knock out a full-sized Bog Troll for hours."

Eve almost giggled. The Elf agent's love for weaponry didn't mesh with his peaceful aura at all. She bit her lip as she tucked the gun into the back waistband of her skirt and covered it with her cardigan. "Thanks. I owe you, Rannin."

Rannin lifted his pale palm in blessing. "May all the luck of the *Seelie Sidhe* be upon you forevermore. I'll remain here until you return."

Eve and Rannin bowed to one another, and then Rannin pressed a knot in the tree trunk. As the door slid open, Eve conjured up the invisibility Glamour. When Rannin gasped, she smiled.

Eve stepped into the lift. As it began to descend, she slipped her right hand into the pocket of her cardigan, making sure the bottle of herbs meant for Lorcan was still there.

The lift stopped, bouncing gently. Its doors opened. Eve hurried down the marble corridor. When she reached the locked door, Eve placed her finger on the reader and Glamoured a copy of the fingerprint of the previous entrant—a trick she'd perfected as an agent of the Faerie Guardians. The door opened.

Eve walked into the humid, leafy hothouse. Her Glamour hid her completely—including the sounds of her careful footfalls. Nearby, someone chanted familiar words.

The Ceremony of the Cup.

Eve ran.

Behind a templelike structure, under an archway of woven branches, the officiant lifted the chalice and spoke. He looked familiar, sounded familiar to Eve.

"Let it be done, as from ancient times, this the Greening of the Blood everlasting, with the drinking of this Third Cup of Fortune. Let this once human be human no more, but a member of the Faerie tribe of Leprechauns, sealed by this Cup and his solemn oath. Let him love gold and silver above all. May his greed blossom and his rainbows span from east to west, evermore and evermore."

Tommin lay prostrate at the officiant's feet, heaving with sobs. The officiant turned slightly, and light from above struck his face, revealing the snub nose and wide brow of the gold-son Alby. Apparently, he'd not only managed to finish his conversion, but also advanced to the ranks of the Lep elite since Eve had last seen him during the terrible Troll attack.

Gloria was right when she said that wonders never cease.

"Rise, Tommin. Rise and drink. Rise and be made whole, a Leprechaun until the end of time or the end of your luck," Alby said grandly, holding the Cup high.

Eve moved closer, concentrating on keeping the Glamour steady and strong.

Lorcan Reilly came into view. Lorcan, leaning on Gladys and looking proud as a new father, standing beside Shamrock Jimmy. What surged through Eve's veins was stronger than hatred, sharper than fury—and she almost lost hold of her invisibility.

Lorcan and Jimmy heaved Tommin to his feet. They stepped back, leaving Tommin swaying like a landlubber on a storm-tossed ship.

"Place your hands on the chalice and repeat after me," Alby the officiant said.

Tears streamed down Tommin's cheeks. He cradled the Cup. "Please," he begged. "Please."

"Oath first," Lorcan grumbled, rolling his eyes.

"Repeat after me, gold-son of Lorcan Reilly," Alby said. "I take this Third Cup of Fortune of my own free will."

As if entranced, Tommin stared into the chalice. "I take this Third Cup of Fortune of my own—"

Eve sprang at him like a lioness, knocking the Cup and Tommin to the ground.

"What foul magic is this?" Alby took a few steps backward. "Have you brought invisible demons here, Lorcan Reilly? Have you no respect for the sacred Cup? By Croesus, man, that was the last of it!"

Tommin turned his face to the ground and tried to lap up the spilled elixir as Alby bent to retrieve the dented chalice.

Holding her invisibility steady, Eve grabbed Tommin and yanked him to his feet. "Get it together, Tommin," she whispered in his ear.

"Penny?" Tommin turned his head one way and then the other. "Penny! Where are you?"

A sharp blow struck the back of Eve's head. As she fell, her Glamour fizzled out. Her head hit the floor, and Lorcan laughed.

"What have we here, Gladys? Why, it's our darling gold-son Eevar, come home again!" he said.

Another blow to the head drove Eve into unconsciousness.

# Chapter Twenty-Six

## *Ag Cleasaíocht ar an gCleasaí*

## (Tricking a Trickster)

"What happened?" Tommin asked from where he lay sprawled on the floor. He lifted his head and pointed to a facedown woman. He knew her, didn't he? She had Penny's voice, but the red of her hair, the shape of her shoulders—they belonged to Eve. *Impossible.* "Who is that, Jimmy? Lorcan?"

Lorcan Reilly cursed and kicked the body hard. "Useless brat. Here I thought she'd been dead the last two hundred years."

"You know her?" Jimmy asked.

"My sixth gold-son," Lorcan said.

"Son?" Jimmy snickered. "Are we looking at the same body?"

Lorcan whacked Jimmy in the shin with Gladys. "You'll keep your opinions to yourself, lad."

Tommin looked from Jimmy to Lorcan to the motionless girl. "Eve?" He scrambled to his feet and stumbled toward her. He had to see her face. To touch her. To know if this was one of Lorcan's tricks or a gift from heaven.

And then she vanished.

"No!" Tommin cried.

"Oh my gold," Jimmy said. "She's gone!"

"Eve!" Lorcan shouted. He shook his fist in the air. "Show yourself, you she-devil! You witch! Come and deal with me face-to-face—or are you too afraid?"

Where was she? Tommin opened his mouth to beg her to return, but that would be wrong. Stupid. "Run!" he called out to the unseen girl.

Lorcan swung Gladys and struck Tommin hard in the gut. He bent over, groaning with pain.

"Bind him and take him to my old place on Assets Lane, Jimmy. Be quick about it, lad." Lorcan pointed Gladys at the officiant, who stood cradling the damaged chalice like a baby. "And you. Find more elixir. Now!"

"But there isn't any more," the robed fellow said.

Now, undistracted by the Cup, Tommin noticed how much the officiant resembled Alby. He'd seen his face so many times in his night-mares of the long past. "Are you—?"

Alby sneered. "Your old schoolmate Alby, in the green flesh. Pleasure's all mine, and so's the treasure, Tommin Kelly. I guess this is another one of your unlucky days. No elixir for you. None left in all the world."

Jimmy took a length of rope from his bag. "Good thing I was prepared for your nonsense," he said as he pulled Tommin's wrists behind him and tied them. The rope dug into Tommin's skin, but he did his best to ignore the pain and pay attention to Lorcan's ranting. The Leprechaun might give away some bit of information, some clue Tommin could use to escape.

He'd come so close to surrendering. Blast the elixir and its allure! Lorcan twirled Gladys in his fingers, his expression dark as a thunder-cloud. He narrowed his eyes and said to Alby, "I don't care if you've heard there's no more elixir. That's what's been said since the Neathlands War, and yet bottles keep appearing on the black market. So, you just go ask your friends and your enemies and whoever else you need to until you find some. Agree to any price. Just bring me enough elixir for one Cup, or I'll end you myself—the painful, slow way."

"I'll try," Alby said. "I will try, sir. But only because it's my sworn and sacred duty to convert all Newlings. Not because of your silly threats, and certainly not as any favor to you or that worthless gold-son of yours."

"You have two days," Tommin heard Lorcan say as Jimmy tugged him down the path and away from his gold-father. "Two days and no more."

# Chapter Twenty-Seven

## *Ag Leanúint*

## (Following)

Eve silently berated herself as she watched Jimmy drag Tommin out of the hothouse. She ought to have been more careful. How could she have dropped the Glamour? What a foolish, foolish mistake!

Her heart begged her to follow Tommin, to make sure he was safe, but her head commanded her to stay close to Lorcan. One: she needed his blood. Two: she needed him dead. Three: now that Lorcan knew she was alive, he'd likely stop at nothing to convert both her *and* Tommin. Keeping an eye on the enemy seemed the best way to preserve both their lives.

While she watched Lorcan, she'd try to figure out what her next move should be. At the moment, she didn't have a clue.

She trailed behind Lorcan as he tramped through the long-abandoned streets of Neathdublin, his feet pounding the earth as he swore and mumbled, calling down ancient curses. After a while, he sat on the edge of a wall and drank from the same silver flask he'd used back when she'd been his little niece.

Weary, Eve crouched nearby on a crooked doorstep. She took out Gloria's packets and measured the powders into her palm. Not much medicine remained, which meant not much time remained for her to act. When the powders ran out, so would her powers of Glamour and Charm.

Lorcan coughed and scratched like an old man. Had she not known his history, she might have found him pitiable, sitting there in his filthy red coat and dusty shoes, his hair a wild tangle. But there was no wisdom in pitying the devil.

She lifted her hand to her mouth and funneled the bitter medicine onto her tongue.

# Chapter Twenty-Eight

## *Teach an Éadóchais*

## (House of Despair)

Tied to a wooden chair in a dark room that smelled of mildew and misery, Tommin could do nothing but think.

What in the world had happened in the gardens?

Lorcan Reilly, that was what. The beginning of all Tommin's troubles, and possibly the end. His palms itched, and he suspected his temperature had started to rise. The back of his head throbbed. The coma might come soon.

Maybe falling into the coma would be a good thing. A way to escape Lorcan's plan. Comatose, Tommin couldn't be converted and used as a stepping stone to the throne . . . although he imagined Lorcan would be waiting whenever he woke up, standing over his body with a Cup of Fortune and Alby the officiant.

The sacred elixir.

Curse the foul, wonderful stuff!

One whiff of its essence had completely obliterated his resolve to resist conversion. The very *memory* of its aroma sent a chill through him now, followed by a twinge of longing. *Grand,* he thought. *Remind me again how weak I really am.*

Tommin mentally changed the subject.

The young woman with Penny's voice. She'd had Eve's hair, Eve's shape.

Lorcan *had* called her Eevar and said he'd thought her dead. She'd acted like Eve, charging in to save him. It was true Eve had possessed a talent for Glamour and could have made herself appear as Penny—but to vanish altogether? He'd never heard of a Glamour like that.

Besides, Eevar—Eve—*was* dead. Tommin remembered poisoned arrows piercing her body. He remembered mourning and regret and being forced to leave her unburied. He'd much sooner believe in invisibility Glamour than a Leprechaun-cursed girl coming back from the dead. For Eve to be alive, wouldn't he have to believe in both impossibilities?

Another thing. If Penny had been Eve in disguise, why hadn't she said so back in Pennsylvania? If she'd ever loved him, why would she have played such a cruel trick on him, making him fall in love with her, making him sick?

Had her gold-father been watching the whole time, spurring her on and praising her feats of malice?

Saints, his head hurt.

Elsewhere in the house, a door slammed. "Where's my tea, Copper?" Lorcan's voice shouted.

"Almost ready," a young boy's voice replied.

"Gladys will teach you the difference between 'almost' and 'done' if you don't hurry, boy!"

"Yes, sir."

Copper? Wait. Copper had died the same day Eve had. None of this was possible. Lorcan, Eve, Copper, the Cup . . .

Tommin doubted his own sanity. Maybe that's how a second gold-deficiency coma started—hallucinations and warped perceptions. Maybe this was *it*.

One last time, he tested the strength of the ropes binding his hands and feet. They held firm.

He shut his eyes and waited for oblivion.

# Chapter Twenty-Nine

## *Dhá Thaibhse*

## (Two Ghosts)

"Don't scream, Copper," Eve whispered as she wrapped an invisible arm around the boy. She'd followed him on his errand from Lorcan's house to the grocer's shop, thrilled to have found him alive—and sad he'd been kept slaving for Lorcan Reilly throughout the two centuries since they'd been together.

Copper swore and lifted his hands in surrender. His basket of mushrooms tumbled onto the ground and spilled. With Glamour-covered hands, Eve guided the trembling boy into a dark alley behind an abandoned building. She lifted him easily (he was skinny as ever) and set him on a wooden crate.

He covered his mouth with both fists, the skin beneath his freckles gone whiter than milk. He rocked and shivered, moaning quietly.

"Please don't be afraid, Copper. It's me. Eve."

"If you're Eve, then you're a ghost! Oh, heaven save me!" He made the sign of the cross and mumbled a prayer as if he were a human boy and not a shape-shifting Faerie.

"Hush now. I'm as alive as you are, just covered in Glamour. Meet me in the shed behind Lorcan's house after dinner, and I'll explain everything."

"Meet a *ghost*? Do you think I'm mad? Get away with you." He slid off the box, fingers raised to form a crooked cross. On unsteady legs, he backed into the street, squashing a few of the mushrooms beneath his boots.

Eve followed slowly, trying not to spook him further. "Copper, please. This is important. Remember how I promised to get you away from Lorcan? I'm here to keep that promise. It's going to be soon. But I need your help."

"I don't know about that. How do I know this isn't a trick? How do I know you're really Eve?"

"Remember the time you and I stayed up late and ate all of Lorcan's ginger biscuits? And how you fast-talked him into believing he'd finished them off when he was drunk?"

Copper swore, then exclaimed, "It *is* you!"

"Such foul language seems terribly wrong coming from the mouth of a little boy," Eve said, bending to pick up Copper's basket. She piled the undamaged mushrooms inside and offered it to him.

"I'm older than you," Copper said, his face blossoming into a grin. "By Croesus, I wish you could teach me how to be invisible like that."

What a joy it was to see that in spite of two hundred more years with Lorcan, Copper's sprightly personality remained unchanged. Eve smiled. "Somehow I think I'd regret it. Now, promise you'll meet me," she said. "And if you get a chance to, please tell Tommin not to give up hope."

"Tommin? You mean *our* Tommin?"

"Have you not seen him? He's in Lorcan's house."

"Well, chop me up and put me in a stew! Both of you was dead, and now neither of you is. The world's a funny old thing, isn't it?"

"Truer words were never spoken, Copper. One last thing. I need you to snitch a knife. A big sharp one, with a silver blade. It must be silver, not steel."

"I know the very one. Lorcan keeps it under his bed in case of robbers or Trolls or such."

"Good. Now, go on. And don't forget to meet me. Together, we'll figure out the best plan of attack against Lorcan and his comrades."

"As if I could forget such a grand thing as that," he said, still grinning from ear to ear. "As if."

❧

Eve couldn't help herself. She missed him too much.

While Lorcan slept off his liquor and Jimmy was out for a Take, Eve conjured up the strongest Glamour of invisibility she'd ever made, and she paid Tommin a visit. She promised herself she wouldn't linger. The way her supply of powders was dwindling, she couldn't afford to stay long.

The sight of him—chin on chest, hands and feet tied to a chair—wrenched her heart.

The only light in the room came in through the door she'd left open a few inches. The damp air sat heavy in her lungs. She approached him cautiously, loath to startle him, and knelt at his feet.

"Tommin?" she whispered. She reached up and lightly touched his cheek, finding it far too warm. "Tommin."

He gasped, sat up straight, and opened bloodshot eyes.

"Don't be afraid," she said. "It's only me, in a Glamour."

"Me? Me *who*?"

"Eve. Can you not remember me?"

"I remember Eve, but I don't know if you're her. Anyway, whoever you are, I hope you're here to cut these blasted ropes."

His cool greeting stung—but not as much as the response she had to give him. "I can't. Not yet."

He turned his sickly face away from her as if he could see her and didn't want to. "Get away with you, then. I've no use for tricksters or the so-called dead."

"Tommin, please. I wish I could explain, but there isn't time. Jimmy will be back soon, and Lorcan could wake up—"

"If you're really Eve, why didn't you come to me sooner? Why did you let me think you were dead?"

"I did come to you. But I couldn't tell you it was me. It was too dangerous. I—"

"My gold! You *were* Penny, weren't you? You let me fall in love with . . . with a lie. An illusion. You used me, and now you won't even set me free?"

"It isn't like that. It's complicated. Listen, I have to go, but I'll be back. I'm going to rescue you."

"You're a liar, just like the rest of the Leps. For all I know, Lorcan sent you in to trick me again. To add to my suffering. To torment me like some Neathlands cat batting about a wounded rat."

"I'm sorry I deceived you, Tommin," Eve said. "Truly I am."

"Not as sorry as I am." His head wobbled as he spoke. She didn't doubt that he could fall into a coma at any moment, that his words were tainted by exhaustion and illness.

Eve stood, feeling none too well herself. To leave the boy she loved in such agony was like stabbing herself in the heart, but she had no choice. She felt the Glamour fraying at the edges. "I'm not giving up on you," she said as she headed for the door.

"Perhaps you should," Tommin said, his words as bitter as her medicine.

*Never,* she promised silently. *I never will.*

# Chapter Thirty

## *Ag Fheiceáil sa Dorchadas*

## (Seeing in the Dark)

Gripped by fever, Tommin gritted his teeth to keep them from chattering. The floor pitched and rolled like an ocean under his chair. The black walls of the black room pulsated in time with his slow heartbeat.

He'd not allow himself to be sorry for what he'd said to Eve. He wanted to stay angry. What strength was there in sorrow and regret?

He ought to have expected treachery from her. After all, she'd been brought up by an "uncle" who specialized in the art of deception. She'd had no other example to follow. She'd been cursed and she'd sipped the Leprechauns' Cup—same as any other thieving Lep.

Same as he had.

They both should have turned out better, but curses were curses—not things you could simply toss aside like apple cores.

From now on, he decided, he'd look out only for himself. He'd take the Cup if he felt like it, revel in its magnificent flavor and magical gifts, and be converted. He'd forge a life of his own. A Leprechaun life, devoted to gold.

No more lotion girls, fake or otherwise. No more girls ever. No more broken hearts and broken promises—only Bliss and rainbows until the end of time.

*If* he ever woke up from the coma that threatened to overcome him within the hour.

# Chapter Thirty-One

## *Lá Nua*

## (New Day)

"Ha!" Lorcan Reilly's loud exclamation filled the house, waking Tommin from a sound sleep. "Get Tommin ready, Jimmy. Our day has dawned!"

"You've got the elixir?" Tommin heard Jimmy ask.

"Scalby? Ally? Whatever that officiant's called—he's found enough to do the job. We're to meet him at the temple right away."

Alone in the dark adjoining room, Tommin lifted his chin from his chest. He was ready to drink. Or die. His head pounded, his hands and arms itched and twitched and burned, his bones ached, and his heartbeat skipped and galloped in fits. He'd had enough of the gold-deficiency sickness, enough of the soul-scraping longing for a Take he could not acquire.

He was done wrestling with the decision to convert or refuse—even if it did mean he'd help Lorcan gain the throne. Anything to end the hellish pain racking his body.

The door flew open. The light streaming in from the kitchen stung his eyes, and he cringed.

"You look like a dog's dinner, brother," Jimmy said. "But you're about to feel a thousand percent better."

"Untie me, Jimmy," Tommin said. "I couldn't run even if I wanted to, and I don't want to."

Jimmy shook his head. "It's not so much *you* we don't trust. It's your invisible girlfriend."

"She's not my girlfriend."

"Well, I'll undo your feet so you can walk, but I'll be keeping hold of you until the ceremony. Lorcan's orders."

"Fine," Tommin said. "Let's get on with it."

Jimmy knelt and used a knife to slice through the rope that bound Tommin's ankles together. Tommin stood, wincing as the room spun. He listed like a foundering ship.

"Steady on," Jimmy said, putting an arm around Tommin. "Eyes on the prize and forward march, brother."

The prize. The fizzing, glowing blue elixir. Sweeter than honey, richer than butter cake, more invigorating than a sea of coffee.

Leaning heavily on Jimmy, Tommin hobbled out of confinement and toward his destiny.

# Chapter Thirty-Two

## *Ag Caitheamh Rúin*

## (Wearing Secrets)

Underneath her Alby-shaped Glamour, Eve shivered. The blue liquid sloshed inside the pitcher she held. It had been easy to tranquilize Alby with a dart from Rannin's gun, simple to help Copper haul his body into the thick, neglected underbrush of the hothouse forest. Those things had not raised her blood pressure one bit. But standing beside Lorcan unsettled her, no matter how many times she reminded herself she had the upper hand. She straightened her spine and squared her shoulders, pushing the fear out of her body so she could focus.

She had to focus. She'd taken the last bit of Gloria's powders, and heaven help her if they wore off too soon.

If any one part of her plan went awry . . . well, they'd be finished, then. Clay in Lorcan's hands to be fashioned into what he wanted.

Jimmy and Tommin came down the path to meet them. Tommin's face was all wrong: pale gray and empty of emotion. And he came so submissively, gaze cast downward, matching his pace with Jimmy's.

"Have you finally seen the light, my gold-son?" Lorcan asked.

"I'm ready," Tommin replied. His gaze moved to the pitcher. He licked his lips hungrily.

"Let's get started, then." Lorcan nodded to Eve the officiant—without a hint of suspicion.

Eve beckoned Tommin to stand at her side. Lorcan took a step back, pride beaming from his green-tinted face.

Nearby, Jimmy leaned against a tree and crossed his arms, looking well pleased. He barely flinched when the dart lodged in the vein of his neck; his fingers clawed at its fletching for only a second before the tranquilizer sent him slumping silently to the ground.

Eve swung hard and smacked Lorcan in the head with the pitcher. The elixir splattered everywhere: in his hair, on his clothes, her sleeve, the ground. Stunned, Lorcan stumbled sideways, lost his grip on Gladys, and landed on his back. Copper burst out from between two bushes and pointed the gun at his head, saying, "Don't you move a muscle unless you want to die within the next five seconds. I have a dart here with your name on it."

Green blood trickled from Lorcan's ear and meandered into his matted hair. He growled but kept still.

Tommin whimpered as his knees buckled and he sat down hard on the ground. Head in his hands, he muttered, "The Cup, the Cup, the Cup."

Eve dropped the Glamour and placed a beautifully shod foot on Lorcan's chest. "You'll never be king, Lorcan Reilly," she said. "It's time you paid for what you've done to Tommin, and to me."

"Me as well," Copper added.

Lorcan coughed and sputtered. Smiling like a crocodile and wasting a great deal of Charm, he said, "Darling Eevar, my favorite among all my gold-children. Let's talk about this, shall we? See what power I have given you? The throne awaits us, my queen!"

Eve drew the long silver knife and pressed its point into his chest. "Shut your mouth."

"Yeah. Don't tempt me, either," Copper said, kneeling beside Lorcan and jamming the barrel of the gun against his temple.

"Now give me your hand, and don't try anything tricky," Eve said.

"Certainly, my child," Lorcan said. "Anything for you. We are family, aren't we?" He chuckled nervously.

Eve gripped Lorcan's fingers. With a quick stroke of the knife, she sliced his palm. She handed the knife to Copper, then pulled the jar of herbs from her pocket. She uncorked it with her teeth and spat the cork onto the ground.

She counted the drops of blood as they fell into the jar. *One, two, three.* The cure for the curse bubbled and hissed, sizzled and smoked, smelling like burned sugar and smoldering leaves.

"In the arm, then, Copper," she said.

An almost inaudible pop sounded as Copper injected a dart into Lorcan's bicep. "Good night, former master," he said. He grabbed Gladys from the ground near Lorcan's body. "It's the end for you, too," he said to the thorny stick as he got to his feet. With a shout of triumph, he whacked the stick against a stone column until it splintered into pieces.

"What is all this?" Tommin said, hugging his knees, eyes wild with confusion and fear. "What are you doing?"

"We're saving you," Copper said, grinning. "Don't you recognize me, Tommin? Your old friend Copper?"

"This isn't real," Tommin said. "None of this is real."

Eve emptied the bottle into the chalice. She lifted the cup with both hands and carried it a few steps, finally kneeling beside Tommin. This, then, was the moment she'd dreamed of for two centuries. Time for Tommin to be restored to humanity. She only hoped he wasn't too far gone, too overcome by the gold-deficiency fever to accept the remedy. "Tommin," she said gently. "Look at me. I need you to answer a question, and it's important. You must say yes, my love. You must say it clearly and quickly, or I'm afraid you're going to fall into another coma."

Tommin looked at her blankly, as if she were a table or a lamp. Tremors shook him. "I'm listening," he said in a faraway voice.

"Good." Eve held the chalice up and said, "Tommin Kelly, will you take the remedy for the curse, renounce the ways of the Leprechauns, and accept a human life as your own?"

Tommin sobbed. "I don't know," he said, covering his eyes with his forearm. "I don't know."

# Chapter Thirty-Three

## *An Rogha*

## (The Choice)

Everything was moving at the wrong speed, Tommin thought as he watched Eve hand the chalice to Copper. Like the film projector needed fixing. On her knees, she came closer and rested her hands on his cheeks. Her palms were soft and cool, and he felt a little better at her touch, although he still wanted to be angry with her. Wanted to hate her for making a fool of him.

"Please, Tommin," she said. "This is probably the only chance you'll ever get to break the curse. To be free."

"I don't know how to be free. I don't know if I can be happy without Taking." He gripped her wrists and removed her hands from his cheeks. "And why should I trust you, anyway? You tricked me as much as Jimmy did. Maybe that's a cup of poison you're offering."

He regretted the words as soon as they left his mouth. Her heart-shaped freckled face, her earnest blue-gray eyes, her fiery hair—the sight of her as she was centuries ago—brought back the boy he'd been the day they met. A shoemaker who lived with his granny and wanted to do right, even though he often did wrong.

"I still love you," Eve said. "I won't stop, whether you take the remedy or not. I'll never show you my face again if that's what you want, but I can't promise not to watch you from behind a Glamour now and then, just to be sure you're safe."

"Come on, Tommin," Copper said, crouching next to him. "I'd swim the seas the world round to have someone care for me like that. Even if the 'always being watched' thing is kind of scary. Anyhow, think of how happy your granny would be to know you've come clean."

"I'm afraid you don't have long to decide," Eve said. "The potion is only good for an hour."

"I just don't know." Tommin felt himself fading, but he kept looking at Eve. His mind swirled with memories of their time in Neathgillan and his times at the mall with her as Penny. And kissing her at the carnival. But darker thoughts and feelings intruded: a burning physical hunger for gold, an unsatisfied lust for treasure, and a deep desire to bury crocks and raise rainbows.

"King's cats! Look at his neck," Copper said. "The spots. Looks bad, that does. All those colors . . ."

Tommin's vision blurred. He leaned forward on his hands and knees, gasping for air. His heart slowed and rumbled in his chest.

"Hold on," Eve said. "Tommin, please. Say the words. Tommin, say you renounce the Leprechauns and want to be human—before the coma comes!"

She took his face in her hands again and made him meet her gaze. "Say it now." Where her fingers pressed into his skin, a little strength flowed from her into him—or at least it felt that way. Like static. Like magic.

Like love.

Eve loved him. As bad as he'd been, as bad as he might be in the future. Gold was sweet, but its thrill never lasted, and it would never love him back, no matter how devoted he was to it.

Eve had loved him for over two hundred years. She'd spent her more-precious-than-gold *life* on him, and he loved her for it. And for a hundred more reasons his unraveling mind couldn't list at the moment.

He couldn't keep his eyes open anymore. The coma was snaking through his veins like ice water, numbing his feet and hands, numbing his lungs and brain.

"I do love you, Eve," he whispered. "I renounce. The Leprechauns. I want to be. Human. Good. For you. For Granny." He collapsed against her, only conscious enough to notice the warmth of her body. It was too late for him. He'd hesitated too much. *At least,* he thought, *I get to die in her arms.*

"Copper. Help me," he heard Eve say.

Tommin felt his mouth being forced open. Something cool and briny rolled over his tongue and seeped down his throat. With his last bit of strength, he swallowed.

"Is he dead? Oh gold! Tell me he isn't dead," Copper said, moving to kneel beside Tommin's still body. He patted Tommin's cheeks and tried to pry open his eyelids.

"Leave him alone, Copper. He'll be fine," Eve said. "He's just unconscious. His body has some changes to make. If he were awake, I reckon it would hurt pretty badly."

Eve stood and glared at Lorcan where he lay snoring on the ground, limbs splayed so he resembled a grotesque, beached starfish. He didn't deserve such peaceful slumber. To wake up and go on terrorizing servant boys and cursing babies. Now was her chance to keep him from doing those things—and worse—ever again. She put her hand in her pocket and drew out the little bottle of poison. The carved stone chilled her palm.

"What's that?" Copper asked. "More medicine?"

"It's the end of Lorcan Reilly," Eve said as she moved toward the Leprechaun. "Poison for the blade to bring his death."

"Sweet silver!" Copper stood and moved to her side. "Are you really going to kill him?"

"Of course I am." Even as she said it, she began to question her plan, the plan she'd contemplated for centuries. To back down now would be absurd. Ridiculous. "He ruined my life, Copper. And yours, and Tommin's. And who knows how many others'."

"Eve?" Copper's voice sounded almost tearful.

"Yes?" Her hands shook a little as she crouched down beside Lorcan and set the knife on the ground, preparing to anoint it with the poison.

"I don't think you should do it. I don't think you should kill him." He squatted beside her and rested his hand on her wrist.

Incredulous, she met his gaze. "What? After he tortured you for hundreds of years, Copper?"

"He did that. And I hate him for it, every bone and tooth of him. But if you kill him, you'll be more like him and less like yourself. Oh, that sounds stupid, but what I'm trying to say is you're better than that. You're better than the lying, thieving, conniving Leps, and you're certainly better than a murderer. The way I see it, if you turn him over to the Faerie Council or Guardians or whatever, they're going to put him to death for his crimes anyhow. You'd be the hero, then, wouldn't you? And there'd be no murder on your soul."

"I've been an agent of the Faerie Guardians, Copper. It's a little late to worry about murder on my soul."

"This is different, and you know it. This is personal, your own story. Not some police job."

Clutching the bottle to her breast, she closed her eyes. What good had hate ever done her? It was love for Tommin that had brought her here in the end, not revenge. Not hate.

Eve knew Copper was right, as much as it irked her.

She shoved the bottle into Copper's hand. "Take it before I change my mind, oh wise one. You know, you're probably the only one in the world who could have talked me out of killing him."

Copper pocketed the bottle. “Full of surprises, I am.”

Eve reached over and tousled Copper’s red mop of hair. “Always were, always will be, I think.”

“Now what do you plan to do with the two great louts and your passed-out boy Tommin?”

Eve pressed the gem on the ring Rannin had given her. “Help is on the way,” she said. “Fancy meeting an Elf?”

Copper stood and fake-glared at her, hands on hips. “I *have* met Elves before, you know. You forget I’ve been around a good deal longer than you.”

“Sorry. I didn’t mean to offend one of my ancient elders.” Eve smiled. She got up, went to Tommin, and sat beside him on the ground. Gently, she lifted his limp hand and held it against her cheek. His skin was cool and pale instead of green tinted and feverish. For that, she was grateful.

“It is a shame, though,” Copper said as he walked toward a stone bench, “to have to put off Lorcan’s execution. See, I can’t go back to Underantrim till he’s dead. After he lost you and Tommin, he laid down extra enchantments to keep me inside the borders of the Leps’ lands for as long as he’s breathing.”

“I’m sorry, Copper. I wish I could help you somehow. But it won’t be long, I’m sure. Meanwhile, you can raid his pantry and cupboards and use his clothes for kindling.”

“Well, that doesn’t sound so bad. I could do with a bit of ham and cheese right now, matter of fact.”

Eve shifted to make herself more comfortable while she waited for Rannin. The chalice, left upon the ground on the other side of Tommin, caught her eye. She’d take it with her as a souvenir, to remind her of the day she’d saved Tommin from the Leprechaun’s curse.

“Do you mean to marry Tommin?” Copper asked. He’d lain down on the bench with the dart gun across his flat belly.

“Time will tell,” she said. “Anything’s possible, isn’t it?”

"I'm only asking because if you do mean to marry him someday, he's a human now, and you're still cursed. You'll be young and lovely forever, and he'll get to be an old man someday, all grizzled and wrinkly. And he'll die, but you won't. How might that work out, I'm wondering? Seems like a sad ending, that."

Eve grabbed the chalice A bit of liquid sloshed in the bottom. Would it be enough? And was it what she wanted—mortality and no more Glamour, no more Charm, no more clandestine adventures?

Beside her, Tommin stirred, whispering her name. Her choice was made. She'd made it long ago. She closed her eyes and recited the words to renounce the curse, and then she drank every last drop of the cure.

# *Chapter Thirty-Four*

## *Idir Dhá Domhan*

## (Between Two Worlds)

Rannin drove the Mini through a hairpin curve. The tires squealed, and in the backseat, Tommin's head gently lolled against Eve's shoulder. She slipped her arm around his back and held his unconscious body as still as she could, treasuring his closeness.

"Sorry," Rannin said. "You wouldn't believe how skilled I am on a horse. Cars are so . . . uncivilized. They simply don't understand me the way a good horse does."

"It's fine," Eve said.

"So how does it feel to be human?" Rannin asked. Eve was glad he'd regained his Elfin serenity after the shock she'd given him. The poor fellow had come Below to fetch the muscular black woman he'd dropped off and found a slight, fair redhead in her place. Fortunately, Copper's detailed, rambling speech had convinced him that Eve was who she claimed to be.

"Strange," she said. "Like I shed a layer of myself. But in a good way."

In the front passenger seat, Lorcan snored, dredging up Eve's memories of living with him as his niece—unloved, hungry, and kept silent by magic.

"What do you think they'll do with Lorcan Reilly?" Rannin asked.

"World's shortest trial," Eve said, "and then execution, I'd say. The evidence against him stretches back three hundred years or more. Him and his mad scheme to be Leprechaun king. Anyone else would have given up on it after the war. Even if he had become king, he'd have had almost nobody to rule over, hardly any tribute coming in, and a palace so decrepit a Bog Troll wouldn't live in it. Such a wicked, foolish creature he's been—and all for naught."

"And his gold-son Jimmy?"

"Probably a short prison sentence. His biggest crime was being stupid, and unfortunately, that's not really against the law. We left him in good hands with Copper and his tranquilizer darts. The Guardians should be picking him up within the hour, by my reckoning."

"That boy would make a fine agent," Rannin said. "For one so small, he possesses great bravery."

"You know, that sounds like the perfect job for him." It was easy to imagine Copper chasing down a delinquent Gnome and tackling him with a victorious shout. Yes, Copper would make a fine Faerie Guardian—as long as he was assigned to the Neathlands. There probably wasn't much need for a little brown bat agent in the world above.

Eve turned her head to watch the Irish countryside speed past her window. Green and more green, sheep and rock walls, houses and trees. The homeland she'd not realized she'd missed until now. She'd almost fallen asleep when a road sign caught her eye: **Loughgillan, 22 Kilometres.**

"Rannin," she said. "I need you to make a detour."

# Chapter Thirty-Five

## *Beannacht*

## (A Blessing)

The first thing Tommin saw when he awoke was Eve's face.

She sat in a chair close to his bed, reading. She looked up from her book and smiled, and he smiled back.

By the saints, she was pretty. Her shiny ginger hair had been trimmed to chin length, and she wore a yellow dress that made her skin almost glow. He noticed her eyes, the silver edges of her irises, the one part of her that suggested Faerie instead of human teenager. How young she looked for someone so very old.

But he felt young, too, didn't he? New and clean.

Eve's hand reached out and held his. He squeezed her fingers gently. Her skin was soft as a peach. He shut his eyes again—not because he was tired, but because he wanted to memorize how it felt to hold her hand. Because it was nothing but good, and goodness was a precious thing to him.

After a while, he opened his eyes. Eve adjusted his pillows so he could sit up. "Where am I?" he asked.

She went to the window and opened the curtains. Outside, a lake sparkled under a cloudless sky.

"Is that Lough Gillan?" he asked. He sat up straight, wanting to see every inch of the view—of the lake *and* the girl who was standing with her back to it, smiling.

"It is indeed. Gloria—you remember Gloria from the mall, the security guard?—she made me take part of the reward she got for turning Lorcan in. She's a bit of a catastrophe, as agents go, but she has a kind heart. Anyway, the long and short of it is, I bought this house for you. It's yours. I mean, if you want it. If you don't, that's fine, of course."

"That was a speech almost worthy of Copper," he said.

She looked down at her folded hands, blushing. "Sorry. I didn't mean to run on like that. I'm just so happy you're well. I've missed you. Awake you, that is."

He got the distinct impression that she fancied him.

Suddenly, he felt far too healthy to lie about in bed. It was criminal to stay under the covers when there was a beautiful lake just outside, and singing birds, and fresh air.

Tommin kicked off the blankets and swung his feet to the floor. When he realized all he was wearing was a pair of striped pajama bottoms, he grabbed for the sheet. "Any real clothes here?" he asked, his voice cracking like a twelve-year-old's.

Eve laughed. The sound warmed him through like sunlight. She left the room and returned with neatly folded jeans and a shirt.

"After I'm dressed, would you walk with me around the lake? For some reason, I feel like I've been in bed for a hundred years."

"Well, it's only been three days," she said. "But a walk sounds lovely. I'll wait in the kitchen."

"Good," he said.

Eve smiled like he'd promised her the moon.

❧

The lake sloshed against the shore. A few tethered boats bounced in the little waves at the edge of the water. The sun began to set, staining the sky pink and gold as Tommin and Eve walked the well-worn footpath.

They had not spoken since leaving the house. He did not take her hand, although he thought about it more than once. To do so seemed to him like asking for more pie when you were already full, like being greedy and unappreciative of all you'd already been given.

"You're quiet," Eve said when they stopped to stand on the edge of a wooden pier. A pair of ducks swam past. "I'm afraid to ask, but are you still angry with me for pretending to be Penny?"

"No. Not angry. Only . . . I don't know. I don't *want* to blame you for deceiving me. I know you did what you had to. I just . . ."

He reached for her hand then and led her back onto the path. Their footsteps aligned as they passed a few empty benches and a closed concession stand.

She wiped a single tear from her cheek and gave him a wobbly smile. "I wanted to tell you the truth. I *will* from now on. Always."

"I'll do the same," he said, and he forgave her completely. He felt a little ashamed that he'd not done so already. The number of lies he'd told in the name of the Take!

"Well then, I have to tell you something. Remember when I said I'd never give up on you, and I'd be watching from behind a Glamour to make sure you were all right?"

"Yes."

"I won't be able to do that."

"What? Have you changed your mind about me, then?"

"No. Never. But after you drank the remedy, I drank the rest. I knew that if I loved you and wanted a life with you, I had to renounce my own Leprechaun gifts and take the cure. When I did, I lost all my Charm and Glamour."

He squeezed her hand. "You gave them up for me? Eve . . ."

"For you *and* for me. It isn't such a big thing. My Glamour had been failing, anyway. Have you ever tasted dragon-scale powder? It's horrible. And I wanted to be with you. To be human with you."

"For one thing, I have no idea what dragons' powders have to do with it, and for another, you're lying to me, Eve my darling," Tommin said.

"I am not," Eve said. "I did want to be human with you."

He grinned, knowing he looked ridiculous, and not caring. "The lie was that you gave up your Charm. You still have charm, Eve. You charm me so much that I want to kiss you."

"Please," she said. "Please do."

They stopped in the middle of the path, and he pulled her into his arms. She smelled like vanilla and berries and hope. She closed her eyes, and he hesitated. He did not deserve her. "You're sure you want to be involved with a former Leprechaun? I'm not certain what life will be like for me without Taking. I'm not sure who I am, really. And I'm still eighteen or nineteen in some ways, I think. I mean—"

She narrowed her eyes and set a finger on his lips. "Tommin Kelly, I didn't chase after you for over two hundred years to stop loving you now. Quit talking and get on with it."

He kissed her and kissed her, and human bliss filled every part of his being.

Hearing a noisy family approaching, they left the path and climbed a grassy hill. "So, Tommin Kelly, what will you do with your life now?" Eve asked.

"I want to make shoes," Tommin said. "Beautiful, sturdy, trustworthy shoes. That is, if I can, now that my magic's gone. But I think I can."

"Will you teach me how?"

"I'd like that." Movement in the trees caught his eye. He pointed as a pair of black-and-white birds took flight from a high branch. "Look."

The birds soared across the lake and then disappeared from view among the trees on the other side.

"Magpies?" Eve said.

"Magpies," Tommin said.

"No one can compare you to them anymore," Eve said. "You're an honest man, and I mean to keep you that way."

He leaned over and kissed her forehead, remembering how Granny had kissed his. Remembering how she'd called him Magpie and loved him in spite of his sins.

"Nora," he said. "Nora Dolan."

Eve took a step back and looked at him as if he'd lost his mind. "That isn't my name. Are you feeling poorly again?"

He laughed. "I'm fine. And I know your name, my love. Nora was my granny. I want to name the business for her. Nora Dolan Shoes."

"It's a lovely name," Eve said. "And fitting. 'Nora' means 'honor.'"

"Well, that's settled, then." He looked into the distance at another familiar hill. "I'd like to see one more thing before we go back to the house, if you're not too tired."

"You're the one just back from the brink of death. I could walk to Bantry Bay and back again if you're up to it."

"Come on, then."

He recalled the way as if time had stood still, as if he were nine-year-old Tommin. The hill was every bit as steep as it had been two hundred years ago, but the edge of the forbidden forest looked softer now, bordered with berry-covered bushes and tall grass.

Eve stopped to watch a hedgehog amble past in the weeds. She exclaimed with delight at its two babies scurrying to keep up. And then she quieted as she noticed where they were.

She squeezed his hand and gave him a skeptical look. "Are you sure you want to go in there? The sun's going down. And then there's *that*." She pointed to a sign that promised trespassers would be shot on sight.

He squeezed her hand back. "Just this once, Eve."

"Well, at least we know Lorcan won't be joining us," she said. "All right. Lead on."

It was just as he remembered, and yet nothing like it. The trees seemed shorter and more widely spaced, the shadows less menacing.

And now there were happily chirping birds, and squirrels leaping from branch to branch, and little flowers nodding among the ferns.

"Tommin," Eve said softly, drawing his attention away from a tiny yellow bloom. "The tree."

He looked up and beheld it: silver-gray trunk soaring heavenward, majestic branches spread wide, heart-shaped leaves greener than green.

They wept then, as mortals must in the presence of the Nameless Tree. They knelt for a time, felt its gnarled roots beneath their knees, and breathed the strange, spicy scent of its ancient bark.

"I was born here," Tommin said to Eve, when he found his voice.

"You were," she said. "And I won't say I'm sorry for it, no matter how much trouble we've known between then and now."

He kissed her cheek, and a single leaf fell from high above, twirling and tumbling until it came to rest on Tommin's head like a blessing.

# *Acknowledgments*

Thank you, dear reader, for spending some of the precious hours of your life with a reluctant Leprechaun and his heroine.

Thanks to the bearded fellow who strolls past my house every day with a walking stick and a faithful dog—because he made me ask myself, "What if he's a Leprechaun out looking for new places to bury his gold?" and thus inspired the beginnings of this tale. (When I catch you, sir, I'm going to give you a copy of this book. Maybe you can read it to your dog at bedtime.)

Thanks to talented editors Courtney Miller, Adrienne Procaccini, and Marianna Baer for helping me and my story grow, and to everyone at Skyscape and Amazon for everything you did behind the scenes to help create and market the book. You're all amazing!

Thanks to Mike Corley for the glorious cover.

Thanks to John Feeney for the Irish Gaelic translations of the chapter titles.

Thanks to gifted fellow writers Amanda C. Davis, Joanne Brokaw, and Roberta Gore for reading, critiquing, and encouraging.

Thanks to Kingdom Writers, West Branch Christian Writers, and my NaNoWriMo friends.

Jenny Brown, a thousand thanks to you for sending chocolate-filled care packages and words of encouragement at just the right time—again and again.

Thanks and so much love to my dear BSF sisters.

Eternal gratitude to my family and friends, and especially to my wonderful husband, John—for fixing the computer (and my car, and everything else) a zillion times, for being my online stalker and review reader, for loving me when I'm unlovable, and for sharing the joys and sorrows of life with me. You're a treasure far better than a thousand crocks of gold.

Last—and most of all—I offer thanks to God: keeper of promises, healer of broken hearts, redeemer of lost causes, and the one who loves you and me more than we could ever deserve or imagine.

# *About the Author*

Carrie Anne Noble is the author of the highly acclaimed novel *The Mermaid's Sister*, which won the Amazon Breakthrough Novel Award for Young Adult Fiction in 2014. She is also the recipient of the 2016 Realm Award for Speculative Novel of the Year. A member of the Science Fiction & Fantasy Writers of America, Carrie Anne enjoys hosting spectacular tea parties, watching British TV, and spending time with family and friends.